T0012644

THE BASS REEVES TRILOGY

FOLLOW THE ANGELS, FOLLOW THE DOVES

The Bass Reeves Trilogy, Book One

SIDNEY THOMPSON

University of Nebraska Press
Lincoln

Library of Congress Cataloging-in-Publication Data
Names: Thompson, Sidney, 1965– author.
Title: Follow the angels, follow the doves / Sidney Thompson.
Description: Lincoln, NE: University of Nebraska Press, 2020 | Series: The Bass Reeves trilogy book 1.
Identifiers: LCCN 2019024357 (print)
LCCN 2019024358 (ebook)
ISBN 9781496218759 (paperback)
ISBN 9781496220189 (epub)
ISBN 9781496220196 (mobi)
ISBN 9781496220202 (pdf)
Subjects: LCSH: Reeves, Bass. | United States marshals—Indian Territory—Biography. | Slaves—Southern States—Biography. | African American men—Southern States—Biography. | United States—History—Civil War, 1861–1865—African Americans. | Reeves, George R. (George Robertson), 1826–1882. | Frontier and pioneer life—Arkansas. | Frontier and pioneer life—Indian Territory. | Frontier and pioneer life—Texas.
Classification: LCC F697.R44 T47 2020 (print) | LCC F697. R44 (ebook) |DDC 363.28/2089960730766 [B]—dc23
LC record available at https://lccn.loc.gov/2019024357
LC ebook record available at https://lccn.loc.gov/2019024358

Set in Minion Pro by Laura Ebbeka.

For all my brothers
and sisters and nieces
and nephews of color,
such as Conner

The white man had the uncomfortable
feeling that I was slipping away and taking
something with me.

FRANTZ FANON, *Black Skin, White Masks*

Methinks that in looking at things spiritual,
we are too much like oysters observing the
sun through the water, and thinking that thick
water the thinnest of air. Methinks my body
is but the lees of my better being. In fact take
my body who will, take it I say, it is not me.

HERMAN MELVILLE, *Moby-Dick*

Contents

Note on Language

A note about the use of the word n——: The policy of the University of Nebraska Press is not to print it, because it "values a thoughtful and ethical use of language." I abhor its casual and slanderous use as well, but my ethical responsibility as a writer of historical fiction is to re-create the past as I honestly see and feel it. Because I want readers to experience the violence, repression, inhumanity, and hate of nineteenth-century America for its teachable lessons, I have chosen to include this word, even if it appears in a compromised manner, as "n——" or "n——s." Neither the press nor I intend to suggest at any time that the characters using the implied epithet are supplying the blanks themselves out of cultural sensitivity. Sensitivity to the contemporary reader is the only concern.

FOLLOW THE ANGELS, FOLLOW THE DOVES

1. Map of Indian Territories, 1869. Drawn by G. Woolworth Colton from maps and surveys furnished by the Engineer Bureau, War Department, U.S. Published by G. W. and C. B. Colton and Co., New York, 1869. David Rumsey Map Collection, www.davidrumsey.com.

PART ONE

GENESIS

2. Bass Reeves, legendary deputy U.S. marshal of Indian Territory (present-day Oklahoma). Courtesy Western History Collections, University of Oklahoma Libraries, General Personalities 87.

1

Bass Reeves

All day long on the day of the great hailstorm of 1838, the sky over Van Buren, Arkansas, had been a slate of soft, even gray, like the neck feathers on a loggerhead shrike, what slaves called a butcherbird. Except for the signs of color and calm, none of the few hundred residents could know that by late afternoon windows would need shuttering, or that tomato and strawberry plants would be lost if not protected by wagon cover, or that at the wharf an anchored steamboat would be put out of commission with bent smokestacks and a cracked paddle wheel, or that lives would be lost, including a foal, a slave woman, and countless dogs and yard fowl.

On the Reeves plantation, the cloud cover came only as a welcome reprieve from the July heat. Slaves in the fields laughed with the overseer and remarked on their good fortune that the sun was absent that day, loafing somewhere with the moon, fishing for stars maybe.

The winds drifted in at midday but not at a violent pitch. Then thunder rolled up, followed by a light rain and distant flashes of lightning buried high in the clouds—not in streaks but pulses, like fireflies—with the sky quickly churning darker and lighter in swirls. It happened in seconds. Hail the size of hen eggs. Some had concentric circles in them, giving the appearance of eyeballs, while others were spiked, resembling enormous brown widow egg sacs. Mostly, they looked like cotton bolls perfectly picked and dropped from heaven.

Pearlalee Stewart watched it commence from the back door of William Reeves's plantation house, where she'd been working in the kitchen, still able in her ninth month of pregnancy to sit and peel potatoes and shell peas. Master Reeves ran from the parlor to join Pearlalee at the door to see what the commotion was—the beating of hail on the ground and on the roofs of things, with the cries of things scattering for the trees, with the shredding of trees. Above all of that, she heard Master Reeves pray.

Minutes later the hail stopped, but the rain lashed in long sheets for hours afterward. Then the calm returned, the rain merely drizzling before it soon stopped altogether at dusk. The temperature dropped throughout the night, so the next day felt like April. That was when Pearlalee went into labor—on the springlike day in July that followed the great hailstorm of 1838. Not in the slave quarters but in the modest comfort and privacy of her parents' cabin, a privilege Master Reeves had bestowed on them due to their age and faithful service, she gave birth to her third but only living child, a son, and named him Bass Reeves. Her father's name.

Bass Reeves the elder was tall, dark skinned, and sinewy and was remembered for his predilection for sugarcane—taking up tobacco only when sugarcane was no longer in season. Each fall, beginning with its first harvest, he'd carry a cane stalk with him wherever he went and would use it as a walking stick, until he'd chewed it all the way down and would start on another and another, till winter, which was how he acquired the nickname Sugar. No one but Master Reeves called him Bass anymore, not even Sugar's wife, Jane Reeves, though when Master Reeves called him, he called him "Ole Bass."

Bass Reeves the infant was first held by his aunt, Totty Stewart, the seamstress and midwife on the plantation, and with Sugar's favorite vine cutter she cut the cord. While she cleaned the baby and swaddled him, Pearlalee's mother began preparing the placenta, boiling it right away with garlic cloves, then later serving it to Pearlalee, cubed with collard greens. By the heft of her nephew, nigh three good cantaloupes, Totty pronounced he'd be as tall as his grandfather and as big and strong as his father, his enormous baby hands and feet clear stamps of greatness.

Pearlalee's husband, John Michael Stewart, had been sold at the beginning of the year to a plantation twenty miles south of them, with assurances from Master Reeves that every Christmas, she and John Michael could be reunited for the day. Pearlalee cried with her newborn as she pressed him to her chest—his soft, warm flesh like John Michael's flesh and the flesh of their two previous children she knew for certain now God remembered. She missed John Michael, wishing she could name their baby after him. But she was afraid that if she did, Master Reeves would eventually sell him away too. Master Reeves took to Sugar, or Ole Bass, like he took to no other slave, better even than he did to most white folks, which was why Master Reeves had invited him, along with Jane, to take his family name, and honored, Sugar and Jane had taken it. So it was settled— Bass Reeves would be Bass Reeves, though she would always say it broke her heart.

◆ ◆ ◆

Once the slaves were at work on the plantation the next morning, their songs rising in isolated murmurs among the mockingbirds and persistent roosters and the random lowing and braying of livestock, Master Reeves appeared on the porch of Sugar's cabin.

The door had been propped open all night and morning by a broken brick to let in fresh air. As abrupt and rapid as a woodpecker, he knocked on the doorframe, and Sugar and Jane, both stooped over the awesome vision of their grandson asleep in the crook of Pearlalee's arm, saw with a start the master's shape.

"Why, Master Reeves, come in, come in!" Jane said, rushing to greet him.

Master Reeves removed his hat and clutched it at his hip. "Mrs. Reeves wanted me to come by, see how everybody was faring."

"The Lord blessed us, he did, Master," Sugar said, smiling wide around missing teeth.

Master Reeves blocked the sunlight with his shoulders and coattails as he approached the bed, and his small button eyes, cravat, and mustacheless beard emerged at once from his silhouette, features so distinctly his. "Well, my, my," he said in a warm tenor. "He blessed us all, didn't he, Pearlalee?" He lowered his hand around Bass's head as if to measure its size. "What a buck this one will be. My goodness, girl!"

Sugar and Jane united in laughter, and it seemed to Pearlalee at such moments, when her family laughed at nothing, that they were laughing at air, just at air, how the air of the cabin was theirs and smelled like theirs and how Master Reeves was breathing it. If she thought of it that way, how it was just air, tainted but nobody's really, and that was all, she could find herself laughing along, because look at little Bass; he was breathing it in too, while only yesterday he'd breathed water and blood. Like a fish for her water and blood. She beamed with pride.

"Congratulations, Pearlalee. Ole Bass. Miss Jane." Master Reeves nodded to each, then turned back to Pearlalee. "Mrs. Reeves will be expecting you tomorrow if you think you're healthy to return."

"Oh, yes, sir," Pearlalee said. "I be fine by then. I be ready."

"Good to hear," he said. "You're missed even for a day."

2

Shoo

Whenever Bass would press himself many years later for his earliest memories, he remembered the human shadows of the windowless slave quarters before sunup, with Auntie Totty helping his mother wrap him to her back so she could tote him while she worked, only taking him out to clean or feed him. It was the not seeing her, seeing only a blur, but hearing and feeling her against him, a cough, a sneeze, her clocklike breathing among the mansion's clocks. He believed this to be a memory and not simply a memory of a story he'd heard repeated. He remembered that security, that faith, that love from a family too sprawling to view clearly from a single vista.

Once weaned, he stayed in the care of his grandparents, watching his grandmother perform culinary magic or his grandfather chew plants he couldn't swallow. His grandmother would bury sweet potatoes in a hole in the dirt floor of their cabin in front of the fireplace, only to dig them up at another time, while his grandfather would hold out his closed fist to young Bass and say, "Huh, got something for you. Hide your eyes." Bass would obediently offer out his hand like a plate and close his eyes each time he was told—his grandfather never more mysterious or magical than then. Bass would feel the leathery skin and ball joints brush his palm and feel something drop, light as a cocoon or a dandelion, and each time, he'd find the anticipation of discovery unbearable. What in the world could his grandfather give him out of thin air, without digging? Sometimes he forgot his grandfather wasn't his father, he loved him so much.

The first time Bass saw the plug of used tobacco deposited in his hand, he thought it was food, something his grandfather had peeled, being wet and smelling of dirt. Until his grandfather laughed and Bass recognized it as a joke. The second time, Bass wondered if it was something that had just died, if the strings were feathers. Because his grandfather wouldn't trick him like that twice. The third time, thinking he was smart, Bass reached for his grandfather's dipper, floating beside him in the water bucket, and held that out instead of his hand. His grandfather smiled too. And from the porch where they stood, he flung his hand open, and Bass watched the plug sail off for the dust of the yard as if it were a knuckle that had come unknotted from one of his grandfather's fingers and was flying away. As soon as that notion had occurred to Bass, for just a moment, he wondered if that notion was so. Maybe he'd been wrong all along about what his grandfather had been holding and letting go—as if his grandfather's hand, gnarled from a life of overuse, had suddenly split open like an old cotton boll and was dark inside instead of white and was flying away, flying away, before stopping short to rest. Sugar would never try him again.

◆ ◆ ◆

His grandparents frequently laughed and smiled, and so did his mother and auntie, even his father, who was lighter than the rest, with freckles on his cheeks, like the ones everyone claimed were passed on to Bass. Bass as a toddler had only seen himself in the poor reflection of water, not yet in glass, so he had to believe they were there. When Master or Mistress Reeves or any white person spoke to the family or came near, the family laughed louder and smiled bigger, and though Bass should have felt happier too, he didn't.

White people never seemed much amused either.

His first memory of Master Reeves was seeing him stroll up a path in clean matching clothes and mistaking him for a relative who was forced to live elsewhere, like his father, and was on his return home. But because Master Reeves seemed unhappy in sharp contrast to his father in the past and his grandfather then, Bass wondered if something wasn't wrong with him. Bass associated Master Reeves's pale skin with the mushrooms his grandfather collected in the woods behind the stable and with the kind of potatoes that didn't taste as good as the darker kind his grandmother buried in the cabin floor in winter to keep from ruin.

Bass watched Master Reeves and his grandfather speak in a way that suggested they knew each other but not well. They didn't speak for long before Master Reeves turned from Sugar and regarded young Bass.

"Hello there, little fella," Master Reeves said.

"Is you kin?" Bass asked, and Master Reeves smiled more enthusiastically than before.

Master Reeves bent with his hands resting on his knees so as to see young Bass at eye level. "Well, in a way I suppose we are."

"Boy, don't be pestering Master Reeves like that with questions. He a busy man."

"Oh, it's quite all right," Master Reeves said, still eyeing young Bass. He was so close to him Bass could see the man really well—his lips like the thin lips on a snake, the teeth in full rows without a gap. "There's a lot going on behind his eyes, Ole Bass. You can tell already."

"Oh, you right, Master. He'll be a good worker."

"Is you sad?" Bass asked Master Reeves.

Master Reeves grinned. "No, young'un, I'm not sad. Are *you* sad? I hope not."

Bass shook his head. "Do you like dark taters better than the other kind? I do."

Master Reeves hesitated before answering. "Oh, I definitely can put away some taters of all kinds, and I'd wager you can, too, can't you?"

Bass nodded, and Master Reeves patted his head and stood up.

"Cute boy, Ole Bass," he said before walking away.

◆ ◆ ◆

Bass didn't speak to Master Reeves again for several years. By that time, Bass knew better than to say more than "Good morning, Master Reeves," unless prodded to say more, but even then never in the form of a question, because that would have been insolent. He learned to respect white people's time above all else. They were busy running the plantation. His grandfather explained how such work required the focus and patience of a fisherman. Bass knew about fishing from the times Sugar had taken him to the river to catch catfish and stripers. His grandmother, though, compared white people's work to making a stew, how she didn't like a lot of carrying on around her either, how it looked easy at the end when she was just stirring a pot but Bass mustn't be fooled. Auntie Totty presented yet a different perspective by using her needlework, the truth of the backside of a pillow cover versus the front, while his mother prepared him for bondage by telling Bible stories. Jonah and the big fish. ("About nothing but patience. Waiting things out.") Job and all his heartache. ("Patience and more patience.") Abraham and Isaac. ("Just trust the knife won't fall. Pray, son. You praying for patience.") Jesus on the cross. ("If that ain't it, what is?")

Bass prayed for patience nightly. He knew he needed some, a whole lot even, because he wanted to kill bad guys, like those in the Bible stories, with urgency. He could feel the call to set things right and couldn't stand doing nothing. He'd lie awake at night making up songs about it:

I had a butcher knife hid and dug it up
Cause I seen Abraham with Isaac and knowed a boy
    needed hup
Lickety-click I did run and I throwed that daddy off
"Never again," I said and cut off his head
Then I and Isaac hid the body in a trough

Pearlalee discouraged such song singing, afraid he'd grow up to be an outlaw, and to offset his songs and the games he organized with other boys in which they'd act out his songs, she would dream up a random task for him and then complicate it. "Iron this here pile of clothes while I finish up them frog legs," she might tell him, making him think she was about to fry up a batch, when her intention all along was to sit in front of him lazy as you please and eat a batch of frog legs and not save him any, or she'd let him think so. Until he stopped flinching outwardly about what was right or wrong or unfair. Sometimes they talked about these lessons after the fact, but usually they didn't.

Never under the daily tutelage of his grandparents or in the nightly care of his mother and auntie when among the slaves in the slave quarters did he hear anyone utter what they were. As far as Bass knew, there were white people and there were Negroes, and they had separate duties, all important but different, with white people simply being busier in the head with invisible work, which explained why it was harder to do and demanded more peace and quiet and standing and sitting still. Not until late summer after he turned eight, at cotton-picking time, was he confronted with the notion of slavery. Everyone in the cabin had groaned about it more and more as the time grew closer, until the night before the first harvest, when everyone grew quieter. Uncle Moseley, who was not his uncle, sang a song in the dark after everyone settled down for sleep. He sang low and deep, as if to a baby, and verses grew longer as he went along:

> You gone pick that cotton like you be told
> You gone pick that cotton till you be old
> You gone pick that cotton like they balls a snow
> You gone pick that cotton, be wishing it be cold
> You gone pick that cotton, tweet tweet like a lil' robin
> You gone pick that cotton cause wings broke and you
>   tired a sobbin'

Bass snickered initially, thinking others would too or might sing along, but Uncle Moseley was on his own tonight. So Bass stopped listening to the words, and Uncle Moseley's voice became an easy lowness to fall asleep to.

In the morning, Pearlalee announced to Bass that he wasn't staying behind anymore but was going to the field because he was a man now and needed to work the fields like a man. Bass would remember clenching his fists to feel what the fists of a man felt like as he ran ahead of his mother to tag along with older boys, who were not much taller as a lot, some shorter. And he would remember recognizing how out of place the overseer first appeared because of the expression of boredom on his face, even as he stood at the corner of a cotton field in full bloom, the most beautiful thing Bass had ever seen. The whiteness seemed to have no end to it. He would also remember wondering how anyone with a whip tucked into his belt could appear that bored. On the ground near the overseer was a pile of burlap sacks, and each of Bass's friends and neighbors from the quarters grabbed a sack before entering a row. Bass ran to pick one up before they were gone.

"Bass, son," his mother called, "come here, boy."

Bass hung the sack around his shoulders like everyone else was doing, and it dragged the ground between his feet as he ran over to her.

Pearlalee took his hands and pulled him in closer. "You make your family proud today, Bass. You got a job to do, and that's all that matters. You be patient at it and perfect at it, you hear me?"

"Yes, ma'am."

"You a slave, and this is slavery. And what that means is Master Reeves have the right to tell us what to do because he own this whole plantation and everything on it, including me and you and everyone. That be why he's so busy, why we respect him so much. He take care a us, make sure we eat and get by. Now it's your turn to do your part, you hear? We here to be thankful."

"What about the cotton?"

"What about it?"

"He own it too?"

"That's right, son. Every boll."

"And that white man yonder too?"

"No, none of the white folks. Only colored folks is slaves. Now, listen to me," she said, "don't be aggravating nobody. You growing up today, and that's that."

"Yes, ma'am," Bass said. He would remember smiling at his mother, while she looked about to cry.

"Come here," she told him. She held him tight against her apron. Then shooed him away.

◆ ◆ ◆

Bass chose a row with plants so tall they looked like trees growing out of the ground without trunks, and the first boll he picked was so soft and thick as hair he wanted to pick it all just to touch it all. But the more he picked, the more he had to pick, as if he wasn't getting anywhere. There were branches behind branches, bolls behind bolls, and husks and sticks stuck him from every direction. Cotton wasn't all soft, like how a rose wasn't all rose.

As the day grew hotter, more and more mosquitoes stirred. He started picking with both hands to keep the mosquitoes off and to fill his bag sooner and speed up the day, but the sun refused to move. It just sat there and swelled.

He didn't think much of being a slave or a man. He wanted to run to his granddaddy and grandmammy and do anything they said. He didn't want to cry, but he didn't care if he did. He missed being theirs.

3

Peas in a Pod

Bass worked as a field hand until his teens, when his reputation of having a way with the livestock led to a position as a stable hand—feeding, watering, and grooming mainly but also assisting in castrations and deliveries. Most impressive was the manner in which, within weeks of his new position, he could coax a horse to lift its hoof and remain still while he used a pick to flush out debris. After a couple of years in the stable, as his size and strength grew, he was moved again, to serve as an apprentice to the blacksmith. Bass had developed an appetite for learning, having adopted the primary lesson of his family: if he remained positive and productive, the ultimate overseer in God would look after him. If not in this life, the next. Eventually.

He witnessed less patient men attempt to break free long before they'd learned where even to go or how to get there and before they'd earned enough trust in their duties to obtain a sufficient head start.

It was his patience that attracted Master Reeves's attention one day. Bass had spotted him leaning against the oak tree near the stable, wearing black riding boots and watching Bass hammer horseshoes and punch nail holes, one after another without break. What else would the master have been watching? If not Bass's patience, his perfection, because his shoes were getting prettier and prettier and more uniform, as if he were using a sawed-off horse hoof the way some would as a guide. Eventually, Bass was able to ignore Master Reeves's long-distance supervision. Before he knew it, with his eyes down on his work, Master Reeves walked up on him, boots first.

"You sure remind me of Ole Bass, you know that?" Master Reeves said.

Bass smiled. He nodded. "Thank you, Master."

"Except you don't smile so big."

"Sorry, Master."

"No, I like that you don't. I trust Ole Bass because he does, and I trust you because you don't."

"Yes, sir, Master." Bass respectfully kept his eyes lowered, on Master Reeves's tall black boots.

"You seem to smile only when you want to."

Years later Bass would remember telling himself not to smile then at all.

"Are you happy here?"

"Oh, yes, sir, Master. I be happy anywheres." He smiled but not big, as that was his way, that was true, to be restrained, and watched Master Reeves's boots pivot with grace in the blackened dirt of the shop floor.

◆ ◆ ◆

In the winter of 1857, when Bass was nineteen and Master Reeves was sixty-three, Master Reeves appointed Bass to be his companion, or body servant, in the same way Pearlalee was Mistress Reeves's companion. His mother had campaigned precisely for this position her son's entire life by bragging on him to Mistress Reeves whenever Master Reeves was within earshot. Now her whole family was considered upper slaves, in the service of the house instead of the field, and with that came the distinction of eating at the house table. Not at the long polished rectangular table in the dining room where the Reeves family ate but the dull square one in the kitchen. Still, what the Reeves ate, they ate. No more getting by most days, like the other slaves, on grits, oats, or ashcake.

Wherever Master Reeves now went, Bass accompanied him. If Master Reeves sequestered himself in his study, then Bass remained that day in the house and performed the duties of a butler. If Master Reeves took leave of the house to inspect the plantation on foot or horseback, then Bass attended him as his valet and escort. Or if Master Reeves had business in town, then Bass served as his coachman and bodyguard, which was why, by March, once Bass had thoroughly familiarized himself with the house and its rules of etiquette, Master Reeves directed Bass to his closet and showed him two Springfield muskets. One was slightly longer and heavier and older and darker than the other.

"Take these down with these ammunition pouches and tack up our horses. It's time you learned to shoot."

"Yes, sir. Thank you, Master Reeves," Bass said calmly, but he couldn't bear to keep his enthusiasm suppressed. "Thank you, sir," he added. Though Bass wished to turn and run, he stepped across the rugs and floorboards with the same evenness his mother had taught him, by rolling his weight heel to toe, so that no dishes rattled and no clocks chimed off-hour. He couldn't remember a day of his childhood when he didn't dream of drawing a firearm down on a bandit or pirate or on Satan himself. At such times as this, Bass wondered if he didn't owe it to God and Master Reeves both to love Master Reeves and say so in his heart. And maybe Bass loved him that way already. Maybe Bass loved him as much as he loved his own father—that much, as much as he could.

◆ ◆ ◆

In a stony meadow on the north side of the plantation, Master Reeves dismounted his palomino and removed his straw hat, which Bass had never seen him wear before that day and rightfully so since it fit him a little small even resting back on his head.

"Hang this on that birch there," he told Bass, and Bass, having already dismounted from his sorrel, took the hat and worked his way across the sun-soaked meadow about fifty feet to a birch standing alone by a stream. The birch was no bigger round than Bass's own arm. Maybe smaller if Bass flexed.

"I never liked that hat. Years ago, when I worked for the state legislature in Little Rock, a friend gave it to me as a joke, his way of congratulating me for a motion I'd gotten passed despite his efforts to the contrary. I suppose we were friends at the time. Anyway, he said I was bigheaded. You like that? I may not be the best shot, but today I will be, by Jove." Master Reeves steadily talked to Bass as Bass broke off the lowest limb, hung the hat on the jagged stob, the red band making a perfect bull's-eye, and walked back.

Master Reeves demonstrated the loading of the longer, heavier, older, darker weapon, an 1842 smoothbore. He explained the percussion cap, the paper cartridge, the ramrod. Then he leveled the musket with the butt plate pressed against his shoulder, pulled back the hammer, and aimed.

"Always aim the muzzle, the end of the gun there, a hair high, because the ball will drift down a hair over space. And always take a breath first. Hold still." He squeezed the trigger, and hiding quail flushed from the edges of the meadow. With the smell of mercury fulminate rising to their nostrils, Bass and Master Reeves watched the hat swing like a pendulum, the .69-caliber lead ball having nicked the brim.

"Hah!" Master Reeves said. "Told you I'd get it. Your turn now, and don't be scared. There's nothing to be afraid of."

Bass proceeded to load the musket how Master Reeves had demonstrated, and Master Reeves nodded. "That's right, that's right," he'd say. But Bass was slow to level the musket, unsure if he should brace it against his left shoulder or right.

"Does it matter, Master Reeves, which side I shoot on?"

"Well, boy, are you right-handed or left-handed?"

Bass looked at his hands and shook his head.

"When you hold your fork to eat," Master Reeves said, "which hand do you use?"

Bass shrugged. "Whatever one's closer."

"Then I guess it doesn't matter. Give it a try both ways."

"Yes, sir, Master." Bass leveled the musket against his right shoulder to be like Master Reeves and cocked the hammer back.

"Remember, aim a hair high," Master Reeves told him, "and hold steady. Easy does it."

Bass stared at the hat until the flat circle of woven straw coalesced into clear view, like the coconut cake he'd recently watched his mother bake and ice in the Reeves's kitchen. He lowered the muzzle even with the top of the circle and took a breath. He held still.

When the percussion cap cracked, Bass took his eyes off his target, and Master Reeves struck up a ballyhoo like no other white person Bass had ever heard. More like a drunken Negro on a Saturday night.

"You did it, son!" Master Reeves said. He clapped Bass on the back. "Look at that!"

Bass had hit the center of the hat's crown, a perfectly round black blot in all that straw white, as if he'd poked a red-hot punch rod through it.

"And you didn't even knock that blasted hat from its roost. It was that clean of a shot. My goodness, boy, you're quite the crackerjack!"

Bass smiled. He was accustomed to success but not praise from a man as important as Master Reeves.

Master Reeves exchanged muskets with him. "Let's see if you can do it again with this one, but left-handed this time." He explained that the barrel on the 1855 model was rifled and had a flip-up sight, and instead of a percussion cap, there was tape primer. He loaded a different paper cartridge into the muzzle, this one with a .58-caliber minié ball, and used the ramrod as before.

The curved butt of the stock fit more comfortably against Bass's shoulder. He took a breath and steadied his aim, lining the sight with the top of the circle, but thinking better of that, he lowered the sight another hair to accommodate the smaller, lighter round being rifled through the air with more accuracy. He thought he could hold the musket still and breathe and nothing would change. That he could remain frozen like this all day if he had to. Could close his eyes if he wanted, and then he did on impulse and eased the trigger.

Louder than the percussion cap was the crack of the birch tree splitting in half. Bass opened his eyes and caught Master Reeves ducking from the sky, his hands shielding his face as if from potential lightning, and once the tree fell to the ground in two pieces, the hat toppled and rolled away like a wagon wheel.

Master Reeves stood upright and howled with laughter. He hopped in the air and ran for the hat, hobbling over the stones of the meadow but hobbling with speed. Bass watched incredulously at the hat as Master Reeves plucked it from the ground and eyed it up close.

"Unbelievable!" Master Reeves said, holding the hat high for Bass to see the singular hole of entry. Master Reeves turned to the tree and on his haunches inspected the trunk's cross sections.

Bass waited for permission to follow, until Master Reeves stood up and waved for Bass to join him.

"You've got to see this, Bass, how one ball's lodged against the other like two peas in a pod. You won't believe it. I don't believe it. It's amazing!"

4

Ice

Master Reeves entered Bass into his first turkey shoot on the first of May in 1857. Lutherans of neighboring Fort Smith had set up the contest as a fundraiser for the construction of their church, and on the site of its future grounds, they hung turkeys by their feet from a clothesline tied between two sugarberry trees. The objective for the contestant was to shoot the head off a turkey from a hundred feet, and whoever succeeded advanced to the next round, and the next, until there was a winner of the twenty-dollar prize. The turkeys shot in the contest were to be roasted over a pit for the jubilee barn raising planned for the following day.

A surprising number of contestants, forty-one of seventy-eight, progressed to the second round, but only three made it past the third: a first lieutenant in the Seventh Infantry, an English wayfarer dressed in tails and a top hat, and Bass Reeves. Four rounds later the Fort Smith officer was disqualified when his shot didn't completely sever the gobbler's head from its neck, leaving it dangling by a string of wattle. Back and forth for over an hour Bass and the Englishman aimed their muskets and shot, while slave women sat nearby on upturned wicker baskets, plucking the turkeys as soon as they were untied from the clothesline and tossed in the mud at their feet—the feathers mounting into a brown heap as high as a haystack.

The crowd gathering behind Bass and the Englishman was estimated at three hundred white spectators, far greater than the town's population, and all about them, quietly perched on tree limbs and fence rails, were scores of crows and blackbirds, while a thick funnel cloud of buzzards floated in rotation above them, no longer startled by the gunfire.

The crowd had been largely polite throughout the event, until someone yelled, "We need an American in the race," which was quickly answered by another fellow saying, "Oh, we got an American. The problem is he ain't human!" Laughter erupted, but it didn't slow or distract Bass, because Master Reeves thought differently, and Bass thought differently. So those people could think how they wanted. They could live like frogs and crickets a body eventually stopped hearing, like water boiling the way water boiled, like water trickling over smooth stones, like thunder even after a while, like birds just waiting. No matter.

But the Lutheran church of Fort Smith unexpectedly ran out of turkeys. All one hundred of them, donated by a local farmer, were dead. The minister huddled with his deacons, while the crowd offered up a variety of solutions, from dogs to chickens they could fetch from home, but the minister broke from his huddle and declared the contest a tie. The crowd moaned, but the Englishman immediately removed his hat in a dramatic show of relief and, appearing much shorter now without his hat, shook Bass's hand.

With more turkeys than could ever be eaten at the jubilee, the minister invited the winners to haul away as many as they wanted. The Englishman graciously declined the offer, but Master Reeves accepted both shares and directed Bass to draw up the wagon. Since he was keeping their portion of the prize money, Master Reeves said Bass could have all but one.

On their way back to the plantation, Bass turned in his seat to eye his bounty, plucked white and dotted with blood, and if he saw flies, he'd remove his wide-brimmed hat and shoo them off. On the ferry crossing the Arkansas River, Bass got down from his seat and dunked each bird off the side to rinse it.

After Master Reeves paid the ferryman, he looked at Bass as they proceeded again on land. "It's like I financed a war," he said.

They rode for a time in the silence of horse hooves and wagon squeak.

"It's not your fault, Bass. I'm not saying it's your fault, but it's not mine either. How could I imagine somebody would match you for so long? You can't imagine the expense of ammunition these days. You just can't."

"No, sir, Master, don't imagine I can," Bass said, and he turned once more to check on his turkeys. He'd never expected to receive any of the prize money anyway. What would Bass do with money? It was reward enough to be given the opportunity to leave the plantation and compete like a free man, but to perform in the turkey shoot as well as the most perfect white man and then get to go home with half a wagon of fresh meat to share with all his fellow slaves so that, for a moment, they could feel free and perfect too—that surpassed what he'd ever dreamed possible.

When they arrived at the plantation, Bass could barely remain seated, eager to begin unloading the turkeys so that he could begin gutting and cleaning them before he lost sunlight. By that time, the slave day would be winding down, and he'd have help preparing the pits with firewood.

He let the horses continue to advance up the lane at a quick canter, but not one dog ran out to greet them.

"Easy," Master Reeves said.

"Oh, yes, sir," Bass said, pulling on the reins to slow the horses to a trot, and Bass spotted a wagon ahead, behind the house, parked in the shade of the oak tree between the stable and the icehouse. Its horses were unhitched, likely feeding in the stable, while Master Reeves's whippets were gathered beneath the wagon licking the grass.

Bass pulled their wagon alongside it, and Master Reeves stood from his seat to peer down into it. Despite the heat, the entire floor of the wagon was dark with water and strewn with hay. Bass could see inside the wagon without standing.

"My ice!" Master Reeves said. He smiled and climbed down, using a wheel spoke as a step. "What do you know? They're early."

Bass watched him unfasten the door to the icehouse and step inside, the dogs scurrying in a bunch to follow him in.

"Come here, Bass," Master Reeves said.

Bass jumped to the ground, and before he'd reached the threshold of the icehouse, waves of cooler air curled out against him. It was his first time to step inside the square limestone structure, which was much smaller than it had appeared from the outside, and darker, even with the door open, because of its thick walls without windows. In the center of the dirt floor were hay-packed cakes of ice stacked as tall as he was.

"This'll make summer bearable," Master Reeves said. He patted Bass on the back, and Bass had to catch his breath from the surprise of his touch. "This was once a pond in Massachusetts, but we'll make something much sweeter with it, you'll see."

"Yes, sir, Master," Bass said, politely smiling.

Master Reeves turned to go, and Bass backed away to let him have the lead. Following the dogs, Bass latched the door.

A man as well-dressed as Master Reeves, only younger, in his thirties, and sporting a red vest and a dark mustache, was exiting the rear door of the house and laughing as he spoke to two poorly dressed white men who were trailing behind him, their shirts rolled up at the sleeves and drenched with sweat. The well-dressed man seemed vaguely familiar to Bass, with familiar small dark eyes darting back and forth between him and Master Reeves as he walked in their direction.

"Well, goodness gracious, George," Master Reeves said, "why didn't you send word you were coming? I wouldn't have gone off to Fort Smith today if I'd known." He and the well-dressed man met each other with a hug, and Bass knew now it was Master George, the master's son. Bass had seen him over the years passing through the plantation but always unexpectedly, ghostly, a momentary sighting—the black sheep of the family, Bass had heard his mother say, and not in a good way—then off into a carriage or on a horse, his mystery always a fast one.

The other white men quietly stood back and waited like Bass to be addressed.

"It's a good thing I showed when I did," Master George said, "because no one was around to take charge and help these men unload their ice. Don't you have an overseer? Mother didn't know."

Master Reeves nodded. "Thank you, son," he said. He turned to the men. "I suppose I owe you."

Master George appeared neglected for the moment, and his eyes wandered along the ground, snakelike to Bass's shoes, going up his trouser legs and linen shirt to his now down-turned face.

Bass took his hat off and wiped his forehead with his kerchief, pretending not to notice the attention.

Master George walked up to Bass and stood so close to him that he met Bass's still down-turned eyes.

"Mother says you're quite the gunslinger. Let me rephrase that; Mother says Father says that. But what do *you* say?"

"Oh, no, sir. No gunslinger. Not atall."

"Do you think my father is wrong about you?"

Bass stared at the ground. "No, sir. He knows a lot about a lot."

"Then how do you explain this ability you have?"

Bass shrugged. "Can hold a gun up straight is all. Don't know enough to explain, sir, Master George, sir. I just do as I'm told."

"I see." Master George kicked at the ground with the heel of his boot and rested his hands on his hips. "Shooting a man is not the same as shooting a turkey."

Bass nodded.

"Art thou a silkworm?" Master George asked with heat.

Bass's back stiffened as he looked up at him. Master George appeared as sincere in the framing of his eyes and mouth as a preacher, but Bass understood about as much as if Master George were a Mexican.

"Dost thou spin thy own shroud out of thyself?" Master George said. "Look at thy bosom!"

Bass prayed for patience and understanding. He had to say something—it would be expected—but he could think of nothing. He could think of Sugar, what Sugar would do, what Sugar would say, and nothing else. So he grinned wide and said, "I know you a busy man, Master George, so can I do something for you, maybe get something for you?"

Master George inched closer by puffing out his chest. "That was Herman Melville, boy. I'm speaking of the great *Moby-Dick*. I want to know your opinion, if what Captain Ahab says speaks to you. You do have an opinion, don't you, Bass? You are *Bass*, aren't you? Ole Bass's grand-Bass? I'm talking to the right n——, I hope."

Afraid of how this man would twist his words if he used any, Bass continued to nod.

"You aren't going to answer me in speech, boy?"

"Yes, sir, Master George. Name Bass, yes, sir."

Master George nodded, then nodded again as if to make his nodding clear. "Melville also says that a whale's case, if the whale is a large buck of a whale, I mean, will yield about five hundred gallons of sperm." He stared at Bass, and Bass eyed him back at a glance, not nodding, not speaking, but looking away at Master Reeves, counting out paper bills into the hand of one of the workmen.

Bass eyed Master George again, then looked away again.

Master George laughed with such small teeth. "Books are funny."

5

Books

Over the next few years, Bass would see George Reeves no more than a half-dozen times. The youngest and most aloof of five children, George lived on a small farm in a sparsely populated area of Grayson County, Texas, near Pottsboro, not far from the Red River northward and the Texas Trail eastward. He'd moved to the newly annexed republic as a newlywed in 1846 and two years later would become a tax collector. At that time, his father-in-law had been elected mayor of Sherman. George would later be appointed sheriff; then in 1855 he began serving his county as a state representative. Because of the unpredictability of his work schedule, he was fond of saying, he usually appeared at his parents' Van Buren plantation unannounced and alone, with little news about his wife and twelve children. He was the first man, and the last man, Bass as an adult ever feared.

Bass had never had a reason before to fear anyone. Since Master Reeves refused to keep an overseer who was heavy with a whip, life on his plantation had been bearable, and bearable over time could seem almost good. The alternative of being sold to much crueler men, or escaping and being caught by them, men like those Bass's father slaved for, kept most slaves in line. As long as everyone showed up on time for work and obeyed without sass talking, the overseer kept to himself, usually napping under a tree.

Bass feared Master George because he didn't understand the meaning of his bookish words or the source of his anger. He only understood that Master George was fond of baiting him, and that was why Bass decided to ask Master Reeves a question.

Bass waited for what he thought was the perfect opportunity. He'd just won his fifth turkey shoot of the year, at the Hunting Dance festival in Seminole Nation, with the highest prize yet of fifty dollars, for being the only contestant to shoot the head off a turkey at twenty-five paces and again at fifty paces, while riding past it on horseback. Master Reeves had taken Bass deep into Indian Territory because they hadn't heard of Bass there yet. In Arkansas, Bass was increasingly being banned because a growing number of people refused to compete against him.

In the wagon returning home—inspired by the sight of Indian men at the festival who were blacker than he was, in plumed turbans and calico jackets and beaded sashes as colorful as flowers, who walked freely and spent money like white men—Bass asked him. In a swath of the flattest land Bass had ever seen, flanked by the North Canadian River and the South Canadian River, which converged far ahead of them, he said, "Master, do you mind, sir, if I ask you something?"

Master Reeves had been stroking his beard mindlessly for some time, and now he slowly stopped. "Well, all right," he said, "so long as you don't ask me for something."

They sat beside one another on the wagon seat, both facing nothing at all—the land, like the wagon itself, was a land of board after board after board, broken only by canebrakes and the random nothing tree. Master Reeves had chosen to take their trip in the wagon and not the coach because he didn't want to attract the attention of bandits. When Master Reeves grew too weary for his age to sit shotgun, he would stretch out in the wagon bed and rest his head on a sack of cornmeal, and this was what he decided to do now, to stand and brace himself against Bass's shoulder and climb back with the supplies.

"Go ahead, Bass. I was having a little fun. I'm listening."

"Yes, sir," Bass said. Afraid his voice wasn't loud enough for Master Reeves to hear over the hoofbeats and the creaking clamor of the wagon, he turned halfway and spoke louder. "I been thinking, Master, how nice it be how you read to me sometimes out the Bible like you do, and it got me wondering lately if you maybe could teach me next how to read too? I sure would love to read the Bible when you too busy to."

"Oh, I don't know about that, Bass," Master Reeves said. "That doesn't seem like a good idea to me at all, not at all. That's the kind of thing can get you and me into trouble."

"Oh, no, sir, Master, I don't want to get nobody in no trouble." Bass waited. He glanced back at Master Reeves staring up, and Bass looked up and saw it too—the steel-blue sky was cloudless straight across, the dull sun showing the only hole in it. He returned his attention to his master, now shining an apple on his coat sleeve. "Can I ask you something else, Master?"

"Really, Bass?"

"Only if you say it's all right, sir."

"If it's the last question I hear from you today, and tomorrow, too, for that matter."

"Oh, yes, sir, Master Reeves. Yes, sir, I'm sorry." Bass turned back around to check their advancement, the condition of the horses and of the road ahead, if in the distance other horses were visible, or clouds of dirt from anyone, and he thought of the box turtle shells the dark Seminole women had worn strapped to their legs beneath their long skirts and how they stomped and shook their legs last night in the snake dance. How the shells rattled from the pebbles inside them. How there were no box turtles along these rivers in October. How those women wore such short blouses that he could at times make out their pelvic lines and belly buttons.

"Well, Bass, go ahead." Master Reeves bit into his apple.

"Oh, yes, sir, Master," Bass said, looking over his shoulder. "I was just wondering, sir, if those was Negroes at the festival I seen dressed like Indians. Some looked like Indians, sure enough, but some looked more like black folks, or maybe some of both."

Master Reeves leaned up on one arm to give Bass a crooked, chewing grin, which made Bass see Master George in him, in his eyes and teeth. "You noticed that, did you?"

Bass nodded.

"Well, the Seminoles keep Negroes, too. They have a different arrangement there, though, living more together than we do, and that causes problems and lots of them. People forget who they are without borders and rules and God's teachings. Would you want to live like you were an Indian and didn't know better?"

"Oh, no, sir, Master." Bass had never considered that doing white people things was a way of living without God, and he would never choose to live without God.

"No, I don't imagine you would. A society of people who forget who they are, well, will forget who they are."

Bass nodded in sad agreement with everything the master had said, because it was all probably true or untrue, and he didn't know which. "Yes, sir. Thank you, Master Reeves."

"I'm in agreement with you, Bass. You deserve something special. I've been thinking about that myself. Maybe I can give you an extra day for Christmas. How does that sound? I'll even see if your father can be allowed to come up and stay an extra day with you and your mama. That would be real nice, wouldn't it?"

"Oh, yes, sir," Bass said, and looking ahead, he shut his eyes. The horses knew where they were going. "Thank you, Master Reeves," he said, not turning but nodding in darkness, as the horses nodded. "That'd be real nice, Master Reeves. Yes, sir, real nice."

◆ ◆ ◆

The Seminole Nation turkey shoot proved to be Bass's last. A widely advertised contest sponsored by a new bathhouse in Hot Springs several months later was canceled the day of the shoot, because many of the contestants had gotten together and accused Master Reeves and his Negro marksman of being professional swindlers and demanded a refund of their entry fees. The humiliation of that event, along with the sheer inconvenience and expense of their trip, discouraged Master Reeves from ever entering Bass in another competition.

Instead, to watch Bass shoot, Master Reeves took him hunting in the Boston Mountains of the Ozarks, along the White River, where they'd track bear and elk and razorback. Master Reeves would keep the bear hides and racks but would let Bass have most of the meat.

At least once a year Bass would ask if he could learn to read, if it was time yet, but Master Reeves always said no. "You'd never read as well as you shoot, so why bother?" he once told him. On another occasion, he said, "Ignorance is bliss, Bass. You don't realize how blessed you are." For a while what Master Reeves had said would make sense. *Ignorance was blessed*, thought Bass, which was how he'd heard it. Adam and Eve had shown that was true, but it was also important to know about such ignorance, why people needed stories to remind them about it again and again. Since ignorance could be good sometimes and sometimes turn bad, Bass waited as patiently as he could for more things to turn.

Sometimes Master Reeves invited Ole Bass to join them on their hunts, usually when teal was in season, since Ole Bass and Master Reeves were getting too old to trek in the woods for long at a time. They would seat themselves on a ridge and have a picnic of whiskey and sugar cane while watching Bass and the whippets work on the riverbank below.

Bass never asked about reading whenever his grandfather was present, because his grandfather would never have approved of the question and would've promptly answered for Master Reeves himself.

◆ ◆ ◆

Sometime between Thanksgiving and Christmas in 1860, in the middle of the night, Master George appeared at the slave quarters, rousing everyone to a fearful, hushed clamor by calling Bass's name in angry slurs from his saddle, while his horse snorted and stamped and scratched its hooves at the door.

Bass jumped out of bed, making the corn husks in his mattress crackle, and the orange ember glow of the stove showed him his mother's outstretched hand. He took it, letting her squeeze him. "Don't worry, Mama," he said. Barefoot and in long strides, he reached the door and slipped the rope off its catch. Wearing only long underwear, he peeked outside.

"Get dressed, n——! Jesus, I need you to come quick."

Once Bass had buttoned his pants and slipped on shoes, he hurried outside, afraid something had happened to Master Reeves or the mistress.

"I need you to run up to the house," Master George said, "and wake my father and tell him I'm here. Understand?" He wrenched the reins in a violent twist of neck and mane, and the black Morgan, splashed white on its legs and chest, recoiled with a whinny. With a grunt, Master George whipped its flank to bolt ahead.

Bass ran after them through the kicked-up dust and, for a moment, thought he might catch the Morgan's tail, believing he saw it sweep half-white, half-black just past his grasp, before the horse with Master George vanished at a gallop.

Up at the house, he found Master George sitting in one of the porch rockers with his feet propped on the rail. The steed was tied to the rail and panting.

"Tell my father I'm down here."

"Yes, sir," Bass said.

Bass crept upstairs and knocked on the closed bedroom door. "Excuse me, sir, ma'am, it's Master George," he said. "He here. He outside on the porch. He told me to come announce it."

Master Reeves rustled from the bed into clothes. A belt buckle clinked, and the floor shimmied from his footsteps to the door.

"What is it?" Master Reeves said. The shutters to the windows behind him cut the starlight into trim.

"Don't know, sir," Bass said.

"Is he alone?"

"Yes, sir."

"Okay, thank you, Bass."

Bass stepped aside and followed Master Reeves through the darkened house.

"Light a lamp in the kitchen," Master Reeves said. "He'll be hungry."

Bass hoped for bad news—not another war in Texas, not death or harm, but something reasonable to explain the state Master George was in. Bass lit the oil lamp on the table where he and his mother and Auntie Totty took their meals. He hoped Master George was broken, had gotten kicked out of office and was about to lose his house and farm, and was here to beg for help, and Bass would be here to see it.

Bass stood out of the way, in the shadows by the back door, and watched Master Reeves and Master George enter the kitchen from the other doorway.

"I can't sleep these days," Master George said. "That's why I'm here—just can't sleep. I rode straight here for the excitement."

"Are you hungry?" Master Reeves surveyed the table, the counters, the stove.

"I guess," answered Master George, taking Bass's seat at the table against the wall and facing Bass.

Master Reeves shuffled his feet in a rotation to face Bass too. He shrugged. "What do we have?"

"War's imminent," Master George said. He let his arms drop hard on the tabletop, and the light dimmed and flickered across the room.

"Will see, sir." Bass opened a cabinet above the stove and removed a covered plate of leftover fried chicken and biscuits his mother had made for dinner.

"Their president-elect doesn't give a damn," Master George continued. "Is oblivious to it. It will happen."

Bass turned with the uncovered plate in his hands and caught sight of Master George glaring at Master Reeves and waving a finger at him, as if they'd changed roles when Bass wasn't looking and war had actually commenced. Bass stood still and watched Master Reeves, unaware, half-asleep, pull out Auntie Totty's chair on the opposite side of the table from his son and ease himself down into it.

"Nuh-uh, no sir, Father, you've got to shave off that beard pronto or grow a damn mustache. One or the other."

Master Reeves looked at his son. His hands rose up, almost floated through the lamplight, to his beard, the same beard Bass had always known him to have, only grayer, longer. Never a mustache. Master

Reeves gently searched the skin above his upper lip with the tips of his fingers. "What do you mean?"

"You're not a Mennonite, Father. My God, you look like Lincoln himself."

Master Reeves smiled and lowered his hands to his lap. "Oh, well."

Master George pressed his chest against the edge of the table. "Oh, well?"

"Well, let me assure you, son, I'm not Lincoln."

"And let me assure you, Father, you look just fucking like him."

"Whoa, now!" Master Reeves stiffened. "Let me remind you that your mother is in the house."

Bass stepped up to place the plate on the table between them, believing he would knock Master George flat back out of that chair if Master Reeves were to give him the word to.

Master George leaned back in that chair and threw up his hands, almost daring Bass. "He never once campaigned in our Southern states. This from a man who said public sentiment was everything." He reached forward and grabbed a chicken leg. "Be prepared is all I'm saying. You could lose everything you have."

"I'm reading the papers."

Master George stood up and, swaying, ripped the cap of meat from the bone in one bite. He eyed Bass, then his father, and chomped.

"I know you trust this Jim here," Master George said, "but maybe you shouldn't." He swallowed twice and tossed the bone on the table.

"Have you been drinking, son?"

Master George reached for more chicken, biscuits, stuffing his coat pockets full. "Just wanted to come and warn you." He stepped toward his father and gave him a pat on the shoulder. "Tell Mother I'm sorry I missed her this time."

"What, son, you're leaving?" Master Reeves watched Master George turn about and walk away. He glanced at Bass, then jumped to his feet and stepped quickly to catch up to his son already in the parlor, in the foyer. "You can't be serious, George."

Master George let the front door swing wide behind him, and Bass reached and caught it before the brass knob banged against the wall.

"You need rest, son. Be sensible."

Master George untied his horse and hauled himself into his saddle.

Bass stood behind Master Reeves. He wondered what books had done to that man.

"Think about what you're doing," Master Reeves said.

Master George unsheathed a saber with a ring and a flash. "Sabers up, gentlemen!" With his sword still raised, he spun the Morgan and charged for the road across the front plantation lawn—the black of the horse dissolving, with the lower splashing of white churning away like a cloud.

6

The Pussytoes

Days later Bass noticed whiskers growing out above Master Reeves's upper lip. Master Reeves had also begun to keep to his study more. And whenever the mistress brought up Master George in conversation, Master Reeves changed the subject or sent Bass on an errand.

The winter wildfire of Southern secession was followed in the spring of 1861 by news of war and further secession, including Arkansas, just as Master George had warned, prompting Sugar to give a speech one night in the restless slave quarters. He hoped to calm everyone's fears of the unknown. Liberty could mean abandonment and starvation. It could also mean a path to riches, to cities where Negroes talked and dressed like white folks, where they could walk into a store or bank on a weekday and have business there. But it could also mean a glorious path back to Africa. Yet this night no one wanted to hear about the land of palm trees and yam barns, even if cotton didn't grow there, because Africa meant ships rowed across oceans, and they'd all heard stories of their back-broken ancestors being fed like Jonah to the water. They had to remain calm in the meantime, pleaded Sugar. To do their work to keep hold of what little they had.

It was April. Bass was twenty-two and awake one night when everyone else was asleep. He was thinking how, soon, in July, he'd be twenty-three. He didn't remember why he woke or for how long he'd been awake, only that he'd been awake long enough for his eyes to have adjusted to the dark and for him to see the seams of the cabin—stars and moon filtering in between the logs in long slivers of gray and silver and blue, like a cage of light. He didn't know how late or early it was when he felt the ground vibrate, as if being pelted by hail. A gradual drumming thunder that grew like an approaching galloping horse.

He rose up in the corn of his bed, and above the musical breathing of his friends and family, he heard with certainty a horse blowing and stamping almost at the door. From habit, Bass looked in the direction of the door's knothole, obscured with cloth, and stared, frozen.

When the horse's hooves scratched at the door, Bass ran to open it.

Master George sat atop his horse, and he was erect and calm like his horse.

"Yes, Master George?"

"Get dressed and meet me at the stable. We're going hunting. And don't call me Master George. I'm Master Reeves to you now. You're mine now, get it?"

"Yes, sir, Master," Bass said, waiting for him to take off so that he could take off himself.

"Are you stupid, boy?" Master George demanded. "What are you waiting for? I said get dressed and meet me at the stable."

"Yes, sir, yes, sir," Bass said, scrambling away inside. All but the youngest of children were now awake and asking questions. "Going hunting with Master George all I know," he said, his fingers fumbling, feeling too big in a hurry to manipulate the buttons on his shirt.

"Master Reeves ain't going?" Pearlalee asked.

"No, ma'am," he said. "Don't reckon so. Master George said I was his today."

"You do exactly what that Master George say."

"He want me to call him Master Reeves today," he said, tucking his shirttail into his pants.

"Then that be what you do."

"Yes'm," he said.

"You can't trust that man for nothing," Auntie Totty said.

Bass leaned low and kissed his mother, then stepped on to the bed beside hers and stopped to kiss his auntie. "I don't," he told her.

At the stable, he found Master Reeves waiting for him also, standing beside his son, who held two rifles.

"I'm sorry to have to lose you, Bass," Master Reeves said, "but I believe your service is needed more with George during these troubled times. Y'all go hunting today; get to know each other and trust each other. And when you come back, I want you to pack your things and go with him to Texas. And wherever he goes in war, you serve him and protect him as I know you know how, all right?"

Bass stared at his mustache, refusing to feel anything at all, anything at all. Nothing at all. "Yes, sir, Master Reeves."

"No, n——, I told you, *I'm* Master Reeves."

"He can call us both that, you don't think?"

"That's ludicrous!"

"Yes, sir, Master Reeves," Bass said, nodding to neither of them now, just nodding to nod, already turning to his horse, or the horse he'd grown to believe was his. Strawberry, the n——'s sorrel.

Strawberry nickered before Bass could reach out good to lay a hand on his nose so that he wouldn't nicker—his whiskers trembling from hot breath. His eyes as big, Bass thought for the first time, as the black marble eggs that sat in a wire basket on the mistress's dining room table, which his mother had to move out of the way before each meal and polish each night. Bass stroked Strawberry's nose as if to calm him for the bridle and looked into those eyes once more as if he wouldn't ever again.

◆ ◆ ◆

Master Reeves spurred his Morgan from the stable in an unseemly manner, kicking up dust all over Bass and Strawberry, which Master Reeves, the other Master Reeves, most certainly would not have done. Bass waited for the air to clear, then followed, loaded with the provisions and supplies, everything but the rifles. The sorrel was taller than the Morgan by three hands and made longer strides, despite the added weight, so every so often Master Reeves had to jog ahead a bit to stay out of the way.

Every so often, too, not at every crossroads but at some, Master Reeves would turn back in his saddle to see which direction Bass would point him in, whether this way or yonder way. It would've been a whole lot easier, it seemed to Bass, if Master Reeves simply let him lead from the front. And when Master Reeves spoke, Bass could hear him better. Sometimes Bass said, "Yes, sir, Master," without a clue why.

Not long after dawn three white men appeared on horseback, creeping down a slope in their direction so slowly, as if they were sitting on limbs of distant trees and not horses, as if the horses hauled a wagon each, but nothing of the such followed. One of the men, the smallest but with the biggest hat and wearing a vest, asked Master Reeves where he was headed, where he was from—the questions of patrollers, not slave traders, and a posse would have shown a badge. They eyed Bass but didn't speak to him.

The padded sounds of breathing and feet tamping in the shadows behind the horses drew Bass's attention—a Negro man with shaggy gray hair, stooped and bloodied in tattered clothes, swayed on legs paled with mud. A rope bound the old man's arms to his chest and his chest to the saddle horn in the hands of the smallest man, who did the talking, fifteen or so feet away.

It wasn't his business to injure the old man's pride any further, being caught, a runaway with a bounty, but Bass allowed his eyes to trail back to the old man, and he caught sight of him looking back. Bass blinked, trying to make out his face, if the old man was someone he knew. He blinked again, and the old man's eyes continued to shimmer in the scant light with prolonged helplessness, as if he was just too tired to blink or simply saw no point to it. Flies lit on the old man's shoulders and lips, lit and unlit, a constant flourish.

Bass averted his eyes straight ahead, at the hindquarters of the Morgan, and prayed the old man's master wouldn't abuse him any further, simply because he was old and torn and broke-looking from being dragged for miles.

"So how can I help you, gentlemen?" Master Reeves said with a bluster.

Bass realized he hadn't been paying close enough attention.

The smallest patroller, the talker, curled forward almost into a ball and squinted. "You ain't one of them Kansas jayhawkers, is you?"

His company laughed, but the talker remained quiet and still and rounded over. "You got papers on yourn?"

Master Reeves snickered, and the two patrollers laughed again. "I don't blame you for being suspicious," Master Reeves said. "It's the best of times, indeed, because you and I still wield the power of repression—the only lasting philosophy, regardless of what some John Bull like Charles Dickens desires to behold as true, am I right? But it is, yes, the worst of times, when n——s and upstanding citizens alike are stopped for paperwork, you bet, men. So, please, allow me to dip in here," he said, moving cautiously to unbuckle a saddlebag, "and show you a few papers about *my* identity. Fuck the big n——'s identity. Let's talk about mine, gentlemen."

Bass slipped his shoes from the stirrups in case he should need to drop down any moment and hightail it for cover, but shoulders up, he didn't budge. Didn't need to to plainly see that Master Reeves had produced a roll of papers, but instead of handing it over, he clutched it like a torch. The patrollers twitched, maybe to touch their guns, but not to raise or cock them yet.

"I'm George Robertson Reeves, a member of the Texas House of Representatives, Grayson County, and son of William Steele Reeves, retired member of not only the Tennessee House of Representatives but also, more recently, more pertinent to you, at least should be, the Arkansas House of Representatives, Crawford County, and that man operates a little plantation down the road in Van Buren. Maybe you've heard of it. It ain't too damn far from here if you know your way around. So go there if you wish to be the Good Samaritan. Inquire from the actual source if Mr. William Steele Reeves himself considers his slave, Bass Reeves, to be a fugitive—you know, the one he has given on loan to his son and is actually, lo and behold, accompanied by his very son even as we speak and dispute. Or you can press your luck right now, gentlemen, if you so choose to delay me any further on my righteous action of taking said slave on a goddamn hunting expedition. This is a free country still, is it not?"

The main patroller stiffened in his saddle as if both to draw away from Master Reeves and to make himself appear taller. "Free so long as we out here doing our part," he said. "Just see to it you keep hitched what should be, hear?" He tipped backward, with his feet raised, like a boy in a swing, then drove his heels down fast to spur his horse.

The other two patrollers laughed with anticipation, twisting in their saddles to watch what their small friend was temporarily leaving behind. The rope whipped the air in the quick motion of hummingbirds, and Bass saw nothing else of the old man than this—just him taking flight, with his pale muddied legs and the pale soles of his feet sailing and dissolving into the dust cloud of the horse, further hidden now by the two patrollers galloping to catch up.

Later in the morning, hunters also passed them by on the road. They spoke to Master Reeves but did not stop. And a stench of death trailed behind the muddied wagons piled with deer, hog, beaver, and bear like a long rope, thought Bass, that dragged the ground.

Bass would've chosen to work for Master Reeves, the other Master Reeves, all his life over anybody else in this world. He'd finally allowed himself to think that all the way through. And if freed, he would've chosen to live close to the plantation, to see his family but also to still see Master Reeves come and go and even shoot with him if he wanted. But to be given away like a word to somebody, like a peach, on loan or not—what was the difference? Eventually, every time, whether heated up mad or sad, he had to change the subject to no subject at all—to the Morgan's shorter, softer stride. A constant catching up and falling behind, over and over. Just that. Or the sun blooming off the Boston Mountains like an oxeye daisy, if God could be a daisy—and why couldn't he? God saying to Bass in his flower speak, *Don't forget I don't forget.*

Petals fell into the tree cover, and then they were there under it, Master Reeves and then Bass, at the brow of the White River, sparkling like ice. Where Bass had always come to pitch camp with Master Reeves—the other Master Reeves. The best campsite to sit high enough above spring floods yet near enough to them, the best hunting grounds for you name it.

It'd be easier not to believe in God, believed Bass. Not to believe in God, he could pull Master Reeves off his saddle right here right now right quick and strangle him, weigh him down in the river with easy-as-you-please stones, then blaze his way northward for Kansas, shooting dead every white man who crossed eyes at him. All of that would be a whole lot easier than this. This fear in place of nothing. But wouldn't his mama and auntie and grandmammy and granddaddy Sugar be proud of him for the magic of keeping his fear buried deep and safe inside him like a tater?

At the bank in a lacy patch of white pussytoes, Master Reeves dismounted and stretched himself as the Morgan, blowing, almost purring at the tiny, fuzzy-headed blooms, nosed closer to the river for a drink. Bass walked Strawberry close but not too close to Master Reeves, a little off into a tighter spot between tupelos, and dismounted.

"Boy, what are you up to?"

Bass whipped his head in his direction, wondering what he could've done wrong. "Master?"

"Are you so fatigued by your own laziness that you think I'll stand by and let you nominate yourself master over me?"

"No, sir, Master Reeves, I ain't tired," Bass said. "Not atall."

Master Reeves took off his hat and wiped a kerchief across his forehead as he trod toward Bass, his boots sinking in softness.

"Then why are you planting yourself upriver of me?"

"This my usual place, sir."

"Your usual place, is it? My father let you go north of him?"

"Well, yes, sir, *here* he did."

Master Reeves smiled and balled the kerchief in his fist. "The chick that's in him pecks the shell."

"Sir?"

"*Moby-Dick*. You haven't read it yet?" He stared at Bass. He started to say more but paused with his jaw lowered, which made his mustache stand out darker and thicker and sharper, the ends angled down, and together with the strip of hair growing from his bottom lip past his chin, Master Reeves appeared to have a spearhead mounted on his face. The tip of it pointed to his nose, as if to say he smelled the musk of everything, that he belonged to this forest. And then it vanished as he spoke: "N——, you know what I'm asking you. Don't play dumb with me."

Bass feared maybe he was dumb. He believed that if he said what was on his mind, he'd be answering a totally different question.

"Are you declaring allegiance to the North by going upstream of me?"

"Oh, no, sir, Master," Bass said. "I just don't cotton to no spot so thick with stick." Bass pointed to the pussytoes. "Like stepping on spiderwebs."

Master Reeves grinned. "Bass, are you scared of spiders? A big n—— like you?"

"No, sir, ain't scared a no spiders. Just don't cotton to no stick."

"I reckon you don't cotton to cotton then."

"No, sir, don't much cotton to no cotton."

"A lot of work, cotton," Master Reeves said.

"Don't mind work, Master," Bass said.

"Don't mind work, huh? Then why are you lollygagging along, boy? Move your black ass downstream of me this very damn instant."

"Master Reeves," Bass said, rapidly nodding his head the way he'd gotten in the habit of doing when the circuit preacher came out to the plantation and gave a Sunday service in the quarters. Bass would stand in the back, along a wall, and listen with his eyes closed, nodding to the rhythm of what he heard. But that was all in the past now. Now his eyes were open and aimed at those pussytoes up under Master Reeves's boots.

"Don't be begging me. Are you having a conniption? You want the whip?"

"Master Reeves," Bass repeated, not meaning to.

Master Reeves laughed but wasn't happy. "I may have to give you back. You think that's what you want, but it ain't what you want, boy, I promise you. You won't go back pretty."

"Master Reeves, sir," Bass said, still nodding, praying God smelled his fear and felt it knotted up in his belly the way Bass felt it. He watched Master Reeves tuck his kerchief back in his pocket and set his hat back on his head. He watched him open his coat, as if Master Reeves might have a whip tucked into his pants, but he didn't have anything of the kind, as if he was showing Bass he had nothing, that there was nothing to fear, n——, so go ahead, as if Master Reeves finally smelled his fear, too, and was saying nothing to give him room to talk, as if he was waiting, praying, too, that this would end, that they could go on back to the peaceful world of earlier. So Bass nudged himself to go on and step up to the words, to go on and speak. "I think, sir," he finally heard himself saying, "I think I recall Master Reeves, the other Master Reeves, your daddy, sir—"

"Get on with it, for heaven's sake!"

"I think I remember him saying it flow backwards, the White River, sir. Towards north way, like the Nile do, like they was maybe the only two."

"Like the *Nile*?" Master Reeves turned to the clear open space of the river and strode closer to it.

Bass began to wonder what Master Reeves could have been thinking or seeing or even smelling after standing there for so long at the edge, his back to Bass, staring off at the wide road of silver water sliding slowly up.

It's some world when a n—— ain't as free as a ant or a frog or a butterfly, who can all find their way north to the tupelos to get away from the stick of pussytoes without having to explain why or risk being whipped or dragged or sold or given away or killed. That was what Bass wished Master Reeves was thinking or seeing or smelling.

"Yep," Master Reeves said, turning to face Bass with a face surprisingly at ease, more like his father's than his own, "that's a beautiful river. I've been away for too long. Let's enjoy this respite, Bass. My father is a wise man. Let's learn to trust each other, you and me, and have a high time on the fat of this land. Then when we get to Texas, you need not ever say 'I think' this and 'I think' that in front of the other slaves, or I will splay you open like a clam. Oh, you'll be bleeding like a pig, but you'll look like a fucking clam. If you have thoughts, I recommend you pretend you don't."

"Yes, sir, Master," Bass said, suddenly flushed with exhaustion. He told himself to get used to this crazy man. He was crazy and always would be.

"You see," Master Reeves said, "my slaves know about Ralph Waldo Emerson. That's right, I read or recite to them sometimes. To give them a glimpse into that vast realm of all they do not know. Do *you*, Bass, know about Ralph Waldo Emerson?"

Bass shook his head and lowered his eyes as Master Reeves inched his way from the river.

"He's a Massachusetts preacher and philosopher. An abolitionist. You know what an abolitionist is, don't you, Bass?"

Bass nodded.

"'So far as a man thinks, he is free.' That's what he says. Let that sink in. 'So far as a man thinks, he is free.' So just by thinking, Bass, you make yourself free. Now, I can't keep you from thinking, not completely, but I can damn sure slow it down. And if you go around bragging about it, I'll have to take issue with you, understand?"

"Understand, Master," Bass said.

"And do you know what else Emerson says?"

"No, sir. Something about ice?"

"Ice? What the fuck?"

"Master Reeves, the other Master Reeves, your daddy, he buys his ice, he told me, from Master Chuchess."

Master Reeves looked away and bared teeth as he lifted his top lip. "No, you'll like this better than anything about ice, because it's about you, boy, about all slaves. He's an abolitionist, my natural adversary, right? Oh, the fun of learning what my adversaries believe! But he's your natural ally, remember. So it's important to you, too, what Emerson says, and he says, 'Nothing is more disgusting than the crowing about liberty by slaves, as most men are.'" He reached out and patted Bass on the arm, but hardly a hand, hardly any strength behind it, not the strength of God that Bass had behind his own, and something like that, which made no sense, could startle him. "Most men are slaves because they have no thoughts, are helpless, which is why we thinking men put y'all to work," Master Reeves said. "Well, you aren't helpless or thoughtless, or you'd be working a field, so that makes you freer than a lot of white men who work fields. That's part of what he's saying. The other part is he wants you to stop crowing, boy. You don't need the North, and they're tired of you believing you need them. Which means they're tired of helping, too. You want liberty, or more liberty than what you have, then think more." He raised his hand up to Bass's head and, with a fingertip, drummed his temple, making Bass blink. "Use your damn head more. This thing," he said, repeatedly drumming. "But by God, Bass, you better keep that shit to yourself. You do that, and I'll let you be free. My gift to you."

"Why, thank you, Master," Bass said. "Thank you, sir. Thank you, thank you, sir." His palms drained sweat to hear himself pronouncing every syllable Sugar sweet, precisely how his grandfather had taught him and how Bass had never wanted to sound, and like magic, Master Reeves at last, satisfied, stopped drumming Bass's temple and stepped away.

Bass leaned back against Strawberry's flank to catch his breath before unloading the supplies to make camp and watched Master Reeves tramp back through the pussytoes. The sorrel twitched, so Bass twitched with him. And he began to think on that, how one thing can start another thing into doing the same thing and taking no thought at all, how that wasn't freedom. But what was it?

7

The Wallows

By late morning, camp was made, including a fire Bass had built from dead tree limbs and old bird nests he'd climbed up and found in the pin oaks just upstream of the tupelos. Master Reeves sat nearby on the bank, his back against a rock, with his boots and socks off, smoking a corncob pipe and reading a red leather-bound book no wider than his hands. Sometimes he looked up from the book as if to watch his pipe smoke vanish over the water, and sometimes he read aloud, as if intending Bass to mull over those words with him. Those beautiful sounds strung together to form inexplicable thoughts—"Smote the mighty Mishe-Mokwa," "Lest from out the jaws of Nahma," "Minnehaha, Laughing Water."

Master Reeves, the other Master Reeves, had read passages to him from the Bible and had always kindly explained whatever he'd read, but only the Bible. Nothing by someone alive who walked the earth like anybody else. It made Bass reconsider this Master Reeves's gift of permission. This Master Reeves might explain a thing, but usually he wouldn't. He preferred to let thoughts bang against Bass's head like birds blind to window glass, which could very well be the best way and worst way both to look at freedom.

Once the flames had latched onto the wood and could be trusted to seethe into coals for a later roast, Bass led Master Reeves downstream to the wallows. Like on the road, Master Reeves insisted on following in front with the rifles and knives and being humbly told with a grunt or hand motion to turn at the trees rubbed hog high nearly barkless and smeared with mud, to squeeze there into that thicket and follow the hog path underneath that way.

Before crawling out of the thicket, Master Reeves leaned in and whispered pipe breath into Bass's face. "How close are we?"

"Close, Master." He guessed his was just plain n—— breath.

Master Reeves pinched his eyes tight like the tight spot they were in. "Don't you dare shoot if I'm in front of you."

"Oh, no, Master."

"Don't shoot scared. Shoot smart."

"Yes, Master." He nodded and looked lower down at the cloven hoofprints in the mud.

"I can't get through there with both hands full."

"No, sir, not good to."

Master Reeves cradled the rifles in the crook of an arm while he reached inside his jacket and untied the buckskin straps from one of the knife sheaths hanging at his hips. Once Bass had knotted the belt around his own waist, Master Reeves gave him the older of the two Sharps breechloaders, along with a handful of spare cartridges and tape primer from his jacket pocket, and pulled Bass in by the shoulder to speak directly into his ear. "Till I see with my own eyes you can shoot straight, you're going first."

Bass nodded, and when Master Reeves let go of his shoulder, Bass dropped to his knees and elbows and held still for a moment, listening. The hogs may have been close but not close enough to be heard above the twittering and fluttering of finches scattering all about, so he stretched to put the rifle through and crawled out of the thicket, looking for sorrel-brown humps. There were more tree trunks rubbed down with mud but no razorbacks in sight. The path sloped to lower, wetter ground, and though the nearest wallow appeared empty, there were other wallows beyond farther thickets. He hoped their talk hadn't alerted the hogs to hide.

Bass waited and helped Master Reeves to his feet before striking out with his rifle raised. He crept to the first wallow from its grassier side, away from its slide of entry, in case a boar sat too deep to be seen and charged out. A veil of mosquitoes hung over it, smelling of fresh shit and buzzing with flies. But there was no hog, not here, not yet.

He continued following the hog path around a meadow completely rooted up as if turned over by man, mule, and plow. He pointed it out for Master Reeves to observe and figure on his own what it could possibly mean. Hearing snorting ahead, Bass stopped and listened to the wallows coming up around the next thicket. It was the range of sound that had stopped him, from low to high, long to short. Like the finches, an impossible number. With the other Master Reeves, the most they'd ever found here at one time was four or five. He motioned ahead, and this Master Reeves nodded—his eyes round and intense.

Bass moved on but slower, nearing the thicket of crabapple trees, which had stopped blooming over the years and had become thickly latticed with honeysuckle vine. It made a good stand from which to shoot the hogs at the wallows, but it was much denser and sweeter than he ever recalled. Reminding him that he missed his mother, remembering her how his father must have, since for his return on holidays she plaited verbena in her hair or wore gardenia or rosebud necklaces.

He tried to peek through the vine to make sure a razorback wasn't inside but couldn't find a break, so he skirted the edge until the wallows came into view, with a dozen or more razorbacks lounging and snorting in the mudholes or sunning beside them in fat rows. A half dozen more rooted in the meadow penned between two creeks, while a striped litter played. Like a plantation of them.

Master Reeves stepped past Bass and leveled his carbine toward the wallows. Bass prayed Master Reeves knew better than to shoot one actually in a wallow. He watched Master Reeves line up the sight and shift his aim, as if he couldn't decide which hog suited him best, until finally he appeared to settle on one and eased his hammer back until it clicked into place.

As if in response to that click, from the thicket behind them, a growl rose so low and deep and sustained, it vibrated the ground—that first—before the air and the hair bristling up Bass's neck.

"Watch it," Bass said, turning his rifle on the thicket and drawing his hammer back.

"What is it?" Master Reeves asked. "What's in there?"

The ground vibrated again, but from the hogs fleeing the wallows for wooded underbrush and the meadow for the creeks. They squealed and thrashed as if they'd all been gutted and were dying, and the dog or bear inside the thicket growled again, somehow even louder and wetter than before.

"See if you can't see what it is," Master Reeves said.

Bass didn't want to move. It made sense—he was safer not moving.

"Boy?"

Bass reached for the knife at his waist and slid it from its sheath. He'd never hunted with a weapon in each hand, but it made sense. He leaned closer to the honeysuckle without moving his feet, but he wasn't close enough to see through the vines and leaves and blossoms. Reluctantly, he stepped closer. Nothing rustled, nothing growled, so he craned his neck and touched his nose to the blossoms but could still see nothing. He stepped aside to try another spot, and though he couldn't see a razorback inside the thicket, he knew now that was what it was, popping its teeth.

"My God, Bass, is that a damn woodpecker?"

The popping stopped. And in a hot breath a razorback burst through the honeysuckle, bigger than three of Bass, the size of a bull, charging and blowing and swinging its long head at Bass to catch him with its cutters. Bass leaped back and jabbed the knife into its neck, and Master Reeves cracked a shot at it.

Bass sat up and watched the hog overrun them, raging away and bucking with the knife still stuck in its neck and shot who knows where. Master Reeves was on his feet and scrambling to reload his smoking rifle, and the hog turned in a spin of dust, popping its teeth and snorting, recharging.

"Watch it. He coming back," Bass said. He wheeled his rifle around, trying to fix an aim. The hog didn't even have a snout on it, just teeth and jaws and slobber bubbling out from where a nose should have been and rocking its ugly head—rocking, ears to eyes, rocking, ears to eyes. It was almost now to Master Reeves, struggling with his primer, when Bass fired.

Master Reeves hollered out Bass's name and dropped his rifle as the hog plowed into him, knocking him flat on his back. The hog's dead weight pinned his legs down, while its motionless, snoutless head settled on his stomach.

"You all right, Master?"

Master Reeves groaned and produced his knife and stabbed the hog in its neck and shoulders. "Bass! Bass!" he called, continuing to stab at it. "Help me get this fucking thing off me, Bass! Bass!"

"Yes, sir, Master. I'm coming."

"Bass!"

"I think you got him now," Bass said, proud after all to have permission for the thoughts he was having. He walked over, and Master Reeves quit with the stabbing but pointlessly squirmed.

Bass admired the bloody entry mark of his cartridge, between the hog's ear and eye. He leaned to pull out his knife but paused to scrutinize the hog's gaping wound where a snout sure should've been, its skin blackened along the edges. He felt around its nose cavity and looked at his fingertips. No blood at all. And he could see no puncture scars from bites, not in it or in the hair close by. As if the razorback had lost its nose to frostbite as a poor runt of a piglet so long, long ago.

"Bass," Master Reeves struggled to say, getting bright red in the face.

"Yes, sir," Bass said. "You got him good. A big'un. Now, let me see if I can't help you haul his carcass off a you."

8

Friends

Master Reeves mostly smoked his pipe and silently read his red book. Only momentarily did he look up to watch Bass fight the ground as if his feet were meaning to plow the ground and not simply trying to find good leverage to drag that hog over a countryside of snags and slopes. With one end of the rope tied around its hind legs and the other held in his fists, the in-between part cut into his shoulder meat, as if Bass were part of the hog and being carved.

Through every step of that hog haul, Bass thought about how that poor old man from that morning had been jerked away behind the patrollers, into the dust of their horses. How that man had waited too long to escape, had put off and put off the way people will put off anything and now found himself too old to do it right.

When Bass finally reached the campsite, Master Reeves instantly took a seat by the river, as if it was his river, with his boots off and feet dipped in. Only occasionally did he give Bass a glance while Bass hoisted the hog up one of the tupelos that leaned over the river, while he gutted the hog and drained it in the water, or even after he lowered the hog into the river and rinsed it.

Master Reeves never bothered to read one passage out loud from his book, as if he knew Bass wanted the distraction, would have enjoyed hearing some word music with that heavenly sunlight soaking up so much blood. Bass dragged the hog onto the firepit, only embers at that point, which was perfect. Then he covered it up with a solid bed of packed earth to lock up the heat.

Bass sat back to catch his breath, and Master Reeves asked him if he was done.

"No, sir."

"I didn't think so." Master Reeves looked at his book and turned a page.

Bass got moving again and built a fire on top of the dirt, to have heat on both sides of the hog.

"We need something in the meantime," Master Reeves said.

"Yes, sir," Bass said. "I kept out the small chitlins for fish bait."

"I see," Master Reeves said without looking away from his book.

"I like the bass here. The bass real tasty, and they'll chase that link a gut like it's a baby snake. You like bass, Master?"

"Then the old man's tongue was speechless," Master Reeves said, reading as if he was just talking:

And the air grew warm and pleasant,
And upon the wigwam sweetly
Sang the bluebird and the robin,
And the stream began to murmur,
And a scent of growing grasses
Through the lodge was gently wafted.

Master Reeves paused as if waiting for Bass to reply, though his eyes lingered on the page as if he might keep reading. Bass didn't know what to do. Master Reeves turned the page and continued to read inside to himself, Bass could only figure, so Bass got up and went to his saddlebag for the spool of horsehair fishing line and hooks that Master Reeves, the other Master Reeves, the father, had given him for the trip. What Bass had always caught here on the White River was bass. His grandfather had taught him how to fish without a pole, holding the spool in one hand and leading the line out with the other. Better to feel the currents and then the fish, the little differences. Master Reeves, the other one, had always sat back smiling as if Bass or Ole Bass was doing it wrong, when the truth of how it looked was Master Reeves didn't know how to do it that way and wished he could but was too afraid to cut his soft white hands, and it probably would've.

When Bass stepped up to the river and tossed his hook of hog gut, he wasn't surprised when this Master Reeves turned from his book to see what else was around him he could claim was his.

Within minutes, Bass caught a striper almost as long as his forearm and threw it on the bank behind him.

"By the shore of Gitche Gumee!" Master Reeves sang.

"How many you hungry for, Master?"

"I don't know. I'm hungry. How many can you eat?"

"Oh," Bass said, loading a new link of gut onto the hook, "I expect three if that be fine with you."

"Four for me then," Master Reeves said.

"Yes, sir," Bass said, almost a whisper, tossing his hook. "Take me minute or two."

♦ ♦ ♦

That night, while eating pan-fried bass, Master Reeves rose up on bare feet and scuttled to his tent as if this were his first attempt to walk, as if he were walking over that hog's bed of coals. At his tent, he wiped his hands on his trousers and leaned down, then returned to his plate by the fire with a full bottle. "Can you handle your whiskey, Bass?"

Bass shrugged.

"Don't bullshit me, boy."

"Oh, no, sir. I dipped my lip in it once, sure enough, long time ago, but that was all. Don't know if I can handle it or not."

Master Reeves reached for Bass's cup, slung out the water, and poured it halfway with whiskey. "Bass, I'm a captain in the Eleventh Texas Cavalry, did you know that?"

Bass shook his head. "Thank you, Master," he said, accepting the cup.

"Bill Young and I formed the cavalry in my own study, in fact. What this means for you, Bass, is that I'm an officer who must watch after his men. I will need someone watching after me while I do that. Make sense?"

"Yes, sir."

"That was some action today with that razorback, but we're about to see a whole lot worse."

Bass raised the cup level with his mouth so that he could smell the whiskey. It smelled how he remembered, and his head shook uncontrollably from revulsion.

Master Reeves smirked into his mustache as he poured whiskey into his own cup. "Bass, this won't be like the disordered Mexicans in our little skirmish in Texas. This will be hell." He set the bottle down, then raised the cup to his mouth, eyeing Bass over the rim, and sipped it calmly.

"That's how you need to do it eventually, but for now, just kick it. That's the only way at first. In one quick swallow."

Bass touched his lip to the cup.

"It's not water, boy. You can't dip your toe in it. It's whiskey, from rye. So be like a horse and kick it. Kick it, boy."

Bass told himself, *N——, now you is ordered*, so he squeezed his eyes shut and kicked it.

"Nothing to it, right?"

Bass tried to smile but coughed from the burn in his throat.

Master Reeves laughed. "Next, I'm teaching you how to play poker. You can't serve gentlemen properly without knowing how to be one, can you?" He stretched his arm and tipped the bottle over Bass's cup until it made swallow sounds down the bottle's neck better than Bass could. "Let's see one more try at it."

Bass took a deep breath and kicked it like he ought, but he coughed faster too. Master Reeves laughed again. But this time his laughter was longer, deeper, like real laughter, and that made Bass laugh with him, as if for the moment he'd forgotten they weren't friends.

◆ ◆ ◆

Four days after dragging that snoutless boar clear from the wallows to the pussytoes, his shoulders were still stove, as though they'd never forget. Not easy to the touch but nagging some for sure, even now in the saddle while doing nothing, just riding Strawberry back to the plantation.

If the white men they passed on the road south to Van Buren could smell under clothes and skin and perceive that Bass's belly was still packed tight like a hog in a pit from all the savory pork he'd been feasting on for three straight days, they would surely want to string him up a tree like he'd strung that snoutless hog. For that reason alone. For eating like a hog and a master both, which was clearly better than how they ate who weren't masters, those hang-dog men with engraved crow's feet and matted hair who refused to acknowledge him directly because he rode in his master's shadow. Because you didn't covet your neighbor's slave in the presence of his master. Only if he escaped and was caught, would you.

Whenever he'd hunted with the other Master Reeves, they killed no more than what they could eat or carry back, but this Master Reeves didn't want to be bothered with carrying meat back. "We're done with hunting, I do believe," Master Reeves had said their second morning after Bass had unburied the hog and cut back its crack-ling to expose the hams. Master Reeves declared the right ham was his, that in fact the whole right side was his, and that the left side, where the hog's heart had been, was Bass's.

Once they'd filled up on right ham and left ham, Master Reeves passed a rifle to him. "From now on," he said, "why don't we just kill. Practice killing."

So they trekked back to the wallows and killed what they saw as quickly as they saw it, leaving the hogs scattered, either dead or off squealing to other places. So Bass and Master Reeves went to other places, too, and shot squirrels and birds and deer, leaving a trail of carcasses through the mountains. For two more days they ate pork and shot what they could. Sometimes Master Reeves watched Bass shoot, not asking anything but watching, then later tried his best to duplicate the accuracy, not coming close.

At night they ate some more and sipped whiskey, or kicked it, while smoking and cleaning guns or playing poker. Bass almost managed to relax at times but never when holding face cards, not with white faces in his hands so much like the master's. And no mat-ter how much he hid or guarded his cards, even closing them over themselves, Master Reeves always knew somehow who was there. Sometimes, in the absence of these activities, Bass gnawed a hog ear and stared at the sky, thinking how nice it would be to have an unlimited supply of diamonds, or hearts for that matter. Sometimes Master Reeves opened his book randomly and would say, "Do you know what 'derision' means?" "What about 'splendor'? 'Plumage'?" Sometimes Master Reeves explained the word, and when he did, Bass was grateful, repeating the word and its meaning over and over in his sleepy mind to make it stick.

These moments of odd leisure with Master Reeves culminated in an elongated contemplation on the meaning of the word "gift," which began in the mountains but did not end even on their ride back to the plantation. There was the gift he had of shooting a gun straight. The gift of life itself. The gift of Jesus that God gave all people. The gift you got in a name passed down. The gift that he himself had become from one Master Reeves to another, and of course, the gift of freedom—both the thinking kind and the being kind. Yet here he was, after all his contemplation, arriving at the closest sense of home he'd ever had, and for the last time, and he was bearing nothing for anyone, not even rib bones for a wind chime.

Strawberry began to prance in the ruts of the road before Master Reeves turned his Morgan down the lane toward the big house. Bass felt buoyed too, until he noticed he didn't hear song from the fields or hammering from the blacksmith shop. The only movement he saw was the slow sway of treetops. The porch rails weren't even hung with rugs after a beating. The air smelled like home, somewhere in the blend of mimosas, cotton blooms, and river silt, but he feared a trick.

Master Reeves dismounted at the porch, and Bass rode up and dismounted in a flurry to collect both reins while Master Reeves collected the rifles and the knives and the ammunition pouches, which swung behind him like memories, as though they had no weight at all. Master Reeves turned as though he might speak how he spoke eye to eye to Bass in the mountains, but he turned away again in a flourish, taking the porch steps first before turning once again to look down at him. "See to it the horses are refreshed. Cool them off good; then get your things together and meet me back here in, oh," he said, glancing at the sky as if he'd been sick in bed for a week and hadn't a clue what part of the day it was, "about an hour. That's long enough, don't you think?"

"Sir?" Bass said, but was quick to revise himself, saying, "I expect so, Master." But he was bottled up with a sea of misery. He'd assumed all along he'd at least have until tomorrow. Could stay up all night talking with his mother and auntie and have breakfast before sunup like old times with his grandparents in their cabin. He could go off somewhat prepared then.

"I've got a real dolt of a slave at home who'll be pleading for a whipping by the time we get back. You'll see. So hour at the latest." Master Reeves lifted his eyebrows. "I've got goodbyes to say to my family now, so you run along."

Master Reeves stomped his boots on the porch, and dried mud scattered. He opened the door and shut it behind him, his pouches really swinging.

◆ ◆ ◆

Bass led the horses to the stable, removed their tack, and brushed them to a calm. They were cool enough that they could eat now, so he filled the troughs, then bolted outside for the quarters. He didn't even have an hour. Didn't Bass have goodbyes to say? Didn't he?

Too many birds along the path exploded like dandelions from his advance. Beyond the silenced mill in the distance, a departing steamboat blew its whistle, and it occurred to him what Master Reeves, the other Master Reeves, had said about Strawberry without saying it—back before the hunting trip, in the stable, when Bass learned that Master Reeves, after all his years of taking, was actually a giver, and the worst kind of one. That night when Bass had learned that some giving was wrong enough to be evil. That night not long ago, but it seemed like it, being way over on the other side of that snoutless hog and these bum shoulders, before going up that road to the pussytoes and the wallows and back. When the giver had said Strawberry was going with him, with the taker. Bass would have Strawberry almost as his own. Bass wouldn't be left with nothing, even if he learned in just a moment that, after all, that was what he had.

A droning chorus of low vibrations emanated from the quarters, yet Bass still feared he had no family to speak of. That in his absence in the mountains, something had happened. Something he couldn't imagine. Yet above the stamp of his feet on the dirt path, the batted wings going away, the quarters hummed like a hive, as though it were Sunday.

Was today Sunday?

How could a man make another man forget what day it was?

From the darkness beyond the propped door, human shapes emerged—a turned shoulder, a clasped fan, lips, and licked teeth— and like the birds rising, sound rose, human laughter and chatter. "Praise the Lord, it's Bass!"

Although his panting quickened, his legs slowed from the sight of his mother rushing outside in her white Sunday dress, with baby rosebuds plaited in her hair. He had to accept the joy that surged as a weight and just stop his feet and let her come to his bend. "Gracious, you alive, Bass," Pearlalee said, pressing her rosebud plaits against his cheek.

When he opened his eyes again, he saw Auntie Totty standing behind her, waving a fan to her face as if to dry her eyes, and behind her, like peas from a pod, the entire plantation filed out of the quarters. A friend for every reason to have one. The pickers, the bucks, the dancers, the tricksters, the little ones, Uncle Moseley, and finally his grandmammy, coming up slowly with hands to cup his face, and Sugar, smiling bigger than anyone, smiling even with his swollen cheek and need to spit. Last was Preacher Zee from town, in his black tie, holding his black Bible high above him as a reminder of its heavenly purpose. He prayed for Bass, and hands reached for Bass from all sides, laid on his shoulders and arms and back and chest and head or laced with his own, their warm bodies hovering.

"Look after this fine young man to keep him strong in the fight to be your soldier of goodness, Lord, so he don't go escaping or killing and wind up ruined like so many other young Negro men."

"No, Lord," Bass pleaded amid louder Amens.

"Temptation will come like he's back in the garden. The snake will come, saying kill, strike, run, but please, Lord, do remember Bass is your obedient soldier. Hear our prayers to keep him safe and strong and good, through and through."

"No, don't listen to him, Lord," Bass begged, blind beneath their lattice and weeping to be disagreeing.

"And while he away, Lord, keep us safe and strong and good, too," Preacher Zee rang, as if he'd decided to rise up from the wrong path he was on to stand on high in the clouds where birds went, "so Bass won't need to worry none about us here and can march straight to heaven with us."

"That be right, Lord," Bass prayed. "Listen to that, Lord, please just that."

They held on, burying him with love, and he held on back while he could. But desperately, for once, he wanted to be free, and if he had to kill to be, for once he believed maybe he could do it.

PART TWO

EXODUS

9

The Sticks

Within a matter of a few hours, he realized he didn't have any idea where Texas was. He'd heard it was big and down from Arkansas, so he'd imagined that it stretched out below Arkansas like a parlor rug you couldn't miss stepping on, but Master Reeves took him more over than down, to the other side of Fort Smith and into Indian Territory, the way the other Master Reeves had taken him on his last turkey shoot in Seminole Nation. Master Reeves, the other one, had called the road a trail, the Butterfield Overland Trail, but he had quickly strayed from it to continue following the sunset into the flatland that split two rivers, while this Master Reeves kept following it, sliding deeper and deeper into the Choctaw Nation, toward a scraggly crop of mountains called the Sans Bois.

They slept that first night on the trail itself, because Master Reeves said the threat of Indians was too great off it. "It's why I usually ride straight through without stopping to rest," Master Reeves explained while watching Bass gather sticks for a fire to keep snakes and coyotes away. "They hate a white man and a n—— even worse, but we have fighting numbers at least." He gave Bass a rifle, and though Bass was glad to hold it and be trusted with it, the notion of a threat conflicted with his memory of the Negro Indians at the turkey shoot, who looked as comfortable in their skin as white men. Maybe the Choctaw were a hateful breed and nothing like the Seminoles, or maybe Master Reeves was full of mud.

They slept with their backs to each other. Or were supposed to. Master Reeves stretched out on his back and watched the direction they were going, while Bass kept an eye on where they'd been. Or another way of putting it, Master Reeves had the right side, and Bass the left.

It took Bass a while to figure out that right and left depended on how you positioned yourself. If he lay on his belly, it didn't matter if Master Reeves was on his back or not, and that messed up the master's plan good. Now they both in their own ways had the right side.

That was little consolation. Back or belly, he still faced his family at the plantation. As tired as he was, he hardly slept for seeing Master Reeves, the father, that final time. How Master Reeves, dressed and shaved on his neck for Sunday, gave Strawberry a pat on the hindquarters, telling Bass, "Be good." And that was how it closed between them. As if Bass wasn't good already. As if he wasn't owed more words than two. As if touching a horse that was touching a Negro was as close as a white man should ever come to touching a Negro in mixed company, with Mistress Reeves standing aside in the yard and crying into a lavender handkerchief beneath a lavender hat.

◆ ◆ ◆

Crossing the Red River proved much like crossing the Arkansas, another long, flat ferry roped and poled over big water between high banks. And so far, Texas looked a lot like Indian Territory. More land than town, only with more lowing from somewhere he couldn't see.

"Master?"

"What is it, boy?"

"I hear cattle but don't see none." He looked on all sides, through trees and down slopes as well as he could, but Master Reeves pointed up. Bass felt silly looking up in the sky, at the few clouds bumped up together like a clover leaf. "Sir?"

"That herd of steer you hear, their sound will rise up and bounce off the clouds." Master Reeves leveled his arm as if he were now pointing where the sun was setting ahead of them over a forest line. "The Texas Trail is on the other side of those blackjacks. You'll get used to it. At night sometimes you'll think you can't sleep if you can't hear them pass."

Master Reeves kept the rifles in their scabbards as though the blackjack forest was his too, along with the purplish air pocketing the path at every bend. After an hour, the air had turned darker, but that was about all that was different, until the trees finally opened up to a grassland, or what was once that. The grass thinned, and then midway the grassless ground sank into a hard-packed trail—a river bed for an overflowing river of dust drifting by from behind the herd, lowing now from the north.

"Need to make it quick in case another herd's coming," Master Reeves shouted, to be heard through the dust, and they galloped until the dust thinned and they were up on grass again and going into another blackjack forest.

After another hour of watching the moon slide forth, they found a road sparkling with lightning bugs, and that carried the men to an iron-rod gate that was hardly visible until Bass saw the gate match up with the moon with its loops of iron, like lassos, spelling what looked to him to be a sound, not a word: GRR. The lane on the other side of the gate and moon became a lane through pecan trees and then no trees, a yard, and a big white house even bigger than the big white house of the other Master Reeves, which Bass didn't know was possible. All the windows, which were even taller, were lit as if this Master Reeves had more lamps and candles too. The columns holding the roof up were so square Bass doubted he could reach around them and touch his fingers. It was the perfect home for the taker of all takers, with a staircase on each side of the second-floor balcony winding to the porch, like Master Reeves couldn't get out of bed and get to the ground fast enough each morning to take some more.

As Master Reeves rode past the front of the house, Bass saw that the columns didn't end there in the front but continued like a row of ivory dominoes all the way around the house to support even a back-porch balcony.

Master Reeves kept his Morgan straight on the lane as they passed the stable and a stand of trees that smelled like more blackjacks. He hadn't spoken since the trail.

A murmur rose out of the twisted limbs, sounding at first like people moaning from them. Bass looked up to see a cloud that stretched long into the distance, toward the trail. He shook his head at this place and watched an isolated cabin shut up with so much darkness creep into view. The size and shape of Bass's grandparents' cabin, it had no window either, and its door stood open like a welcome. Master Reeves dismounted, and Bass dismounted, becoming hopeful the cabin would be, like Strawberry, almost his.

Master Reeves pivoted and charged at Bass. "Did I say for you to get down yet and follow me?"

"Oh, no, sir," Bass said, reaching for his saddle to climb back up.

"Boy, when did I ever say for you to get back on it? You just stop moving."

"Yes, sir, Master. Sorry, Master." With his head tilted down, he only heard the footfalls on the cabin's porch boards before someone leaped and landed on the ground close to him. Bass didn't see anything about the person until the white man's whiteness was almost on him, dressed like a field slave, with no shirt, no shoes, and no socks even. Wearing only pants and a hat, so his white arms and torso appeared especially white, pale as a magnolia bulb.

"Evening, Mr. Reeves," the man said.

"Sean," Master Reeves said. The two shook hands. "Everything under control?"

"Yes, sir. Been a good week. Calm like you was here."

"Outstanding," Master Reeves said. "Well, this is the n—— I was telling you was coming."

The half-naked white man named Sean circled Bass. "A big n——, ain't he? You think the sticks strong enough?"

"Well, shit, Sean, you aren't too scared to shoot a big n—— if you hear those sticks snap, are you?"

A silence passed, and then the half-naked white man cackled.

"Come on, let's get going. I'm beat," Master Reeves said.

"You got it, Mr. Reeves." The half-naked white man turned away, leaped back onto the porch, and trotted inside the cabin.

Master Reeves eased up on Bass's flank and shot him an elbow. "Listen up, boy," he said. "This is Mr. Hagan, my overseer. Hell, *your* overseer. And for your own good, you better do what he says and instantly, like he's me, you hear?"

"Yes, sir, Master."

"Now, turn yourself about," Master Reeves said.

"Yes, sir," Bass said, turning and praying the Lord sat on that cloud above him, because he didn't want to give his back to Master Reeves and that overseer, not here with the lowing in his ears and that acidic smell of blackjacks swimming.

"Well?" Master Reeves said. "Don't you see the sticks yet? Go to them."

Bass looked deeply into the tree-cleared air, a blue space for something he couldn't figure, until he did find the posts, solid pine timbers, standing straight from the ground like smokestacks. He started walking and heard the overseer's feet sweeping through the weeds to join Master Reeves behind him.

"You don't unlock him until I come down in the morning," Master Reeves said.

"Course. I ain't a dumb n——. I won't move until you say."

Bass walked until he stood between the sticks, because it was the only logical place for him to stand. He could see the chains pegged at the middle and the bottom of each stick. He'd watched those mighty steamboats blowing steam up and down the Arkansas too many times. Every pair of smokestacks he'd ever seen were tethered together.

"You've never seen that, have you?" Master Reeves asked.

"Don't reckon so," Mr. Hagan said, striding up white as before but now with a whip and a pistol tucked into the waist of his pants. "Like a damn horse to water."

Bass watched the overseer shackle the chains to his right wrist and ankle before switching sides.

"Spread 'em," Mr. Hagan said, even though Bass had already forked his legs and arms wider than what seemed necessary, trying to help. Mr. Hagan tightened the slack of the wrist shackle by winding the chain around the stick before locking it. He did the same for the ankle shackle before standing up close to Bass, with breath smelling of hard-boiled eggs. "You comfortable?"

"No, sir," Bass said, "but I'll make do."

Master Reeves laughed. "Don't ask him anything unless you want the truth."

"Is that right?" Mr. Hagan leaned in closer to Bass, making him hungry. "You'd like to cut my throat, wouldn't you? N——s love to cut a throat."

"No, sir," Bass said. "I'm a Christian."

Mr. Hagan glinted teeth and snickered. "Yeah, you'll feel like one by morning."

"Give him a little water, Sean, and see to it the horses are looked after. I feel like walking up. Feel like stretching my legs all of a sudden."

"Yes, sir, sure will."

Master Reeves faded up the lane, whistling past the blackjacks, while Mr. Hagan steadily breathed. While the longhorns steadily lowed from the trail. Suddenly, Mr. Hagan shouted with spit, "Henry!" He shouted the name twice, and voices immediately went up yonder from the cabin, from where the quarters must have been, down the lane: "Where's Henry?" "Get Henry." "Calling you, Henry!"

An animal churning took to the lane, and interrupting the shadows was a boy with a small stride running lickety-click. Darker than the shadows and about ten. Wearing only pants himself.

"Henry, take these horses up, then fetch this new n—— here a sup of water."

"Yes, sir, Mr. Hagan." Henry collected the reins and walked the horses toward the stable.

Mr. Hagan gazed in Henry's direction long after he'd disappeared. He raised a hand to his chest and absently stroked it with his fingertips. His head rotated owllike to Bass, and he leaned back as if to let the moon's rays light up his white chest so as to show Bass how he liked his chest to be stroked. "That Henry's as good a n—— as a n—— can get, and honesty ain't no part of it." He lowered his hand to his waist and drew his pistol, aiming it at Bass. "Don't let me hear them chains rattling."

"No, sir."

Mr. Hagan strode away in slow, silent steps, vanishing into the darkness of his cabin.

Of course, Bass still had the longhorns to share his lonely company with.

And Henry, who emerged again, this time soundlessly, carrying a gourd of water. When he was close enough to raise it up, he whispered, "Is you the one they call Bass?"

Bass nodded.

"True you from Master's daddy's place?"

Bass nodded.

"True you knows how to shoot a gun?"

Bass nodded. "Don't nobody here?"

Henry looked back at the overseer's cabin, the doorway still a nothing-filled rectangle. "No n—— do," he said, lifting the gourd while Bass crouched to it. Henry waited until Bass's dry lips were bumped to it; then he lifted it up and back slowly for him so that none was lost. Not a spring water but a stream water that tasted of mushrooms.

"Run along, Henry," Mr. Hagan hollered from inside his cabin.

"Yes, sir!" Henry said. He ran to the cabin, set the gourd on the porch, and churned down the lane.

"I'm watching you," Mr. Hagan called.

"Yes, sir," Bass said.

"You can't see me, can you?"

"No, sir, can't see you." He leaned back until his weight pulled the slack from the chains and from the muscles in his arms. He had to sleep some. If he didn't sleep, he wouldn't keep his patience. There were too many good people in Arkansas praying for him to be better than he felt, and he would need a little rest. A little anyway. He watched the cabin doorway for movement, and when he saw none, he shut his eyes.

"What about now?" Mr. Hagan asked him. "Can you see me now?"

Bass could hear the distance in the voice well enough to know Mr. Hagan hadn't moved, or moved enough to worry himself with, so he let his eyelids stay down and tried instead to pull that calm in his eyelids all the way down through him, until he felt the ball joints in his arms unlock, getting comfortable. "No, sir," he said. "Not now neither."

"What about now?"

"No, sir. Be dark from here as a thousand midnight swamps."

"Then you remember that."

"Yes, sir."

"You hear me?"

"Yes, sir, I hear you. I hear you plain as day."

"But can you see me?"

Bass paused to play along, as if he was really straining his eyeballs. "Well, n——?"

Bass stirred. "No, sir. No, sir, not nary yet."

10

A Good One

By morning the longhorns had forged the river and could no longer be heard, with or without clouds. So went the tart smell of the blackjacks, as if having drifted off into Indian Territory after them. In their place, two Negro women sang low without words by a stream trickling somewhere across the clearing, inside those trees that stretched away like arms from Mr. Hagan's cabin. The women almost cooed to the clothes they wet and wrung.

Bass listened and breathed only, half rousing, half expecting to find Mr. Hagan standing in his face, waiting to see his eyes open first before he whipped him for shutting them for the night. He drew in a long breath through his nose to find out, and when he didn't smell hard-boiled eggs, he fluttered his eyes and absorbed the burn. Eventually, through the glare, the overseer's bony feet appeared across the clearing in the cabin doorway, stemming from a bed out of view.

Bass drew on the chains easy does it like, to right himself without waking Mr. Hagan, and it felt as though he was being hacked up and down his body with a ploughshare for taking back that slack he'd let out last night. Bass thought he wanted to see Master Reeves this morning more than anyone else in the world. The faces he made to silence the hurt. Showing patience with his silence, so much patience from such shallow rest. Only the sweet wordless singing of women rewarded his silence, his patience, and then knowing Master Reeves was coming, hearing now the unhurried hoofbeats of his Morgan. Against the fresh return of agony, his shoulders remembering the hog haul all over again, but now all over him at every crossroads, where his hips forked and joints bent—he unclenched his eyes and unblurred them on the blackjacks, and two comely faces emerged, peering at him from between the trees.

There weren't any pretty women at the other plantation. None, at least, that didn't feel already like sisters to him by the time they'd shown how pretty they could be, but these two were. Especially the darker one. The lighter one too. Both of them.

Not until the two women had begun to sing again, this time with words, did Bass realize they'd stopped singing to eye him. Now, with mouths moving, hooves in the distance, their faces faded deeper into the trees, while their voices defied logic and magnified, with one singing the moving parts and the other the chorus, making a delightful seesaw that refused to scare a single bird into the air and soothed Bass's frets:

> Jesus a-coming and I's a-going,
> Praying for that Heaven place,
> It's a place I'd die to taste,
> Praying for that Heaven place,
> Where it be can you guess?
> Praying for that Heaven place,
> Smack dab twix east and west,
> Praying for that Heaven place,
> Follow the angels, follow the doves,
> Praying for that Heaven place,
> We'll nest in the one safe home above,
> Praying for that Heaven place.

Midway into the song, with the Morgan's stamp beginning to vibrate the ground and the sticks and Bass's heels, Mr. Hagan stood to his feet, buttoning a shirt. Noises of hurried movement stirred toward the slave quarters, so by the time Master Reeves had trotted his handsome black-over-white stallion into view from one direction, the slaves, including Henry, were lining up from the other direction, wearing aprons and hats and bandana turbans to start the day.

Master Reeves appeared as a newer version of himself, with better posture in the saddle and wearing a crisp toast-colored suit with a teal vest and tie. Master Reeves looked more distinguished than Bass could ever recall and not simply because his clothes were clean or perhaps new, and not only because his hair and mustache were combed and spruced with oil, or because he'd shaved his cheeks and neck. He was almost a younger version of his father. Until you looked good at his pinched eyes, hard as marbles, and then you knew which Master Reeves you were seeing.

Master Reeves merely glanced at Bass and the line of slaves before turning his attention toward Mr. Hagan in his doorway, fighting to pull on a pair of boots. Bass noticed movement among the blackjacks and saw the women emerge with baskets of wadded wet clothes. The pretty one with darker skin, darker than his own, whose arms and legs were long and lean like his, gave Bass a look of concern, as if she knew him already and worried, while the pretty one with plumper arms and thighs and lighter skin, as light as his own, whose hair fell from her turban in ringlets, smiled like she knew him and was telling him so.

"Morning, Mr. Reeves," Mr. Hagan said, tucking his pistol into the waist of his pants as he stepped outside, holding his whip. "Long night," he said.

"Is that so?"

"Indeed, sir. N—— begged to be let down. Like a damn cricket, begged and begged."

Master Reeves turned in his saddle, and the Morgan rumbled a breath through his nose. Bass was already looking down at the ground, which stretched between him and that other world where pretty young women love on you and make you king enough to forget people like these in his world.

"Is that what you did, Bass?" Master Reeves asked. "I know you to tell the truth, and that's what I want to hear. Don't lie to me."

Bass relaxed into the chains and took more of the ploughshare, because more than that was coming regardless of what he said, so he better get used to it. He'd lived twenty-three years without ever being lashed, and now he was about to disappoint his family back home that he couldn't keep going.

"Boy, I know you hear me speaking."

Mr. Hagan rushed into the clearing. "Goddammit, boy, you best answer your master when he speaks to you."

Bass clamped his eyes to shut out Mr. Hagan growing toward him, and to suppress the pain of the ploughshare growing, too, as it occurred to him, but also, mainly, the truth, not altogether forgotten despite its diminutive size, as if floating solidly before him like a brass button. Shut so tight, he didn't even know he was crying until the tears backwashed into his mouth and he tasted salt. He'd been too afraid to touch his father's back all those years ago and too ashamed on those few opportunities ever since to look at it straight on, as if his father's back had been the face of his master looking back at him. "You can touch them Xs if you like, boy," his father had told him once, pleading like with sweat running down his face in the cold air, as if he'd wanted his blood in Bass to run down him, too, and touch his wormlike scars now that Bass thought of it. Bass had been four or five at the time. He was looking for his mother and father, and he found them under covers in the dark quarters. It was Christmas night, and everyone else was still dancing and feasting outside in celebration of Jesus and their own day off.

"Hey, you don't need them ears, I'll take 'em off," Mr. Hagan said. "You hear me?"

"Yes, sir, I hear you," Bass groaned because it was a question he could answer how he wanted.

The Morgan danced sideways. Nothing but that. No lowing. No singing. No trickling. Not even eggs. Just the master pattering over closer to make a point.

"Just the truth," he said. "Did you bother Mr. Hagan all night with your weak-minded yammering or not?"

Bass opened his eyes to let the sun burn his tears away. It was in his upbringing to agree, and with nothing else to rely on, he embraced it. "Yes, sir. Sorry, Master Reeves. I did done do that. I did." He gazed distantly, praying he'd answered right.

"I told you," Mr. Hagan said. "The n——'s big, but he's small."

"Well then," Master Reeves said, "let's see how big he feels on the sticks tomorrow morning." He spurred his Morgan back up the lane, and the coattails of his toast-colored suit flapped behind him.

Mr. Hagan spun to the row of slaves. "Well? Ain't the day commenced? Get to it!"

The slaves quickly dispersed, with the women carrying their baskets of wash up the lane, while the others followed the lane in the opposite direction.

Mr. Hagan stepped up to Bass and spat in his face. "Don't let me hear them chains rattling. I'll be listening." He turned away without waiting for a word and kicked the dirt as he tromped down the lane.

◆ ◆ ◆

Bass could feel the droplets of Mr. Hagan's spittle resting on his eyelids and nose and lips and cheeks and throat long after they'd been washed away by sweat. Long after he'd drifted drowsily with half-open eyes into this watery net of midday heat and sticks and chains and spit drops, like buttons.

The heat whirred, and the women sang and didn't sing. Henry brought him a sip of water, and his mother crimped piecrust, turning the pie one pinch at a time with her floured hands. Bass could watch her crimp dough in her easy rhythm all day. Pinch pinch pinch pinch pinch pinch pinch pinch pinch pinch pinch pinch pinch pinch pinch, pinch, pinch, pinch, and then the pie went in.

And then the day, as if devouring itself.

"Stop rattling them chains," Mr. Hagan shouted with hot egg breath, even though the sky had finally darkened and cooled. "Henry," he said, and Henry offered Bass the gourd.

◆ ◆ ◆

Bass had sunken somewhere inside himself. Somebody whispered, so he opened his lips and stream water spilled onto his tongue and beneath his tongue, which he touched to the roof of his mouth. He didn't move beyond that or beyond the swallow. *Don't move,* he told himself. He hurt worse when he moved.

As if the spinning of pies had mustered a breeze, a breeze mustered. A rooster crowed. Patiently, Bass opened his half-open eyes and used them. The pretty women weren't singing. They were passing his way with baskets, looking at him mournfully as if he'd died, as if there was nothing to sing. Then they disappeared like angels among the blackjacks, and their sweet wordless singing rose as it had the day before, floating around like surface water, like water on water, and water on breeze.

Their singing spun without change or pause amid the trickling of water, until, brighter, horse hooves sounded up the lane. Then the spinning stopped spinning, and the two women, identical to yesterday, made a singing seesaw, with one voice answering the other:

Jesus a-coming and I's a-going,
Praying for that Heaven place,
It's a place I'd die to taste,
Praying for that Heaven place,
Where it be can you guess?
Praying for that Heaven place,
Smack dab twix east and west,
Praying for that Heaven place,
Follow the angels, follow the doves,
Praying for that Heaven place,
We'll nest in the one safe home above,
Praying for that Heaven place.

Mr. Hagan stood in the doorway of his cabin, buttoning a shirt, and slaves ran to their row.

The women emerged with their baskets as Master Reeves rode into view in the same toast-colored suit, with the same good posture.

Mr. Hagan stepped off his porch, tucking his pistol into the waist of his pants and dragging his whip. The women were in line. Henry too.

Bass took a breath.

"Morning, Mr. Reeves," Mr. Hagan said.

Master Reeves tipped his hat to Mr. Hagan but was looking at Bass. "Was he any better last night?"

"No, sir. Long night again. Maybe longer."

Master Reeves hung his head with a sigh. "Take him down if he's that small."

"Yes, sir," Mr. Hagan said, tucking his whip into his pants. He unlocked Bass's right side first, and it nettled Bass to be kept in the dark why sides were so important to white people—right like white before left and n——, upriver and downriver, south was south of north but not really.

He crumpled from his weakened joints and thanked the Lord he was spared the whip, saying, "Thank you, Master," without clarification.

Mr. Hagan unlocked the left side and kicked him in the back as if to tell Bass to move it along, but where would he go? Without being told, he wasn't going anywhere. He inched, but that was all.

"Stand up," Master Reeves ordered.

Bass gathered himself on wobbly legs and cast a glance at the line of slaves, at the pretty two on the end. None looked his way, as if they were watching the lane, expecting it to fill any moment with Union soldiers to snuff out a Texas front before it opened.

Master Reeves pulled a red pipe from his coat pocket that could have been carved from mahogany and was twice as long as the corncob pipe he'd smoked on the hunt. Everyone waited patiently in silence, even Mr. Hagan, as Master Reeves found a match and struck it off his saddle. The garlic smell of the phosphorus tip drifted past Bass as Master Reeves stoked his tobacco. "Yes," he said finally. He cleared his throat. "Sean, let's show Bass how big even the smallest ones are on our proud plantation."

"A good idea, sir." Mr. Hagan grinned and looked off at the line of slaves. "Henry, get your butt over here, boy."

Henry ran over to Mr. Hagan. "Yes, sir?"

Mr. Hagan grabbed Henry's arm and led him past Bass to the chains. "You're twice the n—— as the big n——, ain't you, Henry?"

"Twice't," Henry said.

Mr. Hagan unwound a chain from the right stick and locked the shackle around Henry's wrist. "It's loose, Mr. Reeves."

Master Reeves spoke with his mouth pinched around his pipe, his words slow and curving. "You wouldn't try to escape it anyway, though, would you, Henry?"

"No, sir," Henry said. "I ain't a yammering weak mouth."

Mr. Hagan bellowed with laughter, while Master Reeves merely hummed a sound of pleasure through his pipe.

"You hear that, Bass?" Master Reeves asked.

"Yes, sir," Bass said, holding his stomach, as if that were where the pain was. "He say he ain't a yammering weak mouth like this big n—— here."

"You goddamn right he ain't," Mr. Hagan said.

"Finish locking," Master Reeves said.

Mr. Hagan unwound the other chains and snapped the locks, making Henry a little shirtless *X*. Bass strained to lift his shoulders, as if to give himself something to believe in, so unsure of anything but pain. Pain was all there was. He darted his eyes toward the slave line, and theirs darted too. They hunched, too, or squirmed. He lifted his shoulders once more to test their give, wondering if he swung through the pain if he'd be swinging through water.

"Now, whip him," Master Reeves said. "You say he's twice the n——, show me, Sean. Give him two big n—— lashes."

Mr. Hagan stepped back. He took out his whip, letting the leather coil loosely on the ground. Then he reached his arm back and rowed the whip back and forth until the frayed end of it danced on the ground like a cottonmouth. Bass was witnessing his first whipping. The first time he couldn't avoid it. So he watched without a blink. *Let's go, let's see it, by God*, and Mr. Hagan whipped the leather high into the air to make a fierce sapling and, like magic, snapped it down fishlike across Henry's back.

Henry screamed and shook the chains; gasps went up from the line; and though Bass didn't blink, he tensed through his arms, while Master Reeves blew a ring of smoke that smelled sweet as fruitcake.

"One more, Henry," Mr. Hagan said. He dragged his arm back, the whip back, and took a breath.

"Make it a good one this time," Master Reeves said.

This time, Mr. Hagan let out a grunt that outsounded the whip and even Henry.

This time, Bass refused to watch anything but the dirt at his feet. He'd believed he'd seen all there was to see of pain. How could anyone expect dirt to move and ball from a spray of blood shooting that far as if rain?

"That was a good one," Master Reeves said. He wrenched the Morgan's neck so that its head struck Bass in the face as it turned. "I hope you learned you aren't so big here, big n——. Now, follow me." He clicked his tongue to walk his horse up the lane, where the Union soldiers should have been gathering.

11

A Sire Mule

"Keep with me," Master Reeves said, leaving his horse tied at the porch rail and reaching for the brass knob of the front door of the big white house.

Bass fought the ache and buckle in his legs as he staggered up the porch steps. The door stood open for him as if he were the master now, but knowing better, he pulled his feet out of his shoes and brushed his feet together before stepping into air that felt moon born under that high ceiling. He nudged the door, and it shut behind him.

All the lamps and candles burning the first night were now out. It was just Master Reeves's boots tromping through shadows to another room. A room with books and a desk and a desk chair and two more chairs, one on each side of the desk—a room much like Master Reeves's study, the other Master Reeves, the one Bass missed even if he wasn't himself. Bass wondered who was walking though that other house in his place. Whose place was he taking here?

"Shut the door behind you," Master Reeves said.

"Yes, sir," Bass said. He swung it shut and watched Master Reeves remove his coat, exposing a gun belt with an ivory-gripped revolver in its scabbard. Master Reeves hung his coat on the back of the desk chair, but before sitting, he unbuckled the gun belt and laid it on top of his desk. Bass lowered his eyes.

"I suggest, as my body servant, you begin to feel more at ease within my home."

"Yes, sir, I will, Master," Bass said. "Nice house, nice indeed."

The chair creaked beneath Master Reeves as he crossed his legs. In the corner of Bass's vision, Master Reeves rested a hand on his knee and one on the revolver. "Sit down."

"Yes, sir. Thank you, sir."

Bass knew Master Reeves expected him to sit in the chair he was facing, which was to the left of Master Reeves, but Bass liked the other one better, the one by the window, between it and a cherry-colored chest sitting on the floor the size of a six-month-old piglet. And exercising his free mind, as a big n—— ought, he sat in the chair he wanted. "This one suit you, sir?" he asked.

Master Reeves twisted his body. "Why, it's the choice I hoped you'd make. You're supposed to position yourself behind me, following your living lord. As it's my choice to decide if I wish to look back and regard you, to answer or not, to lead or forget." He scuffed the legs of his chair against the floor as he turned to face Bass, now resting his opposite hands on his knee and revolver. "So, now that we've made our choices, I wish to explain my intentions for the last two nights and this morning. I'm not a cruel man, Bass. Every new slave is tied to the sticks. Temptation to escape is just too great at first. You wouldn't want to look special in front of the others."

Bass wagged his head. "Not special, no, sir."

"It's an initiation rite that's come to be expected."

"Yes, sir," he said, no longer understanding the master's words and wondering instead why a washstand stood in the master's study, fully stocked with linen and a pitcher of water.

"No hard feelings, I hope," Master Reeves said.

"No, sir, not atall," Bass said, though he wished the master would stop digging them up.

"At least I spared you a whipping, right?"

"Yes, sir. Thank you, sir."

Master Reeves took a breath but didn't immediately speak, and in his pause, Bass noticed a larger pause, the silence of the house itself. Not a sound of movement beyond any wall, which struck him as very peculiar for a house that housed so many young'uns. Twelve, he'd heard that the master had.

"Since you're sitting in my drinking chair," Master Reeves said, "let's have a drink." He tipped his head, and Bass turned to see what Master Reeves was tipping his head toward. It was the chest beside him. "You'll find an opened bottle of rye and some glasses. Pour us a glass. You too."

"Yes, sir. Thank you, sir." Bass eased up, only to ease down again, kneeling on tender knees. He raised the lid of stamped tin, and inside stood a dozen or more bottles in neat rows. And to their right, also in neat rows, were clear, jeweled glasses. He plucked two glasses out and set them carefully on the desk so as not to disturb the silence of the house. Selecting the bottle with the highest-standing cork, he wrapped his fingers tightly around it—maybe the only bending things on him that didn't ache.

He poured one glass halfway, the master's way, and served it to Master Reeves, before pouring one for himself, a little less than halfway. He reached for the cork to stopper the bottle, but Master Reeves told him not to bother.

Master Reeves took a sip and licked his lips. "Try sipping it now."

Bass could do what the master did. Without a gag, he sipped.

"Good, again," Master Reeves said.

Bass sipped, refusing to acknowledge at that moment how much he hated the taste of that brown thing he loved the wetness of.

"We don't have much time," Master Reeves said. "Texas is about to be called up for battle, and there's one simple thing I want you to do for me to make things right at the homestead before we depart." He leaned back in his chair and sipped, so Bass sipped. "You probably took notice of those pretty gals earlier with the wash. Or heard them, at least. They're always singing. Here, there, everywhere. They serve the mistress and my oldest daughter, so don't be surprised to run up on them coming and going. Well, one's really pretty. The other is pretty enough, though, but it's the one that's really pretty I'm concerned about." He arched his eyebrows as if to indicate something not even he could find words for, as if his eyebrows were caterpillars inching up from his rising flood of concern for the honor of really pretty slave women.

Bass took another sip to show him he could sip without being ordered to.

"I've got a buck chasing her I don't want chasing her," Master Reeves said. "One I've whipped on numerous occasions for just being stupid. The boy who took your whipping, it's his older brother, who's a good worker, no doubt, but he's about as smart as a starved dog. And I'd rather the girl be plowed by a mule than a dog. That's where you come in, Bass. I want you to plow her and the other one, both those gals." He slapped Bass's arm, and dust floated off his shirt into the shaft of window light. Master Reeves grinned, so Bass grinned. Master Reeves took a sip, so Bass took another sip like a man takes a sip. And what man wouldn't want to be a mule to two girls as pretty as those girls, even when it didn't sound right?

"A sire mule," Bass said with a nod, his eyes on the rye, without a hint of question.

The master again slapped Bass's arm. "So to speak. Because when this war's over, I'll need more mules than dogs. I'll need to get back to work. I'll need some good hands. I'll need some miracles." Master Reeves emptied his glass, then reached as if he would pour the whiskey himself, but bypassed the bottle, reaching for something in one of the cubbyholes on the backside of his desk.

"More rye, sir?" Bass asked.

"Yes, please."

Bass cut his eyes at Master Reeves before he could stop himself, and they momentarily met eyes with the same expression of surprise before dissolving to something else.

"Did you hear how the graciousness of my aristocracy rolled off my serpent-pleasing tongue?" Master Reeves drew his lips taut as if to smile and licked his teeth. "*Usus promptos facit*," he said and produced a stack of playing cards. Like a mason with a trowel, he smoothed the edges of the deck with his fingertips in long, patient strokes. "My man needs to know how to keep me company when there isn't better company. So pay attention."

◆ ◆ ◆

Master Reeves had to remind him that a pair meant two of a kind and was never a coupling of a king and queen of the same suit or any suit. A club was a clover, and Bass found diamonds in the design of their heavy whiskey glasses. A full house didn't mean five of a kind, because that wasn't possible, or five of any suit, because that was a flush, which would indeed, eventually, flush the master's emotions into the open better than any other hand. A full house, rather, meant five like a family, how Bass dreamed of having one, with a mama and daddy together under one roof and one, two, three young'uns. So of course, a full house beat a flush, like the random order of the slave quarters, but what didn't make sense, what he forgot again and again, was that a flush topped a straight—that a suit or a skin or a color, whatever you called it, was better than simple, unbroken order among all kinds.

Bass felt himself learning even as he felt his mind drifting away with the rye. He could spot a five by the X hidden in the pattern of the spades or a ten by the pair of Xs and immediately know the card was higher than a six or a three without counting on his fingers. And he could spot a fidget, the little sounds with the master's breathing, the pull of his hand, whenever the master's hand was one to be proud of. Sometimes Master Reeves would pretend his hand was better or worse than it was, usually when Bass's hand was a good one, which made Bass wonder if the master was now reading him.

"Soon we should begin playing for stakes," Master Reeves said, without a word to explain what he meant by "stakes." Then instead of shuffling the cards after raking them into a neat pile, he put them away. "I'm hungry, and I'm guessing you are," he said, rising from his chair. He corked the empty bottle as he crossed the room with it and opened the door. He swayed in place. Without turning to Bass, he said, "Don't make me tell you to follow me every damn time, boy. Keep with me."

"Oh, yes, sir." Bass pushed to his feet overly hard and jostled the room, and the bottles clinked inside the chest.

"Boy!"

"Sorry, Master."

Master Reeves stepped into the hall, and Bass followed him through the house to the much brighter kitchen, where a white woman and a slave, the pretty dark-skinned one, the really pretty one, touched their pretty hands to food. The white woman was pretty, too, with her long black hair tied back like a mane by a pink ribbon, with her hands rolling balls of dough, while the really pretty one, the one Bass couldn't plow fast enough, chopped mustard greens.

"Honey," Master Reeves said, and the white woman turned her head with eyes roving toward Bass, so Bass cast his eyes aside, finding a bucket beside the pretty slave woman's feet, "I want you to meet Ole Bass's Bass."

"Why, of course, hello, Ole Bass's Bass," she said with a laugh.

"Bass, this is Mistress Reeves."

Bass bowed. "Hi, ma'am. Pleasure be your acquaintance."

The mistress floated closer, her aproned skirt billowing back and forth like a pendulum. She rocked to a motionless stance beside the master as she continued to roll a ball of dough between her hands.

"I sure do adore your grandfather," Mistress Reeves said. "He's a sweet man. The sweetest, really."

Bass nodded.

She laughed again for a reason Bass missed, and the master laughed this time with her. "Do you have a sweet tooth like he does, Bass?"

Bass shook his head. "No, ma'am."

"I don't reckon so," she said, "but you do like sweets, though, don't you?"

Bass nodded, allowing his eyes to trail up that pretty slave woman's backside. "Yes, ma'am."

"I'm making rolls for dinner, but maybe we'll make some cookies too. I'll call for you when they're ready."

"Thank you, ma'am," Bass said, nodding again. The slave woman reached down for another bunch of greens soaking in the bucket. The profile of her chin, like the toe of a white woman's shoe, said everything there was to say.

"Bass," Mistress Reeves said, "this is my attendant, Jennie. She's my everything. Jennie, this is Bass, the master's new attendant."

Bass and Jennie gave the other a weak nod, a weak curtsey, hardly a glance, as if they'd never see each other again.

"Yeah, y'all need to get acquainted, etcetera," Master Reeves said, already beginning to walk away. "Come on," he said, motioning with the empty rye bottle still in his grasp, and Bass followed him to the head chair at the kitchen table, clean of plates and silverware. Only a yellow linen napkin, folded into the shape of a boat, sat before each of the six chairs. "This one's mine, and that one's yours," Master Reeves said, pointing the mouth of the bottle at the chair immediately to the left of his own. "This is yours too," he said, handing him the bottle. "I'll hunt you up a candle to plug in it for later—that is, if you promise to be careful and not burn down my stable."

"Oh, yes, sir. Thank you. I be careful, sir." Bass waited for Master Reeves to take his seat, and then he took his. He held the bottle close to his face with admiration. It was his bottle now, and it was as clear as a thing could be. Clearer than a mirror.

"Jennie, when you're done here," Master Reeves said, "hunt up a candle for Bass. He'll need a light tonight."

"Yes, sir, will do, Master Reeves," Jennie said, bobbing her small, round head, cute as a fruit.

Master Reeves crossed his legs at the knee and reached a hand into his coat pocket. "Do you have a pocket anywhere on you, Bass, that doesn't have a hole in it?"

Bass set aside his bottle and checked both of his coat pockets. He rarely had use for a pocket. His hands were too big for them, so he didn't know. He plumbed a finger inside each and ran it back and forth. "Yes, sir," he said, a smile forming. "I do, yes, sir."

"Here then," Master Reeves said, laying a small bundle of matches onto the table. "Use wisely."

"*Uses promptos facit*," Bass said.

The master lolled his head his way and smirked. "That's right. But let's begin with perfection and practice it every time, hear?"

Bass nodded, and the master reached forward, delicately plucked his yellow boat aloft, and, with a pop, unfurled the napkin.

"Go ahead," the master said, so Bass took up the napkin in front of him. But instead of trying to pop it and failing, he carefully unfolded it and likewise tucked it into his collar.

"Come and see if ye can swerve me," Master Reeves said, projecting his voice toward the women.

Jennie turned with hands dripping, saying, "Pardon, Master?"

"Swerve me?" Master Reeves pounded a fist against the table. "Ye cannot swerve me, else ye swerve yourselves!"

The mistress spun around with floured hands. "Be patient, for goodness sakes. We're just about done preparing supper, and then we'll serve you two something. Right quick, you hear?"

"Not *serve* me, Philistine," Master Reeves said. He leaned forward, pressing his napkin-covered chest against the edge of the table. "*Swerve* me!"

"Stop your nonsense, George."

Master Reeves sat back in his chair. "Does no one read *Moby-Dick* anymore?"

Mistress Reeves dismissed him with a wave and turned her back.

"Um, um, um," he answered.

12

The Bottle

He watched Jennie prepare a plate for the master and carry it to him, like a walking fruit tree with that chin of hers, dark and sleek as a pistol grip, or the master's saddle horn. As perfect as she was, she could be compared to anything. His stomach ached for her, and for food, any food, *her* food, and for rest, too long delayed. His head still swam from his move from Arkansas, he reckoned, and from all that came and went with it, and from two nights on the sticks and poor Henry this morning, and from the constant ticktock of thought and burial of thought that Master Reeves's presence forever demanded. And on account of the rye, all of it now was catching up to him in the silence of sitting and waiting. Finally from this, too, his head swam, this sleeve of hope after all the other, this glimpse of Jennie's wrists, those fingers of his future wrapped around a spoon handle, a fork handle, and then bearing a plate for him as her hidden legs crossed the room, for Bass this time, for Ole Bass's Bass—the skin of her fingertips sticking to the plate before letting go. She drifted away and back into his thoughts, long after she'd returned with a candle to plug into his bottle, which wouldn't need lighting yet, being only midday. But Bass was draining fast, and Master Reeves allowed it without complaint, guiding him to the stable himself, to a vacant stall a groom had just freshened with a floor of hay.

"You need your sleep," Master Reeves said, "so get it. But Bass, so help me if you burn down my stable, you will surely burn with it."

◆ ◆ ◆

Bass slept through the heat of the day, believing his dreams were merely dreams. Of horses munching and blowing, of flies flying, of the groom shoveling shit. Even of Jennie saying in a whisper, *Cookies?* And even later of Jennie and the other pretty slave woman taking to song again at the close of the day, their voices carrying over the plantation as delicate as cheesecloth: *Jesus in my heart is a-staying home, a-staying home, so devils beware if you's a mind to roam, a mind to roam.* Jennie was woven somewhere in that lace with the other, but Bass was too weary in his dream to get up and track what was whose or who was where. But with night cooling the stable, Bass slipped into sounder sleep, so only gradually did the repeated call of his name wake him, so harmonized with the singing of the cicadas, a sweetness asking, pleading, *Bass? Bass? Bass?*

His eyes rolled open to the darkness above, and his mind perceived the prick of the straw beneath him. He remembered now a creak of a door, or had he only been dreaming?

"Bass?" he heard again. This time he was certain.

He lifted his head from the hay to find Jennie's vague shape standing in a striped shaft of purpling door light. He parted his lips and forced a swallow to moisten his throat. "Yeah-huh?" he sort of croaked, his tongue sticking to his words, his words merely husks of words.

"Master Reeves sent me to check on you. Make sure your candle work and you don't burn down no stable, he say."

Bass pushed himself to sit up. He licked his lips.

"He say you got eyes for my cousin and me both, but more for me, why he say he sent me. That true?"

Bass wondered how the master could determine that from watching him watch her, if there was a fidget that showed for anything a person thought. He squinted to make out more than just Jennie's outline, which was misshapen by the angular light. He nodded. "Be true," he said.

"Well, I got eyes for you too," she said, "but my heart's with another. If the master want us to be together, then that's that, but I don't need no man. I need a baby, not no man. I got me a man."

"Jennie?" he said, because that was the only name he knew.

The shape without a face or one visible feature went silent as a ghost. "No," she said finally. "Winnie, I be Winnie. My cousin be Jennie. That who you thought I be? You thought I be *Jennie*? Was you hoping that? Tell me."

Bass froze, hoping she couldn't make out his face and fidgets, just as he couldn't make out hers. He didn't want to answer. He didn't know either cousin well enough to hurt anybody. "Sorry," he said, "but it a pleasure be your acquaintance, Winnie. Sure be."

"Praise Jesus," she whispered, her shadow beginning to bounce. "She like the looks a you too. And she don't got no man, and she need one. So you give your heart to her, not me, hear?"

"I hear," he said.

"This is us making do, you and me. Just getting by and nothing more, hear me?"

"I hear," he said.

Her shape stretched taller, as if she were reaching for the roof, and as if to do so she had to brush a horse in slow strokes there in the dark along the way, the way her dress rustled up over her head—a *wish, wish, wish* up into a humpy cloud held high above her—until the long silhouette shrank back down and the dress fell to the floor like the sound a puff of air makes. "I'm guessing that candle work."

"It work," he said.

"You a handsome man, strapping for sure, but I gots me a man," she said, stirring the straw with easy steps. And then one of her feet found one of his legs, and she played inchworm with it up along his calf and thigh.

"You a handsome woman," he said, the words no longer sticking, his mouth producing water now. "Your ringlets, I remember them." He cottoned to the cute cantaloupe of Jennie's head and to her bark-dark skin and tree limbs, but he cottoned to Winnie too. He recalled she was pretty too—not dark, like he wasn't, but dark now in the dark as anybody could be. They both were.

When she reached and found and really took hold of him with her hand, it could have been any girl's hand, so much smaller than his own, wrapped around a fork or spoon, but when she roosted her roundness down on his lap, that fullness he couldn't wrap his blind eyes around as she spilled soft and firm and slid yolk-like through his grasp, he knew he was only with Winnie who didn't need no man, who was just getting by, just making do, just squirming and grabbing and holding on, bucking and scratching and groaning up in his face like she would bite him. But wasn't she trying her best, bless her, to give him back everything that had ever been taken away?

◆ ◆ ◆

"Be good," the old master had told him. His sending-off words. "Be good." As if Bass had ever had much control over something like that. "Be good," Bass heard the horses say under their breath. "Be good," Winnie's feet said to the straw, the wood of the door as it creaked open and shut, each shape to the shadow. "Be good," said the match that lit the candle. "Be good," Bass said alone to himself but not to himself, fully awake and sober now but far removed from the Bass he'd believed in. He was just grand-Bass, the new master's sire mule, who, like a man, held his light aloft to see everything good in his world but didn't feel good at all about it.

Not even the dreamed-for pleasure of being with a gal as pretty as Winnie could please him long enough to feel like one ever took place. Not when it came by command and with no hope for a heart. He felt a kinship to his empty rye bottle indeed, so he must have really owned it. And since it was his, really his, he took the bottle with him as he stepped away from the stall to throw light into the next stall before passing on to the next, until he'd found Strawberry's flank and touched him with his palm. "Strawberry," he said, stroking him until Strawberry nickered. "Strawberry," he said again, and that soothed Bass too. "Strawberry." Close to a whisper now. He hugged the sorrel's neck, and a run of wax gathered in the crook of his thumb.

It was out of habit he returned to his stall to return his bottle to the cast-iron manger, where it hung on the wall with no more than a finger of water left standing in it for the thirsty horse that must have been stalled here only yesterday. A safe place, he'd decided, for a burning candle, where the bottle could stand and wax could run all it wanted except on his hand. But he wasn't ready to be stalled yet, to lie back down in that mashed spot of hay and feel lost in it. So why was he lowering himself back into it?

One day, he'd step back from patience. *Yes, Mama,* he thought he was telling her convincingly, as if she heard him way across the sky and was about to argue. Eventually, it'd be so. Had to be. One day, he'd admit that the time for freedom had come, and he would mount. One day, he'd feel it was time. He just didn't feel it was time yet. The time simply hadn't arrived. He didn't rightly know why it hadn't, but he trusted the Lord to let him know the right day when it came. That it would come to him with a smell on it as a sign and he'd be ready, knowing better where he was, for one thing, and how to get where he was going, for another. All he knew now was up, left, up, left, taking the n—— dogleg to where the Seminoles lived in Indian Territory. Where you went left and how much left, he hadn't a clue, but left was a fair assumption, away from Arkansas, which was up, right.

He would know a whole lot more when that day came, that was for sure, and would feel a whole lot stronger for a run than he did now, that was for sure too. Tonight, he only knew he would run, one day, one night, and soon, before war broke, or after if that was easier, but soon. Maybe tomorrow, if God saw to it to tell him so. Tonight, though, he had no idea, and having no idea made him very sleepy.

13

Rub

He woke to the sound of a nail being wrenched from a post, followed by a slap of wood against wood. The following footfalls told him what he'd heard was the stable door on rusty hinges being thrown open, and those footfalls were too heavy to be Winnie's or Jennie's or any woman's.

Bass sat up with fists balled, expecting who knew what, when the groom appeared at his stall, mostly how Bass vaguely remembered him from yesterday in passing when working his pitchfork. He was in his twenties like Bass but shorter than Bass, much shorter, and stouter and darker, much darker, and wearing the same hat with holes, but instead of the nice face that Bass recalled, the groom bore something altogether different. Different like the bundle of new clothes in his hands instead of a pitchfork, a whole outfit including shoes too big for the groom but maybe just right for Bass.

"Get up," he told Bass, as though he was ordering him.

Bass let his eyes linger on this man's mad eyes and mad mouth, on the pink scar running straight across a cheek as if by a knife. The groom gazed at Bass with such intensity that Bass wondered if doing so had been the fellow's intention long before the moment had arrived.

"N——, you hear me?"

Bass took a deep breath of the bittersweet hay and showed he, too, could see and see and not blink. "I recommend," he said, "you talk to me like you ain't the master. You don't want me in your stall, that it? And you think I do?" He eased up onto his feet, in no hurry at all, rising above the groom by almost two hands. Straw stuck to him, and straw sifted down. He hadn't had to prove himself with a good fight in years. He was feeling about ready for another, a little stove-up or not.

"Master say for you to clean up and put these here new fancy house n—— duds on and meet him at his back door, so you follow me like I tell you cause that be what the master want. And you best not push it with me, cause I ain't scared a you or no one or nothing, you got that?" He pivoted as if he still thought of himself as the master and stepped out of sight.

Bass didn't see the sense of delaying a fight if one was coming anyway, so he didn't budge. He liked his chances where he stood, a place he knew, where the boy couldn't grab a thing in a panic. "If you asking me to bust up the rest of your face for you," he called, "come back so I can bust it. You ain't scared? Well, me neither." He planted his feet through the straw on solid ground, flexing his toes in it, his face busters raised and ready. Surely, the Lord would have given him a smell other than hay if today was really it, if it was all about to start right here, but if this was it, Lord, it was it. "You hear *me*?" he said.

The groom's footfalls returned, and then the groom himself, the hat with holes, the clothes neatly folded and stacked in his hands.

"You ready to start it?" Bass asked.

"You gonna lay with my girl, make my little brother be a man for you, and then try me this morning like I some weak-mouth n—— like you? Shit! All right, then, fuck it." He turned away and set the bundle of clothes on the master's saddle, resting on a nearby saddle stand. "Think I let them clothes get dirty account a you? Shit, you trying me for damn sure, but come on." He spun away from the saddle stand with a bounce and threw aside his hat.

Bass sagged his shoulders. "Henry your brother?"

"Damn is. So?"

"Winnie your gal?"

"Damn is, too, n——. What else you want from me?"

Bass didn't know what to say. The groom bowed up with some meaty shoulders, but Bass no longer wanted to bust him. The master had called this old boy a dog. A starved dog. "The master calls you a dog," he said, and the groom's eyes flashed wide as he charged.

Bass leaned away and, easily outreaching him, shoved the groom down into the straw as he bulled by. Bass jumped back a step and planted for another go. "He the dog, what I was approaching to say. *He* the dog, not you, you see?"

The groom scrambled up, spitting straw off his lips.

"Hellfire, he called me a mule," Bass said.

The groom charged again, and again Bass leaned away at the waist, too easy with his reach to grab and divert the plunging weight wherever he wanted. "Listen," Bass said, "I don't want none a you. I know it ain't right for him to put me in your stable and then gimme your woman. He the dog, doggone it."

The groom sat up on crouched knees as though he might spring for a run at Bass a third time, but he dropped forward on his hands instead, hanging his head down as a slave was taught to and huffing, staring at nothing, straight down at hay and huffing. He struck the ground with a fist. The old green of the hay lingered in the air like a dream, just a hint of its old sweetness in its new dusty coat, but it was there, barely hanging on. It made Bass lonesome to think of it that way, with the groom down in it, huffing.

"I don't want none a you," Bass said. "I don't want none a your woman neither. Winnie a fine woman to be sure, but that it between us. Even if Master put us together again. My word, hear? Got my word."

The groom went silent, huffed twice more, and went silent again. "We in love," he said.

"What she told me," Bass said. "And that a good thing, a godly thing, be sure. I ain't out to trample a thing like that. Be sure a that. Truth be told, my eye on Jennie. Both pretty as can be, but my eye on Jennie. Got my word."

The groom rolled his head side to side, then pushed himself up. Hanging his head, he brushed the straw from his clothes. Bass wanted to trust him. He tried to look relaxed, but he was still ready to bust him.

The groom rolled his head again as if Bass had asked him something. "Took me forever to win her away from ever body, then you come along." He let out a heavy breath, and Bass watched his shoulders sink. "I told her, 'Winnie a good name for you, cause that be what it take, a whole lot a winning.'"

Bass chuckled, because he thought the groom was funny in his way. A bite of the starved dog about him, for sure. Bass held his hand out to him. "We good?"

The groom looked up with that long pink scar as straight as the edge of the world. He looked down and then up again before stretching forward and taking Bass's hand. It was a meaty thing, even if it was small, with a fast biting grip.

"I'm guessing you'll help me with Jennie?"

"I'm guessing, n——, you don't need no help, but we'll see."

They shook hands until their arms went slack.

"Enough foolishness," the groom said, sidestepping him. He collected the clothes off the saddle. "They calls me Rub, so you can calls me that, too, I reckon."

"Bass," said Bass, following.

"Bass Reeves, I knows," Rub said. He swung the stable door closed behind them and led Bass as if he were leading a horse, without a word or glance, as they tracked away from the mansion, along the lane in the direction of the blackjacks and the sticks and Mr. Hagan's cabin. The sky was stretched away from the early sun like a goat hide, with little splotches here and there but mostly with big spill shapes, so the lowing of the longhorns from over yonder of the blackjacks drifted back down here clearly.

He remembered how the master had said at night Bass might think he couldn't sleep if he couldn't hear the longhorns pass, and he wondered why he hadn't regarded the lowing all night or morning until now. Maybe in the stable the breathing of the horses had covered it. And wasn't that a fine difference between a master and a slave—to hear something or not because of what you slept with, more than who?

Rub's stride may have been short, but it was steady and quick, as if he meant to exhaust Bass. But Bass was mostly elsewhere, his eyes on everything but what was directly in front of him. On clouds, on the lane, on yesterday, while his mind landed on every smell that came along, until his eyes focused there on Rub's back, his shirt. How it hung long on him everywhere but the arms and was striped like a woman's, until Bass realized the stripes weren't regular, running this way and that, a reddish-brown crisscrossing, thin and wide. The more Bass looked, the more he saw the bay color was soaked into the muslin, and though knowing now what it was, he saw something else, what the stripes could be, how they resembled cuts or tears, like the one across Rub's face, as if a bay stallion were hiding under his shirt and was bursting out.

It was a sight he wasn't used to seeing at the other plantation, and if the Lord continued to bless him, he wouldn't be sticking around this one to get used to it. As if the Lord were whispering in his ear that it wouldn't be long, the blackjacks fell back in a bend and Mr. Hagan's cabin came into view, and then the clearing where the sticks stood apart like two strangers—all the reasons there could be for a run.

Rub veered off the lane, onto a footpath slithering through grass and into the tart shade of the blackjacks. Rub moved with ease through the trees, merely ducking his head to avoid branches, while Bass had to bend at the waist, sometimes almost crouch, until the trees thinned at a brook, about as wide as Rub was tall.

Rub lowered to set the clothes on a rock at the brook's edge. With the small scoop of his hand he took a drink.

Bass lowered beside him and did the same. The water tasted clean as rainwater, so he cupped for another drink.

"No lollygagging." Rub backed away. "Master expecting you."

"What, hold on," Bass said. "We ain't got no better water to dip in than this trickle?"

"Ain't deep, but it be a good spot to sit down in it and wash off." Rub started off again, as if he was really walking away.

"Hey, what about soap?" Bass asked.

Rub stopped and turned with balled hands, as if he was getting ready for another go. "Ain't you a spoiled n——? Water ain't enough?"

Bass shook his head. "Not for Master Reeves, I don't reckon, and not for me neither."

Rub tilted his head to the side, flexing his hands open and closed. "Look," he said, "doing what I told and that it. Ain't nothing enough? Make do." He stepped away but stopped and turned around. "The womens be down directly with the mistress wash so keep a look out." He turned, and that was it this time. He stepped and kept stepping until Bass couldn't see the bay in him anymore and couldn't hear him.

Bass looked down at the brook and shook his head. The Texas way was puny. In Arkansas he had a river as deep as three of him. He also had soap. It wasn't funny, but it was. He undressed out of his dirty rags and sat down in the water, which hardly crested above his belly button.

He rubbed his hands together and rubbed his hands over his feet and legs and parts, the water clouding up around him as he worked, before it struck him what he was doing, and he cracked a smile. Maybe this was how Rub got his name, thinking this was enough, all rub and no scrub. Bass tipped his head back with an open mouth and became distracted by the black kerchief floating down from the upper branches, a bird descending from one of the blackjacks and landing about ten feet away on the soft edge of the stream—one Bass had never seen before. Something of a crow but smaller, or like a blackbird but larger and with longer tail feathers. It was solid black, or sort of black. Sort of purple too. The bird angled its head and tiny yellow eye toward Bass, then dipped its pointed beak into the water. Bass bent over to soak and rub his arms, moving slowly so as not to frighten the bird, and the bird made a clicking sound that didn't seem animal, appearing purely metallic. Bass stopped his wash to listen to it click, as if in its mouth it knocked two iron rods together. As if suddenly bothered by Bass's presence, the bird angled its yellow eye toward him again and puffed up its feathers, a ruffled plumage that almost doubled its size, as if daring Bass to move toward him and fight, and then it called, or buzzed, or growled, but in a metallic way again, like a chain dragged over a sheet of tin, and as it called, it gradually lost its puff. But then it puffed itself up again and called again, dragging its chain, its yellow eye daring Bass.

Goose pimples formed over Bass's arms and the nape of his neck. Was the Lord telling him to run, not with a smell but with a sound, with a sight, to run right now in that new set of clothes while no one but a queer Texas bird looked on? He shut his eyes, pleading with the Lord to tell him what to do, because Bass was stuck on what didn't seem right, and that was running in the daylight when the master expected him, maybe was already waiting on his porch and lighting his pipe.

The bird called again, as if taunting him, and in the distance, above its dragging chain, a much sweeter call rose up, almost breeze-like, beautiful and wordless, but clearly animal. Bass opened his eyes to see a brown bird swooping past, and the sort of purple-black one took flight following it and disappeared among the blackjacks. The song, the same song he woke hearing yesterday on the sticks, rose and kept rising by step but without the sound of steps. Jennie and Winnie seemed to be aimed precisely for him, as Rub had said to watch for, so Bass decided to do what was expected of him once more, what seemed wise in a rush. Perhaps the Lord's answer of nothing was the answer, to ignore a devil bird's dare for now and hold tight. *Hold your horses*, he told himself, *and be quick about it! Don't be making them doubt you yet.* He splashed his face, rubbed it fast, and splashed again.

A rustling of branches and footfalls in the blackjacks from where the song came made him leap up and stretch for his duds. He didn't want Jennie to catch him like this, like a hog in a wallow. He shook the trousers out, as the rustling grew and the song grew, and then hooves sounded—the Morgan's—in a jog on the lane from up toward the stable, when he realized the rustling had halted at the same time that he'd strained to hear past it. He imagined the women standing frozen as he was standing frozen, unnerved by the sound, too, and peering through the trees at the clearing between the overseer's cabin and the dreadful sticks. Though the women must have stood without rustling, unnerved all the same, they never stopped singing, taking turns with the verses, and just as smoothly eased words into the song without missing a beat:

> Jesus a-coming and I's a-going,
> Praying for that Heaven place . . .

Bass jolted into action, buttoning his shirt in a scramble. He tucked in the tails. The stamps of the Morgan continued to approach, and the women continued to sing where they stood:

> It's a place I'd die to taste,
> Praying for that Heaven place . . .

He reached for the suspenders to begin buttoning them, when a rustling behind him made him jump and expect a deer, but it was a Negro man running, flashing through the trees in a blur of browns, shirtless, hat and trousers, and leaping barefoot over the stream upstream from where Bass stood. The man continued into the blackjacks. All the slaves must have been running to make their place in the line in the clearing, as if today were the day Jesus really was a-coming.

Bass went back to work fastening his suspenders. The Morgan was almost to the clearing now, just outside those blackjacks, and the women were moving again in Bass's direction, still singing and toting fat baskets he could begin to see now, swaying in the motion of cows.

He snatched up the socks and shoes and slipped back into the trees. He'd thought he wanted to hide his nakedness but realized he simply wanted to hide, to spy on Jennie a moment without having to speak to Winnie.

By the time the two reached the spring, they'd reached the end of their words and returned to singing without them. The Morgan seemed to return to where it was before, too, as if Master Reeves had reached the clearing to inspect the row of slaves, or to make sure Mr. Hagan had gotten himself out of bed or hadn't needed to chain a n—— to the sticks for a reason the master needed to know, and then circled directly back to wait for Bass at the big house. He wouldn't wait long.

Bass fixated on Jennie's rope-strong arms and delicate features, her puckered lips as she cooed more than sang, the arch of her back as she lowered her basket by the stream. Winnie knelt by the water, beside her own basket, and submerged a white woman's dress, too lacy and colorful not to be, while Jennie appeared to notice Bass's rags strewn on the ground like stones. His shirt was just within her reach, so she reached for it, but for his trousers, she had to crawl a step. Then she crawled a step back to the stream, where she submerged them together in the water, gripped and squeezed.

He didn't want to speak, but he wanted to. "Pssst," he said, and when Jennie turned, he waved.

She nodded, even smiled, as she cooed without pause, before returning to his clothes, lifting them out of the water to let them drain, then plunging them down again. Winnie, bless her, never looked over, as if too deep inside their music to hear him stirring down the trail.

14

Cracker King

Bass caught the trail of pipe smoke long before he'd made it up the hump of the lane, past the stable but not yet past the master's outhouse and the leafy rose bushes that marked the footpath between houses. A teasing necklace of smells. At some point in that moment or the next, he realized he no longer heard the women singing at the creek and now heard the longhorns lowing much farther away.

Master Reeves sat in a rocker on his back porch with his legs crossed at the knee, his arms resting on the armrests, his hat tipped back as if he didn't really want to wear it. He rocked at such a slow pace with his one foot planted for pushing off that Bass didn't realize the master was moving until Bass stood at the base of the steps and was bowing.

"Master," he said.

"Look at that. Bass, you're quite the civilized dark dandy now, aren't you?"

"Yes, sir. Thank you, sir." Bass smiled about his duds and let his eyes settle on the master's pushing-off foot, the polished shoe. His own shoes were nice, being new hide, but they didn't shine like a wet rock like the master's.

"You must be questioning my breach of etiquette yesterday when I allowed you to join me at my table, to sit among the women folk of my house and eat a meal before you were civilized enough to do so."

Bass shook his head. "Oh, nah, sir," he said.

Master Reeves raised a clasped hand, the mahogany pipe peeking out of it almost birdlike. "Don't mistake that for generosity on my part. It's simply important sometimes, Bass, to remind women how uncivilized a n—— can be." He groaned in his throat as if he were stifling a laugh and chopping it up. "I am keenly aware that I need to thank *you*, Bass. *You*. Thank you." He uncrossed his legs, clamped his teeth on the black stem of his pipe, and stood up. When every wrinkle had fallen out of his pant legs, he stepped toward the door, opened it, and passed through it without closing it behind him, so Bass hurried up the steps to follow, saying to the temptation creeping up inside him, *Never you mind, never you mind.*

Bass eased the door to a delicate click without sweeping much of the light back out. The sun poured through the windows, but the still kitchen nevertheless felt almost cold. Master Reeves had moved on inside to another room, where Bass couldn't hear him. The family hardly bumped upstairs, yet lamps flickered in the parlor and foyer, where no one was, as though there would never be a shortage of oil or money for it. Past the staircase was the master's study, the first room in the hall of doors with its door open. Bass figured he'd find him sitting in his desk chair, his coat hung on the back of it, but he hadn't counted on Master Reeves already shuffling a deck of cards.

"You know where I keep the rye," Master Reeves said, his legs crossed as before at the knee, his top foot bobbing, while his eyes remained on his churning hands, like a paddle wheel, the cards rising and falling. "Open a bottle and start pouring. You know the drill."

Bass shut the door, and Master Reeves said, "Good," without looking up, his hands continuing to churn.

Bass raised the lid on the chest and reached for two glasses, and Master Reeves said, "You are a smart n——."

Bass set the glasses on the desk, one for the master beside the coiled gun belt and one for himself to the right of it.

"But not so smart after all." Master Reeves shook his head.

"Sir?"

"Where will you be sitting this time?"

Bass regarded the chair by the window, where the master had allowed him to sit only yesterday—didn't he remember? Bass lifted his hand to point at the chair as if to prove it was there and still a choice, when he looked at it again and saw straight through the chair to the floor, where the upholstered seat should have been, had been, but was now missing.

"There was an ugly incident yesterday when the mistress observed the filth you left in your wake, like sheep droppings over a pasture, I swear to goodness. But that's neither here nor there, thanks to Jennie. You were as innocent as a lamb anyway. That was yesterday. Today, however, I ponder how you could have neglected to notice such a relevant detail in your surroundings. My man needs to be on guard at all times. Now, if you prefer to sit vigilantly on the edge of your seat, well, by all means, Bass, proceed to the right of me. But if you prefer the choice of comfort over, say, pride, then proceed to my left. It's your choice either way. Just be alert and smart in everything you do—for me and for Texas, for our way of life, and for *you*, too, for God's sake. A drill is never just a drill."

"Yes, sir, Master," Bass said, agreeing, sinking, feeling shorter. He picked up his glass, walked around Master Reeves, and set it on the desk to the left of the gun belt. That quickly, the master could remove the sky if Bass was flying. He stepped aside, almost stumbling, it seemed, as he returned to the chest, bending for a bottle of rye. As if blind, his eyes roved right and left, absorbing nothing. He felt too dumb even to be angry, until finally he saw it, the corkscrew, and plucked it from its leather sleeve and stood away.

"Do you know how Dante Alighieri depicted Satan?"

That quickly, the master could throw sky back under him. Bass brushed off the cork. "No, sir. Can't say."

"With three faces. Can you believe that?"

"Three? No, sir." Bass set the point of the screw to the tan skin of the cork. From the familiarity of how the corkscrew fit in his palm, he loosened his grip to give it a closer look—a twist of polished steel with a decorative wooden handle, smoothed and grooved by a lathe, much like the one the other Master Reeves owned. It was the same one, could be, with a dust brush sprouting from one end of the handle just so, as if the other Master Reeves had offered to give this Master Reeves a fine, strong n—— and this Master Reeves had said a fine, strong n—— was fine and dandy but wasn't near-enough enough and took this blazing corkscrew to boot.

"Logical math," Master Reeves said, shuffling the playing cards, as if he couldn't stop now that he'd started, as with everything else about him. "The evil inverse of the Holy Trinity," he said, nodding, churning. "Father, Son, Holy Ghost, right? And can you guess what race Dante made them?"

Bass closed his hand around the corkscrew. "Wouldn't know where to begin to guess, sir," he said, piercing the cork.

"Try."

Bass turned to indicate in his silence that he had heard him and was thinking. "White," he said.

"White, you say? Why white? What are you saying?"

Bass shrugged. "White the race of being in charge, but that's me being dumb enough to try."

"Well, that's also you being close enough to right to be called right, Bass. The face on the right is white, but with a pretty blend of yellow mixed in it. See, you knew where to begin. Don't play dumb with me."

"No, sir. Sometimes I ain't playing. But I sure didn't know nothing about white man being mixed with no Chinaman. No, sir."

Master Reeves glanced up at Bass without slowing his hands. "You wish, don't you?"

Bass held the bottle with a firm grip and gave a steady pull on the cork until it popped free.

"All right, so maybe white was a lucky guess. What about the other two? What race do you suppose they are?"

Bass cradled the rye and gently worked the cork off the screw. "Black, sir?"

"Very nice, Bass." He smoothed the cards even with his fingertips and nodded. "The face on the left is indeed black, for melancholic people like you. So now you know why I like to keep you west of me."

Bass slipped the corkscrew into its sleeve and closed the chest, the cards flipping by and flipping by, as if a cicada shell had miraculously crackled to life only to rattle its wings.

"All right," Master Reeves said, pausing as if to give Bass time to step back to the desk to hear his words and infernal wings better, "there's one more face to Satan. The middle one, the front one, the main one, the worst one. What color do you reckon it is?"

The only other race of people he knew of was the Indian, so Bass said, "Red."

Master Reeves dropped his jaw as if from the shock of a tooth-ache, his whiskers making that spearhead shape like the shape of spades on his cards. "Damn, Bass," he laughed, twisting at the waist and slapping the deck of cards on the desk behind him, "my daddy was right about you. You're smart enough to think you should be in charge, you know that?" He grabbed the seat of his chair and, while still sitting in it, turned himself around. "You sure you ain't got a little of my daddy in you, boy? I swear to goodness."

Bass poured the master's glass halfway. He didn't like this. He did not like this. He did not want to be a white man's n—— anymore. Any kind of n—— in any way. House or field, with this master or the other master or any other master. Better than killing any white man in his way to get out of being a n—— would be killing the n—— in him first.

Master Reeves raised his glass to his lips. Bass waited for him to taste the rye before backing away.

"Bear in mind now, Bass, the greatest sin is to spill blood, and the Indian doesn't give it a second thought. The Indian protects his land of false idols with fierce aggression and will dance at the first opportunity to spill your blood or mine over his face, as if his own natural red weren't red enough. A white man hesitates to spill blood. A n—— does too. Hell, especially a n——, I'll grant you that. We're almost alike in that way, Bass."

Bass poured his own glass halfway, then set the bottle on the desk and corked it. He sat down and reached for his glass, when Master Reeves reached to tap Bass's arm.

"I received word is what I'm saying."

Bass met the master's eyes, and the master didn't blink.

"The North's a big Indian who wants war, so we're leaving tomorrow to give it to him."

Bass furrowed his brow before he could stop himself.

"What is it?"

Bass lowered his eyes to his glass, now waiting in front of him. "Sorry, sir. Just didn't hear nobody ride up."

"Oh, you hear everything, do you?"

"Oh, no, sir, but I do hear horses good, come and go, yes, sir."

Master Reeves smiled and swirled his glass as if he thought the rye would freeze if he didn't keep it moving. "Well, you didn't hear one this time because there wasn't one. Nobody rode up. It's something I've known. I didn't want to worry you. Wanted you to settle in. You don't need to know everything I know anyway."

"Yes, sir. Thank you, sir." He raised the glass to his lips. Master Reeves watched him swallow.

"So how was it with Winnie last night? Tell me."

Bass gazed at an irrelevant spot on the floor. "She a real pretty gal."

"Oh, come on. Any white man can see that. But does she like to? Some women don't. I'm betting Winnie does. Don't know about Jennie, probably not, but Winnie, tell me, she's special, isn't she? She likes to, doesn't she?"

Bass wet his lips on the rye and nodded.

Master Reeves stomped the floor. "I knew it." He sipped his rye, and then sucking a breath between his wet teeth, he set the glass down and collected the playing cards and cut them. "I'll send Jennie to you tonight, but don't get mad at me if she doesn't want to. Most women don't." He dealt a card to Bass and to himself, then paused. "See what you have to come home to?"

"Yes, sir. Thank you, sir."

"Your pastime can be shooting turkeys like a bloodthirsty Indian or being my Johnny N—— Appleseed. Shit, I know which way my choice would go."

"Yes, sir. Johnny N—— Appleseed."

Master Reeves resumed his deal with a laugh. "I'd be the laziest n—— you've ever seen."

Bass laughed with him. *And I'd be the hardest-cracking cracker this world's ever seen,* he vowed to himself, sipping his rye and this time wanting to, contemplating what cracking like a cracker king would look or sound like—if it'd feel like everything good he'd ever felt but all at once or if he'd rise above feeling altogether, just a shell with a queer metallic song.

◆ ◆ ◆

As with the day before, hands of poker churned with rye, and Bass showed early signs of improvement by learning which cards to discard to prevent himself from winning. Then together they stood up to the rye and took dinner in the kitchen, where Jennie served them. *Was this a glimpse on cracking?* he wondered. The rye had helped him rise above feeling. The knowledge that Jennie would come to him that night, even if she didn't want to, was calming knowledge to possess. The knowledge, too, that he wouldn't be running tonight, even if he should. He didn't know what he waited for, or what God waited for, but running on rye wasn't wise.

Master Reeves led him to the back porch and removed his pipe from his coat pocket. He tipped his head toward the stable. "Take the day to rest up for what comes."

"Yes, sir." Bass stepped off the porch, bowed low in his back, and walked along the footpath, between the rosebushes, past the outhouse, and past Strawberry after giving him a stroke down his long face. Eventually, he laid his head on Rub's hay, believing any moment he'd begin to cry for how stupid and helpless he could be. How pitifully whole, when he needed cracked and mixed and removed and remade in the worst possible way.

The master's cards and rye, the sire-mule business, every word of crazy talk, of course the fancy house-n—— duds—they were all some awfully heavy, hot cracker quilt precisely intended to slow him from running. Chaining him to the sticks without chaining him to the sticks. Tomorrow he'd leave the plantation with Master Reeves. They'd ride to war, and if need be, Bass would shoot the heads off Yankees. He'd do whatever his master asked of him. And tonight he'd be the master's sire mule again, because, well, Jennie was Jennie, wasn't she? If he hadn't cracked himself yet, then maybe he couldn't crack yet. Because, after all, he was a fine, strong n——.

15

Crumbs and Raindrops

Bass drowsed, and the horses munched until twilight, when Rub shut the stable door. He listened for Jennie and Winnie to raise their voices from the footpath. But tonight no song was sung. There was nothing to announce that the women had finished their work, that the door would creak, before it creaked.

Bass sat up at the sound, expecting Rub to have remembered something he'd left behind, a biscuit from his noonday meal or his drinking gourd, or maybe something he'd meant to tell Bass in advance of Jennie. But it was Jennie who appeared before his stall, wearing a different bandana turban, red like the one he'd seen earlier in the day, but this one was ironed.

She carried a bundle of clothes in one arm and a cloth-covered pail by the wire.

"Hi," she said, nodding.

He smiled, and she lifted her pail.

"Brought a bite," she said.

He patted his stomach. "Thank you, ma'am."

"And these clothes you left at the stream," she said, clutching the clothes against her chest, "I washed them."

He hoped it was too dark for her to notice he was blushing. "Thank you, ma'am," he said. "Pretty tattered, huh? You was washing your hands more than cloth, that's for sure."

"You might want them for hunting or such." She took a step into his stall and set the pail down and then the clothes and finally herself, on folded legs. She uncovered the pail and spread the cover on the hay between them. She plucked out squares of cornbread glistening with butter and filled with thick slices of ham. She laid them with devoted care on the cloth, and he admired the generous portions of white-people meat but also her delicate fingers, her wrists, her dark angles. From the bottom of the pail, she lifted a jar of pickled peaches.

"What's that?" he said, taking the jar in his hand and eyeing it closely. "Can't believe that, my goodness."

"The mistress gave them to me," she said. "She's good about giving me something now and again. Even teaching me to read and write."

Bass leaned back as if to halt a horse. "And Master Reeves allow that?"

Jennie shook her head. "On the sly. So I can read to her, because she says it tires her eyes and makes her sleepy. Master gets on to her about not reading enough."

Bass nodded. That sounded like Master Reeves. He handed the jar back to her, watching how she held it and where she put it. The master found Winnie prettier because of her lighter skin, and Bass must have found Jennie prettier for the opposite reason. But it was almost getting too dark in the stable to appreciate her. He stood and turned to the water manger, struck a match, and lit his candle.

He snuck a look over his shoulder and gave her a good soak with his eyes without her seeing him, before easing back down.

"Better," she said.

"Yeah," he said.

"Well," she said, motioning for him to begin.

He smiled and reached for a square and set it on the palm of his other hand and held it out for her. "For you, madam cracker."

She laughed. "Why, thank you, sire," she said, accepting it.

"Not atall," he said. "Got nothing better else to do with my days or even my nights except serve the wonderful likes of you, you know."

"Not until I think up something better for you," she said.

"Oh, yes, ma'am, you right. May I?" Bass asked, reaching for another square.

"Don't be so impertinent to address me directly." She slapped his hand. "I eat, and then you eat. I speak, and you listen."

He cowered in awe. "*Impertinent?*"

"You sound like Satan's left n—— face, who can't pronounce his sins. Listen to me, boy, and shut your trap!" She leaned forward, sneering, and chomped a corner off her cornbread square.

Bass flung his head back in a half-stifled howl, then straightened to see her again. She was too much. Her mouth bulged, and she worked to keep from laughing. She was too cute, whoever she was, this dark fruit tree talking white but laughing black. Bass thought he had to kiss her; whether her mouth was full or not, he didn't care. Now on all fours, he leaned over her nice display of fare.

Jennie jiggled and snorted. She shook her head and clamped her lips, but he was coming for her and was about to plant his first kiss, when she blew a gust that must have originated from her ankles, spraying crumbled cornbread all over his face.

He backed away, afraid to open his eyes.

"Oh, gracious," she said with the lisp of a dry mouth caked with cornbread crumbs. "I'm, I'm, I'm," she stuttered, and he collapsed backward in laughter.

"I'm so sorry," she said. "How awful!"

The horses answered his chortling with stamps and whinnies.

"I'm so sorry, really," she said, "and so thirsty."

His gut hurt, but he couldn't stop. Hearing her slurp a peach and swallow and say, "Ahh," only begged him to continue laughing.

She finally fell silent, so he sat up. "Woo-wee," he said, wiping his eyes and the crumbs and tears away. He eventually hushed.

"I'm so sorry, Bass."

When he saw crumbs stuck to her lips, he couldn't resist laughing again.

"What?" she said. "Stop! That was awful, awful, *awful!*"

"Nah, was funny was all," he said.

"You hate me, don't you?"

"No, ma'am," he said, shaking his head.

"You want me to leave and send Winnie up?"

"Stop that, now," he said, reaching for her and touching her strong arm, like a rope that if she wrapped it around him, he couldn't buck, or if he could, he couldn't shake her. "I want you here and nobody else. Nobody but you, hear me?"

Her eyes softened and shone like raindrops, as though it was morning and he and Jennie were outside far from here, trying to get breakfast made before a downpour.

"You mean it?" she asked.

"Just you," he said. "And my mama, a course, and Auntie Totty—you'd like her—and my grandmammy and granddaddy Sugar, and if you don't mind, my daddy, too, since I ain't seen him for a good long piece."

Jennie smiled.

"But nobody else. Cross my heart," he said, and he crossed his heart.

Her lashes fluttered in the candlelight as if she were part hummingbird. She reached for her corner-chomped cornbread square and nibbled at the rest.

"That don't mean," Bass said, "you and me is gonna be together tonight, though, like husband and wife, just cause Master say it. We will only if we want, right?"

She nodded.

He couldn't make out her expressions behind the shield of her cornbread.

"You want to?" she asked him.

"Course I want to." He reached for a square. "But not cause Master say I want to."

She nodded. "I hear y'all going tomorrow."

He nodded and swallowed, then took another bite. This time, he thought to moan approval, and Strawberry, hearing him, nickered.

Jennie set her unfinished square on the pail cover and reached out past the pickled peaches and continued to hold her hand there in the air, open, waiting. He lifted his hand from his lap and offered it to her, and she took it, a little clamp of a hand halfway around his, as she tipped her head in prayer.

He stopped chewing and tipped his head too.

Her fingers pulsed on his fingers. If she prayed, she prayed silently, so he shut his eyes of her fingers on his fingers and prayed silently with her.

PART THREE

THAT HEAVEN PLACE

16

The Seed

He was dreaming of how she'd fished a peach from the jar and slipped it into his mouth, the syrup running between her fingers, over his lips, and down his chin. How wordlessly she'd watched his jaws move and how wordlessly he'd watched back, until his jaws had gone still, when he thought she might speak, her eyes filled with things to say. But her eyes latched shut, and instead of speaking, she drifted against him, pressing her lips against his. How her tongue, as delicate as a butterfly, slipped into his mouth before he'd had a chance to spit his seed.

He tucked it back quick against his cheek like a wad of tobacco and then rushed to the front to greet his visitor before he'd had a chance to wonder if Sugar had ever kissed his grandmammy this way in the sugarcane off-season. He wondered that now, dreaming. In time, his mouth simply became too sopping wet for him to continue kissing without spilling, so he pulled away and closed his lips to kiss her neck. That's when he chose to swallow the seed, lighter than a rock but hard as one, slicked with moss.

He dreamed that the seed was taking root inside his stomach. Not that he actually feared such a thing could happen. Earlier, he'd thought to himself when shifting on top of her that a tree needs water, so in the dream a similar thought occurred to him, that his seed needed water. He thought of it as his own now, as if it were his own child, and love for it filled him. Not that he called it in his dream mind a boy or girl. But with urgency he prayed for its safety, asking that it be allowed to grow strong from water and be good because of it and not evil.

Below the rhythm he and Jennie made in his dream, the ground answered with its own quiver, as if the ground's heart raced too. God was telling him that his prayer had been answered, that his seed had rooted and would soon grow tall within him, just as the tree inside Jennie had grown within her. In his dream, Bass dreamed of a peach tree growing inside him without sun and rain, without leaves and fruit and bark, only growing into hardening boards to keep him straight.

The quiver grew to a drumming. The Lord was really talking tonight.

Bass consulted Jennie, but as if shy in the candlelight, she kept her eyes shut. Horses snorted in the stalls, and Bass thought clearly, as if awake, *Horses.*

Bass opened his eyes, with the candlelight still shimmering, to find Jennie's turbanless head nestled on his shoulder, an arm across his chest, her legs entwined with his like vines. "Jennie," he whispered. "Jennie?"

She lifted her head in a whip, eyes wide, listening.

"They here," he said.

She moaned and returned her head to his shoulder and squeezed him with her limbs.

The hoofbeats quit up at the mansion.

"I best tack the horses," he said.

"You best tack the horses," she said.

He ran his hands along her back and hips to remember her one more time. He squeezed her until he felt the knots of her spine. "You best wait on me," he said.

She raised her head, her open eyes, and kissed him. "I best wait on you," she said.

He smiled. "You best."

"*You* best."

He nodded. His face warmed. "You right."

He would find shafts of hay and crumbs of cornbread in his hair for days.

◆ ◆ ◆

The body servants to the officers of the Eleventh Texas Cavalry Regiment waited with the horses and mules in the blue dawn on the master's front lawn, when the door opened and the officers themselves filed out onto the mansion's porch, jovial from the sparkling candlelight, all in newly sewn uniforms and polished boots. Those who didn't blow cigar or pipe smoke either spat tobacco or picked their teeth. They mounted their waiting horses and sat tall in the saddle, even those who laughed, and the body servants promptly mounted their horses or mules and followed en masse. The slaves no longer spoke.

From what Bass could piece together from what Master Reeves and the other officers had said in conversation along the way, the regiment's first assignment was to seize Fort Washita from a small housekeeping force of Federals. The military post's strategic position in Chickasaw Nation, Indian Territory, at the mouth of the Washita River, behind a dense forest to the west, had once helped the U.S. Army to protect the Five Civilized Tribes from the raiding Plains Indians twenty years earlier. Just eighteen miles north of Texas's primary entry point, where the Texas Trail and the Butterfield Overland Trail converged to connect Texas to the North, its location proved imminently strategic again. The officers talked openly, as if they trusted their body servants, all of them, as if their body servants weren't slaves and no longer even the enemy.

With so many men and animals and wagons of men assembling at Colbert's Ferry for a muster roll, officers of companies rendezvousing with soldiers of companies, clouding up the trail in the absence of longhorns, Bass found it difficult to maintain many thoughts. He wondered if their milling at the banks for ferry passage could be heard back at the plantation. If they sounded to Jennie like a moan. Otherwise, he watched his total circumference as if he were ordered to watch the world spin, as if his life or the world depended on it, as if he were at the center of it.

They crossed into Indian Territory in a tight formation, with scouts riding out ahead of the infantry, followed by the highest ranking officers, including Master Reeves, and then, caged in the middle, the buglers, color bearers, hospital surgeons and stewards, teamsters, blacksmiths, supply wagons, livestock, and unarmed slaves, all followed by the lowest-ranking officers and a rearguard of infantry. Master Reeves mostly ignored Bass, except for the times he turned his Morgan around and rode to where Bass rode to point out men and their insignia, explaining the bars and stars and sleeve badges, which was a lot like learning poker all over again.

When they arrived at Fort Washita, the fires of the Federals still burned. By signs on the road, the understaffed Federals, a force no greater than a single company of a hundred men or so, had abandoned the fort only that morning and were retreating in a north-western direction, with the likely intention of finding reinforcement in Kansas. The Eleventh's Company B remained behind to secure the fort and the bulk of the regiment's supplies, while Companies A and C advanced in chase. This time, the officers positioned their servants directly behind them and distributed munitions. By orders of Colonel Young, no slave was permitted to fire a weapon; he could only resupply his master. And if his master was to fall in the line of duty, then the slave immediately became the property of the regiment and must serve as ordered or be executed for insubordination.

Once the colonel had clipped ahead to rejoin the officers, Master Reeves slowed his Morgan and leaned Bass's way, when he usually expected Bass to lean his.

"That's fine and dandy until I tell you differently, you hear me?" Master Reeves said. "Don't hesitate to listen, or *I* will execute you."

◆ ◆ ◆

Companies A and C gave chase for two days but never came closer to the fleeing Federals than a day's ride away, so the fighting force made an about-face, immediately seeking sport instead, feeding on the deer, rabbit, and dove that Bass and the other slaves hunted for them in advance of the march.

Throughout the summer of 1861, the Eleventh Texas Cavalry remained at Fort Washita to assist Brigadier General Albert Pike of the Department of Indian Territory in training a volunteer brigade of two thousand Cherokee, Chickasaw, Choctaw, and Creek. But no Seminoles. Clander, Colonel Young's slave, the oldest and darkest and most smiley among them, had seen his fair share of his master's maps and could draw in the dirt the nations of the territory from memory. Five vague clouds bunched together to make a boot, though a boot without a heel.

"A slave's boot!" Bass added, and the other slaves snickered.

The smallest cloud, where the laces started, just east of the toe, was Seminole Nation, and it floated directly above where the slaves sat in the dirt staring, if a body was to drift straight up to it along the Chickasaw-Choctaw border, or swim rather, creek after creek in the low land.

"A body would have to reach his arms out like Jesus hisself to keep the Shawnee Hills pushed to the right and the Arbuckle Mountains and all the townships along yonder way to the left," said Clander. He looked up from his drawing and pointing stick and eyed each slave bunched about him, tight as scuppernongs. He looked down again and tapped Chickasaw Nation. "Emet, Tishomingo, Viola, Stonewall, all of them, a lot of townships, so you gotta keep them arms out the whole stretch and then, once acrost this river here, the Canadian it's called, head left, just left."

"I seen the land there," Bass said, and the full circle looked at him, some in awe, some in disbelief. "Flattest I ever seen," he said. "Flat as a wagon."

"A body be certain to find a Seminole settlement somewhere along the river bank, ain't that right?" Clander asked. His eyes appeared unsure, hopeful, as if he was really asking.

Bass nodded. "That's right."

Without smiling, Clander broke his drawing and pointing and tapping stick in two and rubbed his hands through his map.

The slaves and Indians were never allowed an opportunity for direct contact, but Bass could see by their eyes which tribe hated him. When he passed a Chickasaw, the Chickasaw searched out his eyes. The others wouldn't, as if he were nothing but a wind passing behind his master. The Chickasaw, though, saw him with contempt, as if Bass were a little, lazy cattle egret his master should hoof away a time or two for following along more than working. The Chickasaw owned more slaves than any other tribe, Clander had said. He'd said even the freedmen in Chickasaw Nation weren't free.

To escape to the friendliest of the tribes, a body would have to avoid a slew of Chickasaw.

♦ ♦ ♦

The loyalties of Missouri remained largely divided late in the summer of 1861, despite the legislature's vote not to secede. Sentiment to do so had been growing stronger ever since the St. Louis massacre in May, when Union forces seized the city's arsenal and opened fire on unarmed prisoners and civilian protesters. In the clashes that followed, the Federals gained control of Jefferson City and Booneville, but the pro-Confederate Missouri State Guard continued to battle Union troops in the southern portion of the state.

By August, Brigadier General Nathaniel Lyon had amassed his Union Army of the West in and around Springfield, with intentions of acquiring control of the remainder of the state, if not also to make gains into Arkansas. Brigadier General Ben McCulloch, headquartered in Little Rock, had been raising his own Confederate Army of the West, comprised of regiments from Arkansas, Louisiana, and Texas. By August the troop strength numbered seven thousand, but whenever it rendezvoused with Missouri's renegade militia, consisting of five thousand men, the Confederate forces would outnumber Lyon's by more than two to one. McCulloch hoped to avoid further invasion by attacking first, and by crushing Lyon, he hoped to make a convincing argument to Missourians which side they should all belong to.

Pike's Indian brigade stayed behind at Fort Washita to continue training, while the Eleventh Texas Cavalry set out on the first day of August to join McCulloch's army in Fort Smith on their continued march northward.

Civilian throngs greeted the cavalry as they arrived in Fort Smith. They lined the roads and boardwalks, sat on rooftops and in trees, to wave or hoot or present flowers. So close to his old home in Van Buren, Bass wished that he could rejoice too. He couldn't expect to see his family among the faces. But any moment, he thought, Master Reeves, the first one, the father, would surely appear, with the mistress of course, to see their son off to war, to give him cake and an embrace. But upon their return and upon their departure the following morning, the faces he saw gradually fading past were all so impossibly unfamiliar.

◆ ◆ ◆

McCulloch's Army of the West traveled the same road Bass and his master had taken to hunt hogs in the Boston Mountains only a few months earlier, where he'd seen that captured slave fly away into the air like a ghost. He wondered why his life so frequently repeated itself or if all lives must—how after a while, when you got experienced and really looked around, roads were the same roads and horses were the same horses and masters were the same masters. It was true, even in the case of his two. Just like the sun was the same, like the days of the week. With all the time Bass had on his hands to do nothing but sit on Strawberry and think, while the master spent more and more of his time conversing with the other officers, Bass was beginning to think the key to surviving the world was to simplify it. To ignore the differences that flashed before your eyes in bright, dazzling colors and focus instead on the similarities, those neutral signs coated in dust. To say, *Yeah, I see you peeking. I see you a-coming. I ready. Boy, ain't I!*

He saw the outskirts of Fayetteville for the first time yet did so differently than he would have before and not simply because he was surrounded by numbers far greater than the town itself. Fayetteville, from every perspective he was given, until it fell out of view, was just another Van Buren, just another Fort Smith. It had nice mountains around it like needlepoint pillows, sure, but that was what he had to ignore. It also had rich old white people on horseback and in carriages; it had slaves on their feet; it had poor white people on their feet too. The same could be said about Springdale and Bentonville. More and more buildings and property lines were made of stacked yellow rock, as if there must have been gold in Ozark water. But the barns were made of gray wood like any barn, and the birds off the road took to the air just like they always did.

◆ ◆ ◆

Whenever the army camped, the body servants worked together to pitch tents for the officers, to build a fire or two, and to dig a latrine trench. Sometimes they set up tables and chairs if their masters wanted to study maps and consult or play cards. And of course, they fetched. Food and coffee from the cooks or cigars and matches and rye from trunks called lockers but also corn-cobs and water for their masters caught off guard at the latrine. The slaves worked as usual, but with so many enlisted white men performing the same duties all around them—pitching their own tents, building their own fires, digging their own trenches, fetch-ing this or that—work didn't seem as much like work anymore to Bass and his friends. It was war, and so far, they preferred it to peacetime.

◆ ◆ ◆

According to scout reports, Lyon's army remained camped at Spring-field, perhaps not anticipating McCulloch's plans of crossing into Missouri and joining forces with the Missouri State Guard, com-manded by Major General Sterling Price. On August 8 McCulloch and Price camped their men on farmland straddling Wilson's Creek, located between Fayetteville Road to the west and Telegraph Road to the east, which led northeast to Springfield only twelve miles away. The intention was to rest the men and animals and strike Lyon the following evening.

McCulloch stationed pickets a mile away on Telegraph Road to maintain watch for potential movements by Lyon, while the Eleventh Texas Cavalry, along with two battalions of infantry and a mounted regiment from Arkansas, were positioned at the rear, surrounded by crops of corn and purple-hull peas.

Bass watched soldiers throwing blankets on the ground and piling their pickings on them. He watched so many versions of a white face at work, in the field, in camp shucking and hulling, and every one of them beamed with joy over the prospect of eating not just a plate or a pot but a whole farm. It wasn't a plantation here in Missouri, but it provided them with all they wanted. Bass watched their dirty faces while he picked his own extravagant share. He watched them as if he couldn't stop watching, as if he were a young'un watching kittens. Watching how their limbs were mighty spritely despite their red tired eyes.

That evening, everyone in the rearguard ate like an officer. Bass heard white men say it that way, but he saw something else. The officers were officers and nothing different, but he saw many of the soldiers, after their long supper, pull out writing materials and write letters, more that night than he'd seen before. The only complaint among them was the heat, how it persisted through the night, which seemed the only difference between the soldiers and body servants. The body servants didn't have a care in the world, not with corn and purple hulls aplenty.

The body servants had already been sent away to their bedding when Master Reeves parted from his fellow officers still seated with their feet propped on the table, sipping or smoking. Master Reeves passed through the light of a smoldering fire, heading in the direction of the latrine, but he stopped and leaned against what in the day would have been the only shade tree within a quarter mile of the woods to their south. "I will tell you what makes a vassal good," he said, projecting his voice as his stream trickled over bark.

Facing both the officers' table and the tree, but closer to the tree, Bass shut his eyes.

"What is that?" Colonel Young asked, who never unbuttoned his collar, not even this late in the night, not even when his feet were propped on a table.

"It is judgment," Master Reeves said over his continued stream. "It is never madness. Restraint is worth more than the raw nerve of a fool."

"No, no, no, George," Colonel Young said. "I meant, what is a *vassal*?"

A brief silence was followed by laughter among the officers.

Bass opened his eyes and watched the table shake from the officers' laughter. Either he smelled the master's urine or the trench itself.

"Sorry, gentlemen," Master Reeves said, shuffling away to his tent. "Forgive my little song. But this bird must fly. This ship must sail."

Another silence was followed by more laughter, more table shaking. Then the officers stood and separated. Soon, it seemed, everyone but Bass was asleep. With a hand over his nose, he wondered if sleep would even be possible in this heat.

◆ ◆ ◆

On the humid morning of August 9, McCulloch withdrew the pickets from their forward positions and issued orders to the army to break camp in preparation for a late-afternoon advance. A herd of fat gray clouds drifted in by midafternoon and brought stop-and-go showers. The men simply sat under their hats and coats, until the officers issued orders that they unload the tents from the wagons and pitch them for the storage of their weapons and cartridge pouches. By dusk, the clouds had merged into a sieve, the rain falling without a rush, lightly but steadily. McCulloch revised his plans, deciding to delay their attack until the following evening.

After midnight the rain finally subsided and eventually quit. On fleeter winds, the clouds flushed, and beneath the cold light of the stars the temperature began to drop. Sleep came easily to the men after their second day on purple hulls and corn. The latrine trench, now filled with rainwater, had lost much of its stench.

Minutes after five o'clock, on the morning of August 10, Bass woke from a dream about fox squirrels yet still saw in his mind their golden breasts as much as he heard their claws scuttling across the ground as far away as the woods just south of the regiment. He sat up, wondering why so many had come out so early after the rain.

"Wha—," Clander began to ask, but he immediately clipped himself to listen again for an answer to his own unfinished question.

Bass squinted past the camp of sleeping Arkansawyers, into the far darkness, at the billowing thunderhead that was the woods. Wet leaves turned and shone like stars on water, a row of them. Before the image of raised rifles could ignite articulation, it was as if every tree in those woods suddenly cracked in two.

Minié balls whizzed and, like hail, pelted the soft ground and rent tent cloth, as men cried out. Colonel Franz Sigel's brigade of Missouri volunteers had surprised the Confederate rearguard, while the bulk of General Lyon's army simultaneously attacked McCulloch's army across the creek at its forward position on Telegraph Road.

Despite orders to hold and fire, many Confederates fled, even abandoning their weapons and boots. Amid the confusion, the officers and their body servants worked in tandem, exactly how they'd drilled with two rifles, with the servants reloading them as quickly as possible, one after another, as their masters aimed and fired. After firing twice, Master Reeves gestured for Bass to hold on to the loaded one and follow him, and he ran for the horses, which were bumping hinds as they stamped at their tether ropes.

"Your turn now, boy," the master told him. "I load, and you pick them off. Right in the buttons. Right in the buttons."

Master Reeves worked a ramrod with surprising speed and grace. Bass hadn't known he could work at all, but the master kept pace as Bass found his rhythm shooting white men. You could forget where the Federals were from, that they weren't exactly his enemy. They carried weapons and would kill him, so he learned to see the breast of the coat more than the man and wanted to fill the brass with lead.

He must have pulled the trigger twenty-five or more times and knocked down as many men, the closest ones first and then anyone pointing his way, including a couple of officers surveying, until Master Reeves stopped him amid a lull, or what at last seemed like one, here in this part of the fight. Orders were for the rearguard, beginning with the cavalries, to retreat to the high ground to the northwest, beyond the cow pasture that was beyond the long rows of purple hulls. So they saddled their horses, loaded them with munitions, and rode with heads lowered for the oaken hilltop as the infantry from Arkansas slogged behind them.

Once the cavalries reached the cover of the hill, they loaded their rifles and waited for Sigel's brigade to advance within musket range. Instead, from the edge of the woods below, gunners rolled out artillery. If any of the officers had predicted the lull, a withdrawal of soldiers to clear the way for artillery, no one said.

Bass hated to watch men fall. He'd rather load a musket and even fire one and keep firing, believing each minié ball he sent was a seed of everlasting life direct from God through him, Johnny N—— Appleseed, than stand idly by and watch a man's full collapse, seeing the agony rip his face and knowing that it wasn't so much agony of pain but agony of knowledge that this was it, that fate had fallen on him, and that there was nothing for him to do but fall with it, ready or not.

Bye, Mama. Bye, Auntie. Bye, Sugar and Sugarmama. Bye, Jennie and that Heaven place we never made it to with that family we never made. That's what he thought he might think if God had switched things between him and those white men falling.

◆ ◆ ◆

Even though General McCulloch would neglect to mention in his battle report how his failure to repost his pickets once rain delayed his plans for attack had allowed Lyon to surprise his troops that next morning, he was contrite in the private writings of his journal, believing that only providence had stepped in to make amends for his "grave error." "Providence, apparently," he wrote, "wears gray."

Lying hilltop on his belly in the shade of the oaks, Bass saw it. How bold providence stepped in, no shame at all, right through the front door. Sigel's forces emerged from the woods in a tight formation, appearing to prepare for a quick march for the hill, but the Third Louisiana Infantry, crossing Wilson's Creek, approached Sigel's eastern flank, and Sigel's Missouri volunteers stopped to watch. They relaxed even, leaning against their rifles, or if mounted, lowering their rifles.

Sigel would explain in his own report that his men had mistaken the gray-clad Third Louisiana for the gray-clad First Iowa. It must have seemed like providence to Sigel's men to see reinforcements arriving at the very moment they were needed most. It must have seemed like providence to the Third Louisiana to meet such a hospitable enemy.

In a half hour, the Third Louisiana had decimated Sigel's brigade, killing or wounding at least 250 men and routing the others across the creek, where they vanished into a cornfield. Sigel would unite a small contingency with Lyon's forces north of Telegraph Road, while others simply dispersed, fleeing no one would ever entirely know where.

Bass couldn't believe what he saw. It was something God made for idle men to see, that was certain. But why? He couldn't hazard a guess. Wouldn't.

◆ ◆ ◆

Bolstered by the Third Louisiana Infantry and their four captured cannons, the Texans and Arkansawyers of the rearguard now turned their attention to the opposite side of the hill. Lyon's army was wheeling to the southwest to avoid a direct assault by McCulloch or Price, whose Missouri State Guard now massed on a ridge adjacent to the hill. Lyon pressed with superior artillery, eventually backing the Confederates off the hill, where they found themselves among so many of Sigel's Missourians who had perished in the mud.

An hour later the Confederates repelled Lyon from the hill and remounted it, and for two more hours the engagement ebbed and flowed there, washing on and off the hill, its oak shade now obliterated. The shredded wood of the trees, though, made the ground a hardened floor for improved aiming.

Bass noticed Colonel Young standing a few whittled trees over, as if purposefully making a target of himself, though gazing in Bass's direction. Bass pretended not to notice, but there the colonel was, standing over Master Reeves and hollering down at him. "Not this way," he yelled, pointing at Bass with a pretty fair aim.

"Not this way," he repeated, but Master Reeves remained where he knelt, continuing to feed the tape primer and exchange his ready musket for Bass's smoking spent one. Bass didn't slow either. Master Reeves hollered back, because to be heard a body had to: "He's our best shot. Watch him, just watch him."

Bass scanned the slope, the valley. He was careful and even— *one Mississippi, two Mississippi, three Mississippi*—absorbing the full composition if possible before allowing his eyes to gravitate to the obvious choice, a gunner carrying a charge, an officer rallying, a sniper resetting, a fleet-footed lionheart charging. He didn't like to overthink it. The master told him not to, and he didn't want to either. As long as Bass picked one, there was one less to pick from next time. Before he could think past simple assessment, he found the buttons and drew the trigger. He never looked back.

Even when he scanned for his next shot and saw a body dead or languishing, he never paused to consider if he'd caused it. Later he'd wonder what had happened inside him, how he'd reached such calm. He had, and that realization was enough at the moment, because he enjoyed the feeling and fought to preserve it.

At some point, Young had returned to his tree, little more than a scratching post. Clander helplessly waited for his master to take the ready rifle out of his hands—something Bass witnessed as he reached for another rifle from Master Reeves before pulling another trigger.

When General Lyon fell, his horse shot out from under him, a great cheer went up on the hilltop. And when the general rode out to rally his men on another horse and fell again and this time did not rise, the rebel cheers turned to wolf howls and redtail screams. This was the first Union general to die in the war.

After Colonel Sigel had taken command of the Union army and retreated to Springfield and then to Rolla, where the Confederates unfathomably quit pursuing, no one had yet claimed responsibility for taking Lyon's fatal shot. Perhaps the shooter was altogether unaware of his deed, firing prematurely the providential stray, or perhaps before he could claim credit or blame, depending on which side he fought, he died himself. A wise slave would have much to fear in any circumstance—if he were ever captured, for instance, or if a vengeful Union were to win the war months later. Bass, never calmer than when he was shooting, would have no clear recollection of killing General Lyon.

Master Reeves asked him again and again if he wasn't sure he didn't, almost begging him to say he did. Bass had shot more than one cavalry officer that day and remembered seeing a man in blue on a bay, that was true—the man losing his plumed Hardee hat as he fisted the reins this way and that, as if the rider couldn't decide if he should go forward or back or couldn't because of carnage, so he went side to side instead, and as if to catch the hat hanging on the roiling air as if floating, he raked his saber from its scabbard, not missing it by much, with his brown hair bouncing almost as free as that hat, like only a white man's hair can, a man also with a beard and a mustache, just the way Master Reeves liked a man to wear a beard, and a man with gold shoulder boards on an unbuttoned coat, a double-breasted coat belted at the waist. But with four buttons unbuttoned, how could the man be shot, you know, there in the buttons, without a clear target? So Bass's best guess, he would say, again and again, was, "No, God bless him."

17

What a N—— Wants

Bass had just begun to set up chairs for the officers' meeting when Major General Price walked into the tent and did not sit. His baby face was red. And he turned around as if to speak to others, but he kept turning in a circle, tamping his feet, seeming impatient for something. Maybe for a chair, so Bass hurried to pull one to him.

"Take that away this instant," Price demanded. "We don't need to be sitting."

"Yes, sir. Sorry, sir."

Price turned his red face to the officers filing into the tent. "Stop looking for a place to sit. We shouldn't be here at all except to agree to get going."

Bass folded the chair to carry it back out of the tent. But a black preacher-like suit sleeve came into view, and Bass felt a tap on his arm.

Bass snapped his feet together and bowed. "Yes, sir?" he said, and Brigadier General McCulloch pointed at the plot of grass beside Price, who hung clenched fists straight down at his sides.

"Place that right next to Price," McCulloch said.

"Yes, sir," Bass nodded. He popped the chair open again and set it down so close to Price that he feared the major general would beat him for it, but Price only huffed, asking McCulloch, "Why? Why?" as McCulloch sat down with a cigar in his mouth instead of words.

Bass set up the rest of the chairs, then eased out of the way and found Master Reeves standing in the back of the tent, attempting to suppress a smile that was hardly only a smile.

For a half hour Price and McCulloch, though more Price than McCulloch, argued about what the army's next step should be. Price wanted to remain aggressive and continue pursuing Lyon's routed forces until they were all captured or killed, expunging Missouri of all other Federals. McCulloch was more pragmatic, arguing that since the enlistment time had expired for those serving in the Missouri State Guard, the men needed rest, since many demanded it, and that without them, he believed it best to fall back to Arkansas and finish the fight another time. The generals spoke as if no other officers existed in the tent, though it was clear to Bass by how Master Reeves tossed his head or slapped his gloves or hat against a leg that the master agreed with Price and not his fellow Texan. But McCulloch was commander, and given recent dispatches from the Confederate Citizens Court in Gainesville, Texas, about a Unionist uprising afoot in the state's northern counties, presumably exacerbated by the absence of military authority, he instead ordered the Eleventh Texas Cavalry to return home to defend it.

Price stormed from the tent, his thin tuft of silver hair lifting up in a wave from the top of his head like corn silk, while McCulloch stroked his beard, tapped his ash, and proceeded in a low, church-like tone to discuss the Peace Party. It was, he said, a secret society in Gainesville that was sympathetic to the Union and that comprised at least forty members. Unlike the Citizens Court, whose judge and jury were all slaveholders, none of the Peace Party members were. They held meetings at night in secluded barns and mills but only after everyone in attendance had demonstrated membership with esoteric hand signs of a fox and a dove, followed by a grip and a whispered password—usually a song title, such as "Listen to the Mockingbird," "Old Black Joe," or "Skip to My Lou." Their desire to grow the society with new initiates had allowed a spy with ties to the Citizens Court to infiltrate them. The mission of the Eleventh Texas Cavalry was to arrest all members and hold them for trial.

McCulloch concluded the meeting by calling on Captain George Reeves to step forward. McCulloch stood up, and Bass watched the general's non–cigar hand reach into one of his preacher pockets. Once the master stood before him, the two men identical in height, McCulloch told him to remove his bars. "For your valorous service on Bloody Hill, I'm promoting you to major."

An elbow nudged Bass in the arm, and he found Clander standing beside him. "He getting your major n—— stars," Clander whispered.

Bass heeled him in the shin and watched McCulloch pin his stars on the master's frock collar.

◆ ◆ ◆

Upon arriving at Gainesville, the regiment milled beneath the live oaks on the courthouse lawn and along storefronts on the square, while the Citizens Court privately briefed Colonels William Young and James Bourland and Major George Reeves. The regiment then marched back out of town and set up camp, where for a day and a night the officers strategized on the best manner of dividing the regiment into bands of twenty men, in addition to the timing and place of each arrest. In less than a week, the Eleventh had arrested all members of the Peace Party, except for two who'd attempted to escape and were shot dead. They had also arrested two outspoken Unionists suspected of membership. To the surprise of the officers, very few members or suspected members put up a fight. Many even openly admitted to their affiliation.

Once the Eleventh had corralled the last of the enemies at the regiment's camp, forty-two of them, the trials began. Each morning for a week and a half, five or six of the defendants were loaded on a wagon and escorted from camp to the courthouse, and by the end of the day, they were found guilty of treason and hanged from the oaks.

All but one of the prisoners had ridden up to his noose on a cavalry horse. Barnabas Burch, a seventy-three-year-old too arthritic in his legs to mount one, was loaded onto a juror's carriage. There were no potato sacks for these men, left to dangle long past their death. Five or six men in a tree, until dusk.

Each night Master Reeves turned to the throng of hushed onlookers and stretched his arms wide as if to forgive and embrace them all.

"Merry Christmas!" he'd exclaim. Some would laugh. Some wouldn't. So he'd say it again, louder—"Merry Christmas!" He'd sing it, and he'd keep singing it, as long as it took for enough of them to laugh. Sometimes enough wasn't enough for the master until all of them joined in.

After an hour or so, soldiers rode up on mounts and cut the shit-fouled corpses down with bayonets. Once the soldiers made a show of circling or rearing their horses up on two legs, pairs of slaves toted the corpses away by their boots and noose, buzzing with flies, to an adjacent warehouse, where families, not always dressed in black, collected the bodies for burial.

Nightly that week Bass prayed his gratitude. He was a neglected slave again, merely a shadow following his master in case a thing needed to be fetched. Not a giver and not a taker. Just a doer.

◆ ◆ ◆

Only on the final night of the regiment's encampment in Gainesville did Master Reeves ride home to his plantation, thirty-three miles away.

"I find myself needing female companionship. Don't you?" Master Reeves said.

"Yes, sir!" Bass said, not feigning his enthusiasm.

"I'll even give you the choice this time. How about that? Winnie or Jennie? Your pick."

Bass hesitated, to create the appearance of a debate, to keep some things *his* things.

Master Reeves spun around in his saddle. "Fuck that," he said. "You're too modest a n—— to say what you really want. I know what a n—— wants." He sat forward and didn't speak again on the subject until they'd arrived at the plantation just after dark—Winnie and Jennie already singing in the distance.

The master whistled to the melody and then stopped as he dismounted at his front porch.

"I'll send for Rub to help you with the horses," he said, waving his plumed Hardee hat to sweep away the gnats. "After that, plant your seed, boy, and I'll see you at sunup."

How could a place have no place? Bass was relieved to be back, but not here exactly, yet here exactly, and to have his back to the master. To have a moment with no talking. The singing had stopped, which meant soon he ought to see more than hear. Now, it was just Bass and the horses in a space that moved over land he knew but didn't love. It was here and there, without being here or there. Something he could take wherever he went.

Bass stalled the Morgan and was currying Strawberry, when the stable door creaked. Rub's steps proceeded without his usual haste, as if he were carrying a corpse, but then he bulled around with the Morgan in the next stall, unbuckling straps and tossing the saddle on a stand.

"How do, Rub?" Bass called.

When Rub didn't answer, hearing only Rub's swirling brush-strokes, Bass felt a letdown about what the master's decision must have been. He stepped away from Strawberry.

Rub refused to look at him.

Bass took a step past the Morgan's flicking tail and touched Rub's shoulder, and Rub recoiled.

"You promised! You member your promise, don't you?"

Bass didn't move, and then he did, with the slightest nod. "I hold on to my promises."

Rub stared at Bass's chest as if daring Bass to look down or away and risk getting charged.

"You all right?" Bass asked. "Anything new going on here?"

"I don't be studying *new*," Rub said. "I study staying alive. I study Rub and the only thing Rub got an eye for. I study that, and that be where my studying quit." His eyes bulged, as if witnessing a drag-onfly mounting a horsefly right there on Bass's buttons.

Bass reached out and gave Rub a pat on the shoulder, and Rub withdrew, though with half the violence as before. So Bass patted him again, and this time, Rub let him.

"Who you think gonna win this war?" Rub asked.

Bass shook his head.

"Will it matter to us, you think?"

Bass lifted his shoulders and shook his head again.

"That be why I don't be studying *new*."

◆ ◆ ◆

Rub didn't speak again until after he'd walked out of the Morgan's stall to leave. He stood still first, out of view from Bass, who was now resting on a fresh bed of hay in his own stall. "Holding promises and nothing else, right?" he asked.

"Right."

"Night," Rub said, finishing his walk out.

"Night."

Bass listened to the cicadas singing outside more than to the horses munching and blowing inside. He sure wished a full regiment wasn't camped nearby to track him down if he had a mind to run. If Winnie was the one to come to him tonight, why should he stay? What else could he and she do? What could they possibly talk about?

He sucked on a hay straw, and it occurred to him what he could do. It seemed a childish notion, but it could work. He rose to his feet, collected his candle, and walked to the back of Strawberry's stall. He set his candle bottle on the water manger to give him light and pitched in more hay. He stroked Strawberry's nose and ears and talked to him, saying what a good horse he was. Once Strawberry's eyes glazed, approaching sleep, Bass took a shallow breath, blew out the candle, and crawled beneath the hay.

If he hid somewhere and Winnie couldn't find him, he thought she might discover herself glad and head straight back to the cabin to show Rub and Jennie that nothing had happened. Even if Winnie decided to wait him out, thinking Bass had stepped out to do his business in the trees or tend to the master or whatnot, he could wait her out just the same. It was always easier to say no when a body didn't actually have to say it.

Bass waited for footfalls, but in the dark with his eyes shut against the straw, exhausted, he couldn't wait long after all and drifted to sleep.

◆ ◆ ◆

He never heard footfalls or the stable door open, not even the whispers of his name, nor did he see the light held over him until a blunt object prodded him through the hay. In the arm at first, as if to awaken him, and then in the gut.

Bass shook through his cover to find Jennie, like a dream, leaning low and smiling, her dark skin shining from the light of the tin candle box, which she held dear as a baby, with both hands close to her breasts. A snicker that wasn't Jennie's lured his eyes away, toward his feet, to find Winnie after all, standing upright and clutching Rub's pitchfork. Her lighter skin almost glowed there in the distance, like a mirror's reflection of the box's milky windows.

With a quick motion that made Bass blink, Winnie jabbed him once more in the leg with the end of the handle.

"Hey!" Bass said, flinching away.

"You wake yet good?" Winnie asked, and she stuck him again.

He laughed, and they laughed.

"Dang it," he said. "How'd y'all find me?"

Jennie bobbed her head at something above him. "You mean beside that telltale sign you left, almost like a door knocker?"

Bass tilted his head back and saw his candle bottle sitting where he'd set it, right beside its shadow. Blowing it out had seemed good enough. "Huh," he said. He lifted his shoulders and smirked. "Didn't expect nobody to pay no mind to what's behind a horse." His eyes darted for the shadows beyond the light. "Hey, where Strawberry at?"

Jennie shrugged with a grin, and Strawberry nickered from the next stall.

"Who's you hiding from?" Winnie asked.

Bass looked at her as if he didn't understand the question, and she stuck him again.

"Hey, stop that," he said.

"You ain't hiding?" Winnie said. "You learn to sleep *under* a bed now?"

"You shoot dead as many white men as I done, you learn to do all kind a things that don't seem to make much sense."

Their smiles faded, but he didn't want to talk anymore about killing white men. "So what y'all women up to?"

Winnie stood straight and leaned the pitchfork against the stall wall beside her. "Master sent for us to come down here."

Bass looked at Jennie, standing erect now herself, and though she looked elsewhere, she nodded.

"He say he knowed what a n—— want," Winnie said.

"So what does a n—— want?" Jennie asked, darting her eyes to Bass and holding there on his eyes, cold and hard without a blink, all surface and shine, like her skin. "Master left off the full explanation of what n—— men want, so we gotta ask."

Bass looked back and forth between the cousins, waiting for a smile. When one didn't show, he smiled to smooth the air, and then Jennie joined him.

Winnie rolled her eyes. "Y'all make your mind. Don't matter no which-a-way to me. I can start or step out, or heck, we can go same time. Whatever Master want, what I say. I long past guessing. He do work in a mysterious way, I declare!"

Jennie laughed and shook her head.

"What?" Winnie said. "Master sent for us to seed, so let's seed and get to sleep, what I say, shoot! We make it quick, and Rub won't have no idea, you know?"

Bass nodded, holding a smile back. He eyed Jennie and pointed at her. "Jennie, Winnie, minnie, mo," he said, shifting his pointer from one to the other, "catch a n—— by the toe."

Jennie crossed her arms, and Winnie stepped closer, her eyebrows raised in anticipation.

"If he won't work," Bass said, "then let him go; skidum, skidee, skidoo. But when you get money, your little bride will surely find out where you hide. So there's the door, and when I count four, then out goes—*you*." His pointer landed where he'd known in the beginning it would. "Sorry, Winnie," he said. "Best you step out, I think."

"We'll call for you when we're done," Jennie said.

"You sure?" Winnie asked.

Bass nodded, and Jennie nodded.

"Fact," Jennie said, "you can head back to Rub." She offered the box light, but Winnie's arms hung limp.

"Yeah," Bass said, "that way all us getting what we want."

Jennie took a step closer to Winnie, thrusting the box light at her until Winnie at last accepted it and looked down at it.

"*All us?*" Winnie said, turning away with the light.

"But if Master or Mr. Hagan ask," Jennie said, "you already took a turn, right?"

"Uh-huh," she said, and the stable door creaked open and shut.

Bass didn't wait for his eyes to adjust to what little blue might seep in from outside. He sat up on his knees and reached out for Jennie, finding dress folds and clasping a dress-covered leg. One of her hands came searching for his hand and lay still on his, like a turtle on a log. They held hands that way for at least three good breaths, before she lowered herself on top of him, pressing her face against his chest, her hair tickling his chin, her toenails grazing his ankles, like cute little turtle feet stretching, searching, readying to push off into water.

18

A Revelation

Bass and Jennie never tired enough for sleep, as if each time they stroked the other their only purpose was fire, as if there had never been water and never a turtle, only log on log. Or tree on tree. Only the roosters could separate them and make them stand to dress. Then Jennie ran to the mansion to start breakfast.

Bass grazed with the master in minutes. Once they stood, Mistress Reeves gave Master Reeves a kiss and a hug and clung to his arm.

Bass and Jennie stared into that vast starless space stretched between them, at all that thin acreage, that matter of life and death, which kept growing harder and harder to breathe or accept as natural.

Bass, in tow of the master, rode out at sunup at a gallop. Two hours later they'd caught up with the regiment traveling at a wagon's pace only a few miles north of Gainesville, with a pack of dogs trailing behind for the scraps Colonel Young had ordered the men to throw out behind them. By the next evening, upon the regiment's return to Fort Washita, more than two dozen dogs loyally followed—a fine rearguard, ideally alert to unfriendly Indians or Federals.

Cherokees from General Pike's First and Second Mounted Rifles regiments crowded outside the gate to greet the Texas cavalry, and once the last man of the Eleventh had filed into the fort, including the slaves—all but the dogs, a panting cloud sniffing up meekly— the Cherokees, who hadn't eaten meat in weeks, broke into a run, as if in a footrace.

Those among the Cherokees who had knives unsheathed them and slit the dogs' throats and skinned them on the spot. Those who didn't have knives grabbed the canines by their tails or hind legs and slammed them onto the ground to break their necks. Some dogs scattered. Some hunkered in quivering balls. Some weren't even dead when skinned, howling screams Bass hadn't heard since the battlefield, and for hours, the flayed carcasses cooked over stone fires or in pots of water.

Smoke drifted like fog over the compound throughout the night. It was a smell not unlike any meat-eating fire, and that was the problem. For the first time in his life, Bass lost his craving for meat. Didn't want it. The cooks assured him what they were serving was steer, but Bass ate corn and nothing else. And he ate corn the next day for breakfast.

◆ ◆ ◆

The Eleventh Texas Cavalry remained at Fort Washita throughout the fall, continuing to help Pike train his Indian brigade. When the officers grew fatigued with the traditional training and wanted to sit outside without shade on the first day in October that felt like October and sip whiskey, Master Reeves suggested they defer to Bass's services for target practice.

With the volunteers seated on the fort wall and along the hillside below it, Master Reeves positioned Bass on the shoal of a creek at the foot of the hill. Water that had once rushed was now dammed by beavers and merely trickled past Bass. Upon the master's word, Bass fired into the tangled wood and mud of the dam, about a hundred feet upstream.

When the dam took the cartridge without effect, the volunteers roared with laughter. Their legs, dangling off the fort wall, swung out and back. On the hillside, their backs reclined into the dirt and grass, their feet in the air. Bass reloaded and fired again. The laughter grew wilder as cartridge after cartridge hit the dam with a thud. When Bass had emptied one ammunition pouch, he began another.

He had only had an idea. That morning, when Master Reeves had asked him what he could shoot at if he had a mind to shoot at something, Bass had answered with the dam, because he hadn't wanted to kill anything. "What good would that do?" the master had asked, and Bass had shrugged. "Don't rightly know, sir," he'd said, "but I miss sitting in the creek." The master hadn't been to sleep yet and smelled of rye. The master's head bobbed. "Damn the dam, you say," he'd said. "Hey, why not?"

These Indians had no respect for Negroes. They never spoke to Bass or anyone else among the slaves. But they weren't Seminoles. They were Cherokees, Choctaws, Chickasaws, and Creeks. Bass fired and fired and fired. For an hour and then longer, and though the laughter began to diminish, snickers occasionally circulated. After all, it had been only an idea. To hit two up-and-down lines he only imagined: one left of midway, dropping down from where a forking branch sprouted, and one right of midway, dropping down from where a gnawed trunk came to a point. He shot the base of the forking branch a few times, then gradually fired lower and lower in what he hoped was a straight line. He did the same with the trunk's point. The beavers had packed the dam so densely that nothing ever broke away from it except insignificant splinters and clods.

The late afternoon sun on its slide down altered the coloring of the dam and the shape of every intricate shadow, sometimes giving the illusion that the dome of the dam was moving, was at times drifting closer or farther away, and the door he'd drawn was on the verge of opening. He could only hope his lines fell straight, since what he was doing wasn't a thing that called for praying.

War wasn't what Bass had expected. It wasn't constant fighting. For those without the conditioning of slavery, it was boredom mostly. It was a long, slow gathering. A peace shattered by awful waiting, and a waiting filled with silly things like this dam shooting. So when the fight finally came, it didn't strike you at first glance as being as bad as what you'd just lived through. Bass seemed, with his persistent activity, to be the only person alive—until Colonel Young piped up from the creek bank, complaining that Master Reeves needed to stop his n—— from wasting any more ammunition. Master Reeves came alive, telling his commanding officer to trust him. "Trust me,"

Master Reeves said. "Bass can do it. The collapse of that dam will come as a revelation."

"George, I'm telling you, tell your n—— to stop this nonsense."

"These redskins don't believe in our weaponry, Will. They need a reason to."

"And this is giving them a reason to?"

Bass listened to their debate behind him as he reloaded and as he aimed. Without a direct order to the contrary, he fired and reached into the pouch for another cartridge.

"Not much longer, I tell you," Colonel Young said.

"You hear that, Bass? Not much longer or the beavers win."

"Yes, sir, Master," he said, but he wasn't studying winning or losing—only this feeling, this new war calm based on his old calm from shooting, from doing a thing well over and over. On top of that was this new wartime Master Reeves, trusting and speaking up.

Bass fired a dozen more times, and then from the fort gate Colonel Young yelled down, "Enough."

"You hear that, Bass?" Master Reeves spoke from the creek bank behind him. "Enough."

"Yes, sir." His arms needed a rest anyway. He gazed at the dam, at the orange oversized sun, at the fort wall and the hillside below it, at his now-rapt audience making no effort to rise. The creek trickled past the shoal along the same mark as it had hours earlier.

Bass collected the pouches at his feet and hopped to the bank. He followed Master Reeves up the hill and into the fort, as Master Reeves popped his suspenders and piped a tune with his empty rye bottle, while the vigilant Indians persisted, serene as fishermen.

◆ ◆ ◆

Many of the Indian volunteers resumed their watch the next day, though intermittently between duties, while eating, while cleaning their weapons. Over time more and more of them allowed Bass to catch their eyes. Some offered silent greetings. Bass sometimes helped the least experienced account for distance and wind when aiming, but by the first freeze in November, the most experienced were seeking his counsel. Bass learned tribal words and hand signs, received gifts—a beaded necklace, an elk-antler spearpoint. But the dam held firm. Until that first freeze.

Early, before dawn, came the first yelp—high pitched in the crisp air, like a coyote's. A Chickasaw was calling from beyond the fort wall. Yelps rose in answer from inside the fort. Calls that Bass couldn't interpret went back and forth; then two Cherokees whom Bass had befriended ran to his fireside pallet. They grabbed him by his arms and hauled him free of his blanket, running with him toward the gate and out the gate and down the hill, crunching grass, where at least two hundred volunteers had gathered in dance. They howled for the return of the creek, their breath bursting into clouds.

◆ ◆ ◆

Throughout the fall and early winter of 1861, the rancor between Generals McCulloch and Price escalated into a public feud addressed in numerous newspapers throughout the Confederacy. Price, in command of the Missouri State Guard in Springfield, disparaged McCulloch for remaining down in Arkansas and even refusing to loan him muskets, while McCulloch asserted that he had, in fact, loaned Price muskets but that Price hadn't returned them. Price's opinion was that because he was a major general and McCulloch was a brigadier general, he outranked McCulloch and therefore should expect whatever assistance in Missouri he petitioned, while McCulloch insisted that the national authority of the Confederate army superseded that of any state militia. In a letter to the president, Price wrote, "Please remind poor Benjamin of our position on states' rights."

Jefferson Davis resolved the matter by replacing McCulloch as army commander with someone of indisputable authority and pedigree. Since neither McCulloch nor Price was a West Point graduate, Davis, a West Pointer himself, made the decision to pursue a fellow cadet. After Henry Heth and Braxton Bragg declined the appointment, Davis found a third candidate, who accepted, Major General Earl Van Dorn, whose first official duty as commander of the Army of the West was to select McCulloch and Price as his division commanders.

In preparation for an engagement with a reinvigorated Federal Army of the West, newly renamed Army of the Southwest and commanded by Major General Samuel Curtis, Van Dorn issued orders for Young's Eleventh and Pike's Indian brigade to report to Fort Smith, where Colonel Louis Hébert's Third Louisiana Infantry was already posted. Once Van Dorn joined them from his Ozark headquarters in Pocahontas, they would in league proceed northward to Cross Hollows, where McCulloch's division had been quartered for the winter. Cross Hollows was a well-protected encampment in a wooded valley between Springdale and Bentonville, only eighteen miles south of the Missouri line. From there, McCulloch monitored events in Missouri.

Pike protested the orders on the grounds that they violated treaties the Confederate States of America had signed with the Five Civilized Tribes, which stipulated that the Indian regiments would only serve in the home defense of Indian Territory. Van Dorn initially responded with sarcasm: "The fight for states' rights in Missouri and Arkansas has a direct bearing on territory rights. My estimate of the currency value of these, or any, precious treaties once Indian Territory finds itself bordered by our lawless enemy is roughly: $0.00. To arrive at my number, simply add your yearly salary and then subtract it."

Weeks passed before Van Dorn adopted a more diplomatic approach: "Assure your Indians that if they agree to join our noble cause, they will receive the back pay they are owed. Monies will be issued to them in Fort Smith."

This time Pike relented, though incompletely. He consulted only his least undisciplined regiments, the First and Second Cherokee Mounted Rifles, and presented Van Dorn's offer. Although many of his volunteers refused to fight and returned to their homes, walking out of the dusty fort with nothing but a pocket of hard tack, enough of them, a thousand, reluctantly agreed.

Master Reeves spent these long days on whiskey, while Bass remained in constant watch, ready to steady him or catch him or pluck him, choking, from the creek. By February 1, 1862, Pike's Indian brigade and Young's Eleventh had reported to Fort Smith. They rested their legs and animals, resupplied wagons, received back pay, and waited for Van Dorn to arrive.

Although Price remained in command of Springfield, the secessionists who'd welcomed them to their city had been growing fretful about the Union reinforcements assembling in nearby Rolla, only a two-day march away. Union retaliation for the loss at Wilson's Creek and the death of General Lyon now appeared imminent to everyone. As many as a hundred secessionists emigrated daily to Arkansas, primarily to the safety of the fort or its proximity, evident to Bass from the fort's stone wall, where he sometimes sat alone or with the Cherokees or the slaves and watched the roads of Fort Smith clot with covered wagons and foot traffic. Tents and makeshift tents from clothes and linen made the banks of the Arkansas River look like banks of snow, while thin columns of smoke twisted through town from dozens of riverside and roadside fires.

Midday on February 11, a Tuesday, under clear skies despite colder winds, Van Dorn rode into the fort by carriage with a chest of battle flags, to ensure that none of his regiments ever committed the mistake Colonel Sigel's men had made at Wilson's Creek when they mistook the Third Louisiana for the First Iowa. The flag was shiny and bore a crescent moon and thirteen stars scattered across a red field trimmed with a gold cord. Van Dorn called it the Van Dorn battle flag, but to Bass it looked more like a fancy man's quilt. Van Dorn, certainly a fancy man, fancier than Master Reeves even, with his long rooster comb of hair, had only recently designed the flag himself in previous weeks. In fact, he admitted that the sewing of flags was the reason for his delay. Van Dorn spoke of the seamstress in the fondest of terms: "a shapely old Pocahontas gal" and "a lady's man's little lady." He ordered every unit to carry the colors with pride.

Yep, thought Bass. A quilt it was.

On Saturday the men prepared for departure. The slaves spent the early morning filling in the latrines with hard shovels of winter dirt, but in the late morning Bass found peace at the stream just beyond the western wall. He'd been kneeling for only a moment, had just begun to wash his and the master's clothes, when a familiar voice pitched high behind him drifted down to him, the words hanging above the stream trickle and the din of soldier noise in the fort, as if sung—"My, my, Bass." It was a voice as familiar to Bass as God's.

Bass set his wash on a stone and pushed himself up. A dread and a heartache pulled down through him to his belly. He wiped his cold, numb hands on his trousers as he turned and grabbed his hat off his head. He nodded before squinting into the slanting glare of the sun, before seeing the owner of those words, that voice of Bass's early world.

"You're looking good, Bass," he said. His mustache, now fuller and grayer, nearly hid a half smile.

Bass nodded and looked away to regard the man shapes accompanying Master Reeves, the father. On his right stood his son, a harder version of the elder, and on the father's left was the unexpected, tall, crooked figure of Sugar leaning on a cane, not sugarcane but the leaning kind. "Thank you, sir," Bass said.

Master Reeves, the father, slipped his hands into his trouser pockets. "We miss you—the mistress and I both do."

Bass nodded. "Thank you, sir."

"I hear great things about you. I'm not surprised."

Sugar nodded, and Bass nodded again. "Thank you, sir. I do what I can."

"You'll earn your freedom yet, Bass Reeves."

Bass stopped squinting. He'd never heard Master Reeves, the father, utter his full name. *Bass Reeves*. Not once. And never a promise of freedom. Despite the sting, he opened his eyes wider to take in more of his old master, now the one nodding.

Bass glanced at Master Reeves, the son, for confirmation, and Master Reeves was nodding too. It seemed to Bass that they were becoming something, but Bass hadn't the word for it—not friends and not family. A third thing somewhere in between.

"Y'all have a minute," said Master Reeves, the father, turning away and taking his son by the arm.

"That's right," said Master Reeves, the son, his voice much harder but following. "Y'all have a minute, but finish with the wash, hear?"

"Yes, sir, Master," Bass said.

"Thank you, Master Reeves, and you, too, Master Reeves," Sugar said. "I'll see to it that wash be getting done." With his lips closed, he hummed a certain *uh-huh*.

Bass took a step to begin climbing the slope to help his grandfather down, but Sugar waved him off.

"I got this." Sugar held on to his cane with both hands and eased himself down until he was sitting on the edge of the bluff. With the cane across his lap, he pushed forward with his feet up, until he began to slide down the embankment.

Bass caught him under his cane-thin arms and helped him up and brushed him off, and Sugar in a hurry clutched him with the strength of tongs.

"Boy, you's a sight." He pressed his face against Bass's chest, his words muffled. "Your grandmammy pass, son. She with Jesus."

Bass's vision blurred, then refocused on a bunch of dried garlic blooms, paled past pink on bent stalks. Negroes cooked with their roots. His grandmammy did, but white people didn't.

"She went fast. Sitting in her rocker, peeling potatoes, and faster than I can see, the potatoes come spilling. But I'm making it. Your mama making it. We all making it, son, so don't be worrying none about us."

Bass tightened his arms. He didn't know what to say. He loved his grandmammy as much as he could love or need anyone or anything.

Sugar let go. After a moment, so did Bass, and Sugar stepped back. "Get to the wash, and we talk."

Bass knelt at the stream. He reached for the master's underwear sitting in a wad like a cloud on a stone. Tears burned the corners of his eyes, and he prayed a hello to his grandmammy up in heaven with God, maybe kneeling as he was right now and washing God's clothes. She would want him to do this, to pound it out, to squeeze it out, to be a good slave to good work to the very end of time.

Sugar knelt at the stream beside him. "You listening?" He spoke in a hard, deep whisper.

Bass nodded, but with the pumping motion of his arms and shoulders, Sugar may not have noticed. "Yes, sir," he added in a low tone.

"I don't ever wants to sees you again unless you's free. You hearing me? If you ain't free, son, I don't wants to sees you. Stay hid. I mean this, I don't ever wants to sees you."

Bass slowed, wrung out the master's underwear, and set it aside on a dry stone. His hands had become numb again from the icy water. He reached now for his own underwear balled up on the bank, and he reached for the lye.

Sugar rapped Bass on the arm with his cane. "You can go places, son. You got chances. You's in a better spot than I ever was. You carrying Jesus, for sure, but that be the problem. Time you let *him* now carry *you*, boy."

The colder the water, the smaller the soap bubbles. Bass worked hard to make any.

"When the time be right, son," Sugar said, rapping Bass's arm again, "takes your chances. Don't wait for earning no freedom. Takes it. Fight back or kill if you gotta, but go, go, go. You'lls be a shame to me if you don't."

Bass looked at his grandfather, at the broken blood vessels in his eyes, at the yellowing brown, the silvering black. Though aged, his eyes refused to blink or steer away. Sugar had always been Sugar or Ole Bass, not this man talking with strange words like these.

"Your grandmammy and me wanted you safe and living, but that ain't enough, boy. I sees that now. Look at where I be and what I got." His eyes darted away with the birds in the sky, before lighting again on Bass. "Just clinging to a little a nothing. That all you want, a little a nothing? We was wrong, boy. I wants you free, you hears me? Or I don't wants to sees you. Not in heaven neither, not nowhere. I don't *ever* wants to sees you." He clutched his cane with the knuckles and bones of both hands, and once he'd pushed himself to his feet, the master called from up top. The first master, the father. That familiar voice saying it was time for him and Ole Bass to get along.

19

The Quiet Places

As temperatures dropped overnight, the slaves rebuilt fires and blanketed horses. By morning, needles of ice swirled. By the following evening, northwestern Arkansas was a crackling white mess, and a vicious wind stung. Bass helped those among the slaves and Indians in want of socks by cutting flour sacks into wraps for their feet. By the next morning, on February 14, Price's urgent dispatches for assistance (dated on the eleventh, twelfth, and thirteenth) finally overcame the obstacles of geography, war, and weather and reached the gates of Fort Smith. A snowy man sat as if made in the saddle of the red-dun mustang walking at a dead pace, its nose hanging low and touching the frozen ground as if to brace itself from falling. Bass and Clander were outside at the firewood wagon, breaking logs apart and loading their arms, when they saw the horse and the snowy horseman arrive like two trees floating together in a tangle down a slow river.

Bass realized his own slow pace and hurried to fill his arms. Clander quickened too, but Bass was faster, stomping back inside the commissary storehouse to stack the wood by the officers' fire, to dry it for the night's fire, and to find the master. Bass knew his master, like all the other masters, would want to meet the messenger at the door to lead him himself to Van Dorn.

Bass listened from a corner, watching the logs and the crouched snowman melt, while Van Dorn, the only seated officer, read each dispatch. According to Price, General Samuel Curtis of the Union army had already progressed beyond threatening movement and was marching toward Springfield with an army of at least sixty thousand men. Price announced that his diminished force of three thousand guardsmen had abandoned Springfield in the night and was now retreating along Telegraph Road to Arkansas in hopes of receiving immediate relief from McCulloch. "I doubt Ben is still camped in Cross Hollows," Price wrote, "but am I mistaken? He hasn't responded to my repeated pleas for assistance. I have heard from no one. No one!"

Price kept his final dispatch brief: "Skirmishing at the rear slows our retreat. Fortunately for us, I estimate the Federal force to be much smaller than first reckoned, closer to 10,000."

Van Dorn's small, intense eyes and spade-shaped mustache and beard nearly presented a mirror image of Master Reeves. Van Dorn was only much shorter and slightly older, with deep crow's feet and long hair swept over and piled higher than anyone's. He ran a hand through his comb before ordering all troops in Fort Smith to advance northward to Cross Hollows immediately in double-time to meet the bulk of the army (making a combined force of 16,500). "That is," he said, lighting a cigar, "if you don't mind sporting a sitting duck."

◆ ◆ ◆

Despite exhaustion from the infantry, Van Dorn's troops reached Cross Hollows before dusk on February 15, with the Eleventh Texas Cavalry at the front of the column.

Every cabin in McCulloch's encampment trailed woodsmoke into the sky, causing a dark lake to hang over the valley. If the world weren't so white, Bass could have imagined Jennie lying in wait for him under that lake, lying in the warm hay of the barn there with her dress up and breathing on him in the heavy pulses that Strawberry breathed, but it was much too bright white for a good, clear picture. He'd never seen Jennie in the snow, dusted like a leafless black tree. He'd never seen her in labor either, patted with cold wet patches of old clothes, braving death to give the world another unwanted dark child. Of course, she'd never seen him brave death either. She'd seen him on the sticks bearing up, clinging to a little a nothing, but never standing up to it, not to a white man either.

Never rising much above anything, not like that smoke, that dark lake, or that night that was coming on, which the stars and moon and snow and every fiery light could very well complain about and try to impede but could not stop.

A sea of soldiers greeted the newcomers, who were clanking things they carried and calling as if they all knew each other, before clearing a path to the camp's headquarters. McCulloch stood without a hat, black in his preacher suit, in the lamplit doorway of the largest cabin—the bloody-orange ember of his cigar like a new baby bird rising and falling, breathing, glistening in his unkempt beard. Pickets had communicated with pickets. McCulloch had expected company. Bass knew that much.

Van Dorn dismounted before anyone else dismounted. On the porch, he and the taller McCulloch shook hands. When McCulloch stepped inside, Van Dorn, who seemed taller now, hesitated. He turned and waved for the color bearer to run to him. Van Dorn pointed the toes of his boots over the edge of the porch and smiled as he collected the Van Dorn battle flag into his gray sleeves. He tipped the staff through the door, then his rooster comb, and swung the door shut with the heel of his boot.

◆ ◆ ◆

Within an hour, McCulloch led his rested troops northward in search of Price's Missouri State Guard, while the fatigued newcomers from Fort Smith remained, at least for the night, at Cross Hollows. The officers slept on cots in McCulloch's cabin according to rank, with the highest getting closest to the stove, while the slaves slept in the barn, either in the loft or on the floor between the horses. Bass volunteered to take the floor, between Strawberry and the Morgan, because that was what he wanted. The talk among the others resting above him, up where straw drifted down between boards whenever one of them stirred, was that McCulloch hadn't gone to help Price sooner because he hadn't wanted to. True, McCulloch had never expected Curtis to wage war in winter, just as he'd expected Price to cry wolf all the same, but it was also true that he hadn't wanted to help Price anyway. To Van Dorn, he'd claimed he hadn't received any communications from Price, but his slaves, when vacating their barn to go on the road with him, had whispered otherwise.

Bass reflected on what Sugar had told him at the stream outside Fort Smith when his hands were numb. Bass had always believed that his childhood had been what he had felt it to be, a happy one. How could it not have been? But how could it have been? How could he have been so wrong? Just how does a body start to wipe the map of himself away and start over? How could his grandmammy already be gone?

Bass pulled the Cherokee necklace out of his collar and fingered the beads. He watched his breath frost as he began to sing. He could have been a boy again, a boy wanting to sing but a knowing boy this time, as if he were Uncle Moseley himself on top of being a boy wanting to sing, as if Jennie were the girl he wanted to sing to and were somewhere close by, maybe stepping through snow and within range, so he remembered but also added more than memory gave:

You gone pick that cotton like you be told
You gone pick that cotton till you be old
You gone pick that cotton like they balls a snow
You gone pick that cotton, be wishing it be cold
You gone pick that cotton, tweet tweet like a lil' robin
You gone pick that cotton cause wings broke and you
    tired a sobbin'
You gone pick that cotton just so's they sees you picking
    that cotton
You gone pick that cotton and disappears like you's
    cotton in that cotton
You gone pick that cotton to sews a snowman suit a
    cotton and rides on out like you's white as cotton,
    white as cotton, sho white as cotton, cause you done
    gotten enough a that white cotton, girl, me and you
    both, girl, till we all but forgotten, me and you both,
    girl, that be true, till we all but forgotten

His friends in the loft stirred more in the early verses, and more straw drifted down, slow and white as snow but tumbling more like boll stems, until somewhere in the last verse, the snow and cotton stopped and the loft and barn and camp fell silent and still.

◆ ◆ ◆

An hour before dawn the next day, the world remained deathly quiet, and Bass slept on like anyone else. But another day later, on February 17, a messenger rode in at a gallop, carrying a dispatch to Van Dorn that McCulloch had found Price hiding from Curtis's army in a ravine near Elkhorn Tavern, three miles south of the Missouri line. After a skirmish that pushed Curtis back, McCulloch extracted Price's exhausted guardsmen out of the ravine and was retreating back to camp. "I recommend we fight at full force," McCulloch had written, "unless you advise I stand." Van Dorn sent the messenger on with a fresh horse and a letter of his consent and alerted the troops to prepare for battle. The slaves roused quickly to restock the latrine trough with cobs from the corncrib, because the morning would be a busy one.

The remainder of the day was any old cleaning day, except for the officers who passed the time playing poker. Fewer slept through the night. Soldiers wrote letters by firelight. Alone in the barn, the slaves shared thoughts and memories they wanted passed on.

Clander went first, telling that he'd found his mother hanging naked in a tree with no feet for complaining about her gout. He said he'd found her feet on the ground below, set aside by the trunk like a pair of shoes. Clander told it all quickly, with no story. He was done before anyone knew what to think, so they stared at each other in silence.

Weeton told about a brother losing an eye to a whip snap.

Joe Joe was slow to tell anything. He stammered, "With, with, with," and then said, "cow. Made me, y'all. And sheep. And oncet, oncet my sister, my little sister. Held a gun on me. Said he, he cut it off and shoot us both dead, and, and he would too."

They looked at Bass next, but believing again his childhood had been as happy as he'd remembered, he decided not to tell them a story. Instead, he sang the song that stayed in his mind, like a promise:

Jesus a-coming and I's a-going,
Praying for that Heaven place,
It's a place I'd die to taste,
Praying for that Heaven place,
Where it be can you guess?
Praying for that Heaven place,
Smack dab twix east and west,
Praying for that Heaven place,
Follow the angels, follow the doves,
Praying for that Heaven place,
We'll nest in the one safe home above,
Praying for that Heaven place.

Some closed their eyes, thinking their thoughts, while Clander first and then Weeton and Joe Joe pitched in and sang the chorus, as if they knew what Bass missed.

◆ ◆ ◆

On February 18 the men cleaned their .69-caliber smoothbore muskets and loaded them as if they hadn't already once or twice in the last twenty-four hours. That evening, Bass witnessed the return of McCulloch's division with Price's. From the upper limbs of a hillside sycamore, whose scaly trunk was as wide as a master's bed, he spotted stars where stars shouldn't be and sheets of color moving where they shouldn't. The Van Dorn battle flag, coats, hats, horses, wagons. The glowing ground vanished beneath the men as if eaten.

Master Reeves had led Bass to the tree earlier that day after the two of them had walked past the lumber mill and beyond the range of enlisted men. They were hunting rabbit, the master had told Bass, because his itch for rabbit had grown severe. But he had apparently forgotten all about rabbit and showed Bass the sycamore.

Master Reeves rested his gloved hands on his hips and tilted his head back. "That's one tree like you're one n——," he'd said.

Bass looked up. It was a tree practically naked of leaves but with a fine upholstery of snow on all the branches.

"Let's see you shimmy like a bear, Bass. All the way up. And when you do, I want you to look that way for me," and Master Reeves pointed the way he wanted Bass to look. "You think you can do it?"

"Yes, sir." Bass began to walk around the massive thing, which curved in places like curtains. "I can climb a tree," he said, but he wondered how a body should start climbing curtains.

"Excellent," Master Reeves said. "Well?"

Bass stepped on a knobby root and, with gloveless hands, hugged the narrowest part of the trunk. He lifted his feet to pinch the tree with his knees long enough to hug higher, then pinched higher, reaching up around the lowest limb, snow sifting down over him as he hauled himself up.

"You can climb a tree, too, can't you!"

In a few minutes, Bass stood above all other trees, with a clear view for miles in the direction Master Reeves had pointed.

"How far can you see?"

Bass told him how after the trees thinned, a pasture stretched. There were huddled cows, a farmhouse, a road, a river, and more trees climbing over a mountain.

"I don't know what to think about the leadership we have, I'm afraid," Master Reeves said. "You stay up there, and I'll stay down here. When you see the men returning or, hell, the enemy for that matter, you damn well let me know."

"Yes, sir, Master."

"You keep yourself pointed that way, you hear? To the north. That's the way. Stare at it."

Bass didn't recognize the north, but he knew where it was. "Yes, sir," he called. "Stare at it."

"That's right. Stare at it, Bass."

"Stare at it," Bass muttered, but he looked away. He looked west, where the Seminole Nation should be, hidden yonder behind all those trees, nothing but trees, where he imagined God could still be afoot, waiting for him, and he stared at it. He stared and stared before he ever believed he'd stared at it long enough to look away.

◆ ◆ ◆

In their hasty retreat from Springfield, the Missouri State Guard had abandoned their supply wagons to Union capture. What was stored for winter at Cross Hollows helped replenish only partially what was lost, but not until the Army of the West claimed the stores in Fayetteville would they be sufficiently supplied for the campaign Van Dorn now desired, which was to defeat Curtis's Army of the Southwest and then proceed to St. Louis for full control of Missouri. The advantage went to the Confederates to fight this far south, with the Union at the end of their supply train, but only if the Confederates refrained from giving the enemy any more aid and comfort.

Once McCulloch's and Price's men had rested an hour and the army had begun its slow evacuation south for Fayetteville, the rearguard set fire to the camp, to every structure. Bass, already on the march, could hear the hoots and hollers from the men spreading fire, happy as if they were building something, while McCulloch's slaves, who'd built the camp, grew solemn.

Hooves sucked the slush and mud, while wagons and artillery rolled through it, making a splatter like a downpour, while soldiers endlessly rattled and tramped. Occasionally, an officer laughed, but dependably, the drummer drummed. The world beyond the march became so lost in its silence that it became nonexistent. This was what happened to Negroes. They simply became something else to white folk. A camp behind you with no more use or a river you had to cross. At best, a fish you could eat, once you'd tricked it onto your hook. And if all of that was true, thought Bass, then freedom simply became a matter of sound. Of making yourself heard and nothing else.

Without clear transition, after passing around and over a series of foothills, the Confederate Army of the West finally and quite suddenly arrived at the Fayetteville Courthouse. Crowded streets met crowded boardwalks and crowded courthouse grounds, and full stores soon emptied. The work began civilly, with slaves and Pike's Cherokees loading wagons with military supplies, but away from where Bass worked, deep from within the center of more than sixteen thousand milling infantry and cavalry came the crash of glass and splintered wood, followed by hooting and hollering again and, before long, feathers of smoke. Officers mounted horses and urged the army to demonstrate pride and good manners, but the soldiers continued to loot and burn the town until the town, within hours, had ceased to exist.

On their march southward, into the apple orchards of the Boston Mountains, the officers complained to each other about the ill behavior of their troops. Behind them, in endless lines, the men carried petticoats or rolled-up rugs slung over their shoulders, while others toted sacks of toys and tools and clocks and bells, while others fisted bottles of whiskey or licorice sticks.

"There ain't no hope for a slave life," Bass whispered before sleep.

No slave disagreed, but no slave agreed either. The wood of their fire pretended to speak for them in pops and hisses. So Bass pretended to speak back.

Hello, Fire. He watched smoke swirl up and vanish into the silent night. *I think I sees you. I think I feels you, too, toasting me up right nice on this side. But I got two sides, you know, and the other's calling for you. Let me turn over right quick. But hears you? I sure hears you, Fire. What's that you say? You's what? Feeling burned like a n—— do? I hears you, Fire, but I got this cold side that really needs you. I sure hears you, though. Just give me just a little bit more, will ya?*

◆ ◆ ◆

For two weeks, Van Dorn's Army of the West remained immersed in the faint fragrance of fermented apple, which no amount of snow could completely cover. In fact, snow that had sat on the ground long enough to pack especially tasted of apple. This was the snow Bass gathered in flour sacks to melt for water. The wind carried apple with it, too, though never more than after a tree was felled for firewood or after the fire started to catch.

The infantry rested their blistered feet in this valley of apple, and the officers planned for long hours. They generally spoke less as an army now. They ate and slept and kept warm. With very little space in this valley for so many men to move, they remained posted to their bedrolls. The soldiers who'd looted Fayetteville decked their bedrolls with spoils. At night, under the moonlight, some bedrolls glittered and glowed like the nativity scenes Bass had watched his mother make for the mistress on the master's mantelpiece, while other bedrolls threw large vague shadows, like those in white people's graveyards.

Between their longer hours of planning, the officers played poker, more mutedly than before. They smoked more now, too, at nearly every opportunity, but drank significantly less, while the slaves tended to the officers no more and no less. Only the saddler sergeants worked at an urgent pace and made a sound with it, off at the edges of camp where the animals were tied, to mend hooves and repair or replace shoes and bridle parts. Their racket stirred into the racket of the animals, and it filled up all the quiet places.

Bass was convinced. No one knew what they heard, so they didn't really hear it. Others slept with covers over their ears or talked over it, but he listened. If you walked over to it, you'd never find it. You'd see right through the horses, even the saddler sergeants, to the other side of them without actually getting anywhere. You had to hear it and believe it and sing it first before you could own it and go with it to get there, and he would.

20

Walpurgisnacht

According to Van Dorn's scout reports, Curtis was headquartered on the northern bluffs overlooking Sugar Creek, three miles south of the Missouri state line. Fortified positions were spotted south of Sugar Creek, along Fayetteville and Springdale Roads, as well as a detachment of two divisions under General Sigel's charge, which had advanced as far as Fayetteville to plant a U.S. flag among the charred ruins before retreating northwest to a position on McKissick's farm, four and a half miles west of Bentonville. With Sigel's detachment so far removed from the bulk of Curtis's army, approximately fifteen miles away, the Confederate plan revealed itself.

McCulloch leaned forward in his chair as if to speak, and though that alone hushed the circle of officers, including Van Dorn sitting to his left, he remained silent, chewing his cigar and letting ash fall on the black cloth of his suit. "Somebody," McCulloch said finally, then pausing to chew, "answer me how that German could have ever convinced Curtis to divide his army after that same maneuver last time handed us Lyon's head on a danged silver platter."

Although Bass's attention remained focused on the woven stream of coffee that he was pouring into Colonel Hébert's cup, he heard Lyon's name and saw heads turning his way from all sides of the tent, their necks against their collars sounding like scythes through grass. Master Reeves smiled, watching them turn, as if he and Bass really had become something close.

"West Point don't make every Tom, Dick, and Harry a Napoleon," General James McIntosh said. He sat barrel-tight in his uniform and tugged his beard.

A few murmured and sniggered.

"Only some of us," Van Dorn said.

"Yeah, but if you come in a horse's arse," McIntosh said, "you leaving one too. Guess that's Curtis." More of the officers sniggered, while McIntosh gazed off, repeatedly tugging his beard as if petting it. "If them Yankees are hankering for another Bloody Hill, I say we give it to them right quick before they change their mind."

Price stood and clapped McIntosh on the shoulder. "I second young Marengo."

Throaty turkey-like laughter resounded around Bass, as if real laughter and not an echo, curling like steam. All he wanted was to curl away too. Curl away somewhere like something burnt smelling and dark smelling, like coffee, and curl away just as white, so he would look as normal as steam doing it.

McCulloch cleared his throat, and once the laughter died, he shared what he knew of Sugar Creek. It was shallow, and although it quickly swelled after a rain, providing enough water to quench the thirst of an army, the creek was otherwise fordable at all points. A couple of miles south of Pea Ridge, a township named for the nearby ridge of sandstone mountains, the creek stretched as straight as the horizon. Only McCulloch and Price in the officers' tent were familiar with the ridge and its advantageous 360-degree vista. McCulloch had reconnoitered from the largest of the mountains, Big Mountain, numerous times himself throughout the winter, and Price had recently led his guardsmen around it to hide in a ravine to its east, near Elkhorn Tavern.

"Pea Ridge, you might also recall," Master Reeves said from his chair, "was named for a twining vine called hog peanuts."

The officers muttered around Bass the very words he had used one time or another about the master himself, but he poured as if not listening, roving between those seated and those not.

"Hog peanuts, you say?" Van Dorn asked.

"Yes, hog peanuts," Master Reeves said. "They bloom midsummer, white and lavender and tubular, and in fall produce small pods of inedible seeds above ground, but you have to ignore them. In the soil is where you'll find much larger seeds the plant has cleverly buried. They taste like snap beans."

Van Dorn stiffened his back. "Major, why in God's name are you interrupting our war plans with so much talk about peanuts?"

"Because, General," Master Reeves said, rising to his feet, "we are aware of a resource that our enemy doubtlessly is not."

"Are we starving?" Van Dorn consulted Price, but Price remained expressionless. Shrugging, Van Dorn turned to McCulloch and Pike, who either shook a head or closed their eyes. He returned his gaze to Master Reeves. "Are *you* starving, Major?"

"No, General," Master Reeves said, "but from the gut comes the strut."

Bass poured, pretending not to watch the master's familiar grin creep into appearance and not to see it appear as if in reflection on Van Dorn as the two men eyed each other.

Van Dorn leaned back in his chair and crossed his legs. "Ben Franklin said, you might recall, that he saw few die of hunger. Of eating, though, mind you, a hundred thousand. So I recommend, Major, we remain focused on our primary duty, which is to serve. Not *be* served."

Officers sniggered throughout the tent as Master Reeves took a seat.

Bass sympathized with the master but stopped himself and looked away for the next outstretched cup. He would pour until his pot was all poured out and then slip away for more and maybe keep on slipping like a smell and live on hog peanuts—that's how he'd do it—and really curl away. If the meeting weren't now being adjourned, he'd go right now, or during the next officers' meeting, one of them, if he could just figure out how to curl away without an army seeing. If he could do that, he thought he would. It was a plan as good as any he'd heard, even if it hadn't completely revealed itself. Right when the officers were too caught up with arguing with each other to be studying Bass, he'd slip on out. Because they wouldn't stop a war to hunt for a slave, even if he did serve the coffee. He knew that much.

◆ ◆ ◆

On the morning of March 4, Van Dorn's Army of the West marched toward the fortified positions along Fayetteville Road and Springdale Road, where they met perfunctory resistance, before the Federal battalions each time quickly retreated. Within only a few miles of Curtis's encampment, between Rogers and Bentonville, Van Dorn stopped advancing, and as a ruse the troops cut down trees for fires, as if staging barricades and fieldworks, digging rifle pits, and building log-tied parapets. Instead, for a few hours, they slept around those fires, drying their boots and socks, if they had socks, before continuing to march early the following morning, but this time they marched westward, in hopes of finding Sigel's divisions unprepared for battle and capturing them.

Van Dorn placed McCulloch's command at the vanguard, with the Eleventh Texas Cavalry reaching McKissick's farm first, after scouts had returned with news that it had only recently been abandoned.

Campfires simmered, and though the entire farm was trampled into muddy slush, Master Reeves was the first to find the enemy's trail leading through an old cornfield, aiming north toward a gristmill. Bass grew proud of the master that he was a body who not only knew things that shouldn't be things, like hog peanuts, but was also a body who could spot a trail, saying, *There, there!* A body who could be mocked one moment but gain the upper hand the next was a body to become.

The sky was high, wispy, and gray, and in the hopes of catching Sigel's rearguard, Van Dorn issued orders for his army to proceed with haste. By midday, the Texas cavalry had overrun them, capturing six blue coats on forage duty, three per wagon, loaded with whatever the soldiers could hunt, steal, or pick as they canvassed the periphery of their march. Most of the bounty on the two wagons consisted of rabbit, deer, and dove, but guinea hens from a farm were piled dead, too, with wrung necks, along with sacks of frosted mushrooms.

Stripped of their weapons and kneeling on the ground, the Union soldiers stared mutely at Young and Master Reeves and then at McCulloch, strolling up like a shadow, until McCulloch unbuttoned his coat and, studying them just as mutely, drew his revolver and scratched his cheek with the sight. The soldiers immediately began muttering nonsense, all at once, so that Bass wondered if he was hearing what he was actually hearing.

"English, dammit," said McCulloch, and he fired a round into the ground that kicked dirt and ice across the soldiers' coats and faces. The soldiers jerked back or twisted to the side but did so quietly, without a word, as if too afraid now to speak.

Master Reeves stepped up beside the general. "Pardon, Ben," he said. To the soldiers, he spoke in a way Bass had never heard him speak. Something close to throat clearing, with words as hard and sharp as arrowheads. *Sturm und Drang*, he said. *Weimarer Klassik. Heinrich Faust.* The three soldiers gazed at Master Reeves with confusion and shook their heads, as if they didn't speak the language of stones either. So Master Reeves shifted to English. "What is the plan? Where does Sigel or Curtis expect us to attack?" He stomped a boot. "What do you know? Do you know anything, *Dummköpfe*?"

Bass listened, hoping to learn anything that would show him how to curl away and never be overrun. How would he do it? How did they not do it? He listened and prayed they would find tongues he understood.

◆ ◆ ◆

Two of Price's guardsmen, happy to be off their feet, now drove the forage wagons, with the prisoners huddled among the carcasses and mushrooms. Bass and the other slaves rode ahead of them, and Master Reeves rode ahead of Bass, though at the rear of the Eleventh.

Master Reeves remained close to the prisoners on the occasion his help was needed again for translation. Once, a prisoner asked to piss, and Master Reeves told him no, or something close to it, with a word that sounded more like a number. An hour or so later another asked for food and another for water, each with hand gestures to the mouth. Master Reeves told them no again and spurred the Morgan forward, to resume his position ahead of Bass.

For about an hour, the army advanced in pursuit of Sigel, until sniper fire cracked from the dense forest before them.

Master Reeves leaped from his saddle and, from behind the Morgan's flank, unsheathed his rifles. Bass didn't wait for an order and dismounted, too, steadying Strawberry behind a sweetgum. Master Reeves tossed Bass a rifle and a munitions bag, and together they fired blindly from behind their horses into the opposing fire and rustling branches, until no more fire burst back.

The skirmish between armies lasted only minutes, but it halted Van Dorn's advance for an hour, until scouts confirmed that the Federals had cleared out again. Sigel continued in the same northeastern direction, apparently to rejoin Curtis on his bluffs above Sugar Creek. Once Bass, Clander, Weeton, and Joe Joe had buried the dead from both armies, Van Dorn continued the chase, but with no expectation of actually catching and defeating them.

◆ ◆ ◆

The Army of the West camped at dusk on March 5 within a mile of where Telegraph Road crossed Sugar Creek. Exhausted, they nevertheless chopped trees and lit fires in an east-west line a half mile wide. Master Reeves presented a different point of view in the officers' tent, saying the troops needed rest. "A better ruse," he said, "might be to set no fires and let the Federals believe we're not stopping but still advancing. Let them stay awake all night waiting for us to attack, while we sleep like babies."

"Frozen babies," Price retorted. He stood in the rear of the tent, in a fog of cigar smoke, his ridge of silver hair nearly invisible.

Van Dorn made his decision simply by shaking his head. His plan for the army, the general informed them from his chair, was to take a two-hour respite and, at 8 p.m., leaving the fires burning as they had the previous day, march with mercurial haste around the Federal army's right flank in order to attack them at sunrise on the next day from the north, the least expected direction and, therefore, the least defended. Curtis would find himself not only cut off from his supply line but also trying to fight an enemy of superior numbers while looking over his shoulder. Such an ambitious plan would succeed, said Van Dorn, if they moved swiftly enough for surprise, and to do that, they would carry only enough rations and munitions for two days, leaving the supply train here temporarily, behind this line of fire, and defended by the Second Division of the Missouri State Guard. "Curtis must believe, therefore, Major Reeves, that this location is fortified with many more men than it will in fact be."

Colonel Hébert lifted his cup without shifting or blinking his round, glassy eyes, and Bass, unsurprised, took a step and refilled it, watching the steam rise and vanish. The Louisianan drank more coffee than any of the other officers, so Bass stayed close to him. The Louisianan shaved his entire face daily, leaving no facial hair whatsoever. He didn't even have sideburns. He hardly even had eyebrows. If only Bass could vanish like that once the pot was poured, and then Colonel Hébert's almost invisible eyebrows whispered to him how. If he curled away during the two hours the exhausted army was given to sleep, it could be simple. Whose eyes would even see? They'd hardly be eyes, like how the flour sack for hog peanuts that he now kept folded in his coat pocket could hardly anymore be called a flour sack.

Joe Joe stoked the fire in the potbelly stove, which the officers carried from camp to camp solely for these tent meetings. Clander stood beside McCulloch, holding a map of Washington and Benton Counties that had long been ignored. Weeton was whispered off to fetch this or that.

"Tonight is our Walpurgisnacht," Van Dorn said. "We build our bonfires, and we ration and lighten, with all personal effects inventoried in the manner you see fit."

Master Reeves pretended not to sulk from the tent. Bass saw him walk tall but quietly out, his eyes not seeing anyone, his lips sealed. The master's idea had seemed a good one to Bass. If there were no bonfires, there would be so much less to see.

The officers separated after the short meeting, ordering troops to chop trees and light them in stacks, giving one order after another, while the slaves dug latrine trenches, built campfires for the cooks, and set up tents for their masters. The cooks, meanwhile, skinned the animals that the army had confiscated from the Germans and began boiling them in a mushroom sauce made with coffee and flour.

Bass could feel the time burning and curling away in his place—one order coming after another before the slaves could serve their masters, so that they could at last eat what the troops ate: a corn-and-potato porridge. Then Master Reeves called from his tent. "The prisoners, Bass," he said, sweeping the tent flap aside. "Feed them."

"Yes, Master." Bass moved first, Clander next, then before long all the slaves had rinsed their plates and spoons in the snow and received a ladle of porridge from the cooks. Bass led the way to the Federal forage wagons, but when he found them backed up against a cluster of cedars with empty floorboards and no prisoners to be seen nearby either, only Confederate troops passing back and forth for acres, he consulted his fellow slaves, who only shrugged. He led them back to the master's tent.

A bonfire raged twenty-five feet away and popped like gunfire.

"Master," Bass called.

"What is it?" Master Reeves said from inside his tent, not bothering to part the flap.

"Where have the prisoners been put at, sir?"

After a pause, Master Reeves said, "Where? Where else? At the wagons."

"Master," Bass said, "they ain't there no more. No, sir. Wagons empty."

Master Reeves tossed the flap aside, and smoke swirled out as he looked up at Bass with a cigar plugging his mouth. He grunted and crawled out of his tent. He walked toward the cooks, seated on logs in front of their cooking fires and chewing meat scraps. Bass followed, and the other slaves followed him.

"Where are the prisoners?" Master Reeves asked.

The cooks stared. "Don't know, sir," the sergeant said.

"You didn't have them haul up their animals for you?"

The cooks shook their heads. "No, sir," the same sergeant said. "I ain't seen them in a while. Not since you took them to the officers' tent."

Master Reeves huffed a cloud of frosted breath. "I didn't take them anywhere. I told them to stay with the wagons."

"Well, sir, someone did. They were hanging around outside the tent, looking like they were waiting there as told. I don't know. We had work to do. Our duty ain't watching your prisoners."

Master Reeves turned and scanned the encampment grounds.

"They got to be around," the sergeant said. "We're all over. Where would they go?"

Master Reeves continued to scan the encampment. Bass turned and scanned with him, positive he saw what the master saw. Half the troops wore their blankets around their shoulders like gray shawls, even hiked over their heads. So many men the prisoners could be, right there among them. So easy to have picked up a blanket while everyone was working and meeting and walked away. With no ruse at all—just flat walking away like Bass believed made sense but didn't do. Now, the men looked to pay no attention to anything, unless it was the cold. A few moved their mouths in scattered huddles, but most simply gazed into fires or down at the ground, half-dozing, or off into the bleak, empty spaces between them. Where would the prisoners go? Anywhere they wanted.

Bass sensed a humiliation forming, and a resentment. It had been this easy to escape all along.

"*Dummköpfe*," the master said. Through clenched teeth, he began to huff like a bull. "It's a damn confederacy of dunces, Bass." He turned to Bass, and Bass turned to the space between them and balled his fists. He should have been happy for the prisoners. God was with them, by God. With him, too, holding him back-like but pushing them along.

"Thank goodness the river is frozen," Master Reeves said. He paused as if daring Bass to ask what he meant. But Bass couldn't have cared less what he meant. The river was frozen, whichever river he wanted frozen, and the prisoners, disguised as Confederates bundled up against the cold, something as simple as that, had used it like a bridge and crossed. The master said so. It didn't matter why.

"Otherwise," the master said, pausing again, "our ship would've surely sunk." He took a step away. "Keep close," he said.

Bass kept close. Of course he would.

Master Reeves climbed into his tent. "Let me know if you hear something," he said, his voice muffled with the flap down. "I don't trust anybody but you."

"Yes, Master," Bass said, finding a space by the slaves' fire to curl up with his blanket and wait one last time with it before curling away with it, yes, tonight, before the two hours were up, and no later. Maybe he'd catch up with the Germans, and together they'd reach Curtis with news as to how to turn the tide.

The fire was a n—— fire all right. So wet with sap that it sizzled like bacon, like it was free, free, free to dance and laugh right there but right there only.

"We'll have to rouse soon," the master said, still talking with that flap down as if it weren't down, "so sleep fast."

"Yes, sir," Bass said. He closed his eyes, fearing his trusting master might seesaw himself back into not trusting and just throw open that flap any second only to catch Bass's insolent eye flaps open, too, and spoil the night. Bass could go along a little longer. He waited. He'd have to, with men still moving and muttering enough here and there among them.

"Bass!" the master said, his voice projecting above fire and wind, and Bass rose off his arm and the ground to see the master with his hand holding open his tent flap.

"Yes, Master?" Bass said, afraid he'd fallen asleep and it was already time to rouse. He turned but saw that the bonfires were unchanged, that the field of men was the same field of men.

"On a bone-cold night, there's no other recourse but for me to open up my tent to you."

"Master?"

"As much for me as you. More for me, but we'll both be warmer. Get in here."

"Yes, Master," Bass said. He pushed off the ground, holding his blanket around his shoulders, and ducked into the tent, the master a dark shape like a grave, with his head as the headstone. Bass squeezed into the space beside him.

"No need to face me," the master said. "Look left, and I'll look right. And before you know it, we'll rise, like this didn't happen."

"Yes, sir, Master." On the canvas of the tent, a sea of dark water appeared to wave around a golden ship. "Thank you, Master."

"You're welcome, Bass." The master took in a long breath through his nose as if to smell what smells were on Bass. The coffee. The trenches. The flour sack folded many times over. "We're almost family now."

"Yes, sir. Thank you, Master." He closed his eyes to pray and calm his heart.

"You're welcome, Bass. Good night."

21

Now That There's Space

Sugar's words drifted into his dreams without a face. *When the time be right, son, takes your chances. Don't wait for earning no freedom. Takes it.* Almost like wind or clouds or music drifting over, but Bass wasn't looking up. *Fight back or kill if you gotta, but go, go, go.* As if Sugar were behind those clouds, seeing him in the master's tent—as if the tent were another cloud he could see through. Now Bass was looking up, as if he could see through tents and clouds too. As if Bass knew Sugar was there because he heard him, just couldn't see him no matter how far he could see. As if Bass were held inside his granddaddy's hand, because everywhere was darkness, no matter how much light there was outside with the bonfires. No star or moon showed. *You'lls be a shame to me if you don't.* Bass could have been standing in a cave, because the words echoed.

When he woke, he saw the tent's wall still aglow and the glow still undulating. He listened to the bonfire pop and roar, to the cooks' first rattles. He turned onto his back and watched snowflakes land, hardly there, like freckles, like seeds, which bloomed in an instant before melting away. *Kill if you gotta,* Sugar insisted.

He rolled his head to his right to find Master Reeves looking back.

"Bass," the master said.

"Morning," Bass said.

"Let's win us a war. You and me. Fuck the rest."

"Yes, Master."

◆ ◆ ◆

173

The snow slowed the army's march westward around Curtis's right flank. By nightfall, on March 6, they had covered little more than half the distance Van Dorn had planned. Three miles due west of the Federals' flank, the Confederates camped in a valley along Sugar Creek and Bentonville Detour. The surrounding hills slowed the winds, so the snow fell softly, filling footprints and hoofprints and wagon ruts in quiet minutes. Out of breath, the weary, cold, hungry army collapsed into sleep, officers and slaves included. Only the cooks, who'd dozed on the march, went without sleep, making mounds of hardtack for breakfast.

Two hours later the cooks called for the slaves to distribute the hardtack to the troops, to Price's men first and then to McCulloch's. Then the Army of the West resumed their march in double-quick, with Van Dorn accompanying the vanguard division, led by Price, while McCulloch led the rearguard.

McCulloch's division was not long on the road, marching northward on Bentonville Detour, when Master Reeves slowed his Morgan, now only slightly forward of Bass, and unsheathed a rifle. He stretched it to Bass and unslung an ammunition pouch from around his neck. Snowflakes clung to the master's beard, rounding his hat.

"I won't lie, Bass," he said. "You saved my tail that day with that hellish boar. And on Bloody Hill, hell, you made quite a case for equality. You did." He thrust the ammunition pouch at Bass without looking at Bass, and Bass took it silently and hung it around his neck. "We might be on the wrong end of the surprise if those Germans find their way back to Curtis before we do." Master Reeves turned his head in Bass's direction, though lowered, with the brim of his Hardee hat blocking the wind and snow from his face. "I don't trust many people. I don't." He stopped speaking but kept his head turned as if he might strike up again.

Bass decided to fill the space Master Reeves left. "Thank you, sir," he said.

"Bass," Master Reeves said.

"Yes, sir?" Bass said.

Master Reeves steered the Morgan closer and bumped Strawberry in the shoulder with the Morgan's flank. "Bass," he said again.

Bass raised his head and looked at him.

"Bass," Master Reeves said, also looking without blinking, "when this war is over, I'll make sure Pop frees you, if that's what you really want. You can live off at the edge of the property in your own place and walk over and see Winnie and Jennie all you want most nights, of course Saturday nights and on Sundays, if that's what you want. Or heck, you can go back to Pop and live there in the cabin with Old Bass now that there's space. Until then, though, we have to live, don't we?"

Bass gritted his teeth when he heard him say *now that there's space*.

"It's not debatable, is it? Right, Bass? We're not dogs returning to their vomit, by God, are we? You and I have to live."

For a moment, Bass heard nothing of the mass migration through snow and wind. Then, as though his grandmammy herself had reached down from heaven and suddenly thrown open the gate on sound in order to convince him that Sugar had been wrong, that Bass ought to wait because he needn't run after all, his ears flooded with every intricate friction. Bass smiled for his and the master's war-earned trust—a long, slow gathering indeed. Yes, he nodded. "Yes, sir," he said.

Master Reeves's eyes narrowed on Bass. "I miss home too." He turned forward and prompted the Morgan to jump ahead, giving Bass and Strawberry back their space.

◆ ◆ ◆

The morning sun, even high and on a slant, gradually burned off the clouds, and though March 7 began no warmer, at least the snow had stopped falling in their faces and before their feet. The snow that the vanguard division had packed now stayed packed, and though the rearguard made better progress, reaching Twelve Corner Church at Ford Road by 7:00 a.m., the vanguard appeared to have made better progress, having moved beyond the sight of either Bass or Master Reeves.

Van Dorn's plan was for Price's division to follow Bentonville Detour, in a northeastern direction around Big Mountain, a maneuver that would block the most logical route of retreat for Curtis and cut off his lines of communication and supplies to Keetsville, Missouri. Van Dorn and Price would proceed south on Telegraph Road in order to reunite with McCulloch's division at Elkhorn Tavern at 8:00 a.m., after McCulloch had marched around the opposite side of Big Mountain via Ford Road. Van Dorn's plan was for the army to strike Curtis soon afterward in a two-prong attack.

McCulloch would have to advance his division along the full length of Ford Road and leave its forest cover to squeeze between Big Mountain and Little Mountain, that serene valley Bass admired not for its untrampled snow but for what all that whiteness buried—that wildly sprawling mess of hog peanut vines Master Reeves had spoken of. Dried to brown by now, sure, but nevertheless there, with all their hidden seeds that tasted of snap beans. Bass believed that if his master fell and the army was too busy fighting not to fall, he could curl away yet, under the cover of a blanket. He'd dig up as many hog peanuts as he could find and then run, really run after all. He'd prove to both Master Reeves and Sugar that he wasn't a dog after his vomit. He'd be free, or he'd be free, one way or the other. But before any of that, he had to live—it was true.

Sigel's Germans had indeed reached Curtis in time for him to send a task force north as a first line of defense, under the command of Colonel Peter Osterhaus, who crouched three hundred yards away with 1,500 men for this possible moment, when the head of the Confederate division emerged from the forest. McCulloch's troops marched into the open farmland north of Leetown, three rows of infantry flanked by cavalry, before the first scout spotted the Federals waiting patiently in a line across the field with three twelve-pounder howitzers backed up against a belt of timber. By then it was too late.

Bass had only just emerged from the dense cover of trees when the cannons exploded from the south. It seemed everyone in front of him jumped except Master Reeves and his Morgan. Even Strawberry squealed and danced, trying to turn himself around. Bass worked to calm him, so Bass didn't see the canister balls raining down, only the egg-sized holes they'd made in the snow. Men in the infantry shrieked, and McCulloch shouted for them to countermarch. McIntosh and Hébert and Bourland and Young and Master Reeves, ahead and behind, all the officers were ordering a countermarch.

Again the howitzers exploded.

Bass cantered Strawberry backward, and this time, he did look up, catching sight of the canister balls streaking like falling stars, but dark as catfish, before drumming the things they hit.

Over screams of the wounded, McCulloch called for McIntosh. And before the howitzers could fire again, McIntosh was rallying the cavalry, and among the Eleventh so were Young and Bourland and Master Reeves. Three thousand on horseback from Texas and Arkansas raced from the forest across the field to confront the advancing Union soldiers, with Bass and the other slaves trailing on slower animals. The Federals held their ground for one or two musket shots before either falling or dispersing into the woods behind them.

Bass held the trigger guard of his cocked rifle as he rode out across the farm behind Master Reeves's coattails flapping like wings behind the gray plume of his Hardee hat blown back by the wind in a straight line. He could do it, shooting the master in the back or in the back of his head, but he also couldn't. No, the thing in his heart he could do was to knock the man down who tried to knock the master down and Bass's promise of freedom right with him.

That didn't mean Bass was a dog after his vomit. He halted Strawberry at the tree line, breathing in gunpowder, and Clander looked at him for counsel. Without saying it, Clander was asking if they should follow their masters into the trees bursting with rifle fire, and without saying it, Bass said no.

An Indian caterwauling went up from somewhere, high above the moans of the wounded.

Bass turned Strawberry around to find the cause. Back across the field, the core of the division still waited out of sight behind the opposite tree line on Ford Road. At first, Bass didn't see him. Daring as a sort-of-purple Texas blackbird with tiny yellow eyes and a dragging chain, McCulloch peeked out from the vanguard position, bold in his black preacher suit and hat, perched on his saddle. Down a ways, hundreds of yards away, from what must have been the rear of the division, a regiment of Pike's Cherokees poured out of the forest, springing high with each step to run through snowdrifts and covering land quickly, running at a Union company beginning to emerge as well from the woods behind Bass, though down a ways too. Another regiment of Cherokees broke from the trees, this one mounted, yipping and yowling, the ponies leaping like deer.

Only a few of the Federals stood and fired. The rest darted in a panic for the woods, many of them falling, trying to run too fast through snow.

Bass watched in horror and with envy at how the mounted and dismounted Cherokees crossed the field and without hesitation shot men in the back. Even when they reached those who didn't make it to the woods—eight Federals lying crooked in the snow, some moving, some groaning, some not—how the Cherokees dropped their muskets and drew knives. How they could do all the things they conceived. Knocking hats away and scalping men.

"Lord Jesus!" Clander cried.

Bass turned to Clander, because it was a reason to turn away. Clander looked out of breath. Sick. Sad. And darker than Bass remembered.

"Clander," Bass said, forgetting what he was about to say.

A call for a charge rang out from the road, and Bass searched out McCulloch, still sitting on his horse, still black as a bird or a tree or a preacher or a slave like Clander, like Jennie, like Sugar, while the army poured from the forest to finish the rout of the Federal task force.

By the time Master Reeves finally emerged from the opposite tree line, the Cherokees with scalps had climbed up on the three captured howitzers and were bearing them high as flags. Many more Cherokees danced and sang in circles around them.

Pike rode up on the scene on a sleek black gelding and hollered words in their tongue to calm and quiet them. But the louder he yelled from the crease in his bristly broom of a beard and the more he tossed his head and his long, wavy black locks, the more red-faced he became, and then his Cherokees grew wilder.

Master Reeves smirked for Bass to see him smirk. "Will I, nill I. Right, Bass?"

Bass nodded as he watched the Indians showing no signs of sin or shame. All of them so much darker than he was. So much closer to black.

◆ ◆ ◆

Based on the size of Osterhaus's task force and the fact that Van Dorn and Price hadn't faced a similar confrontation, the east still as quiet as snow, McCulloch insisted that surprising Curtis remained probable. Instead of waiting to reunite with Van Dorn and Price, he sent a dispatch of his decision with two couriers that he would pursue the retreating enemy to its back door, if not right to its hearth, and the scouts galloped away on Ford Road as if they carried the urgent word of God.

McCulloch directed his officers to direct their troops to continue southward through the woods, with two regiments of Arkansas infantry at the front and Pike's Indian brigade positioned as far away as possible on the western flank.

The cavalry dismounted to cross the dense woods, as did their officers' slaves. To avoid thinking of food, Bass looked up. Sometimes he reached down and ate snow. In the distance, beyond the trees and mountains, artillery rumbled like thunder, shaking snow from the upper limbs.

"Probable surprise?" Master Reeves said.

Colonel Young made no reaction, walking beside him between trees.

"Ben missed the Alamo because he had the measles," Master Reeves scoffed.

"What's the meaning?" Young asked. "That was a long time ago."

"Somebody," Master Reeves said, turning to look at others, Bass even, "answer me, How could that German have ever convinced Curtis—or was it Van Dorn? no, McCulloch—to divide his army after that same maneuver last time handed us Lyon's head on a danged silver platter?"

"You're insubordinate, Major," Young snapped.

"You're a real plate face," the master said.

Bass gave Clander an eye, but Clander's mind was down on someone else's footprints, or his master's maps maybe. Or maybe he was past that now. Past escaping and already in that world that was better than this one. One where the Cherokees had never left. Afraid a body could dream for too long and get lost in it and not find his way out, Bass wouldn't, would he? To keep alert of this world, and feel almost happy despite it, he preferred to sing.

So he sang, silently, the first song that came to mind:

Monday's child is fair of face,
Tuesday's child is full of grace,

He didn't know why a song he never much liked entered his mind.

Wednesday's child is full of woe,
Thursday's child has far to go . . .

"Shhhhh," came from someone ahead. Not Master Reeves. Someone ahead of even him. And then another said, "Shhhhh," in a longer way, and so did another. Soon the whole division was hushing itself as the shadows ahead evaporated into light, and not the light of snow but the light of light, patchy and lacy as it was, promising more timberless farmland to open up for the infantry in front. Gradually, the division collapsed into a tight formation. They leaned and slouched in waiting, listening to the silence of the light before them and the rapid crack and boom intensifying to the east, on Telegraph Road.

Here there was neither silence nor skirmish. Men flinched and squeaked snow beneath their boots. Ahead, though, where sound seemed forbidden, a single rifle fired, like a raspy cough that ripped the air toward them and not away.

Some men gasped. Bass listened. Men far away cheered, across the bright field he could not see. What followed would always leave Bass confused. It began with whispers that McIntosh was riding out to retrieve a body, and Bass would always believe that he'd heard men thinking, not saying, *Whose?*

An officer's voice, unrecognizable to Bass, ordered, *Fire*, and a line of Confederate infantrymen fired their muskets in unison. In the break of reloading, as smoke drifted into the trees and thinned the light, an answer came from the Federals—three more coughs from rifles in hesitant succession. The work of snipers firing at will.

On Bass's side, a horse screamed. But there were too many murmurs for anyone as deep in the woods as Bass to hear or know anything clearly anymore. No one wanted to move or decide a thing, the officers only looking dumbly at each other, until the Federal cannons exploded and broke the treetops, when the Cherokees so far on the flank sounded so much closer.

The tight formation of the army quickly became an overflowing river with men ducking and turning to run, scattering. Strawberry bucked as if to escape with the others, and Master Reeves whipped around with a drawn pistol.

The master raised his pistol further and fired as if to shoot the sky through the trees. "Come on, brave men of the Eleventh," he shouted. He threw himself into his saddle but was short in the woods with limbs bending against his back. "Get together, goddammit!" He tucked his pistol away and raked his saber free from its scabbard. "Theirs not to make reply," he continued to shout. "Theirs not to reason why. Theirs but to do and die."

The cavalry gazed at him from the passive stance of trees.

"*Theirs* means *yours*, cocksuckers!"

Bass told Strawberry with his mind that it was true. Weren't a reason why, except in this war between the givers and the takers, he and Strawberry were the doers. He'd mount him, he said, because he had to, and then he did. The entire cavalry, it seemed, was climbing now and getting hunched on their mounts, while the Cherokees lost their minds around them, running and ranting in circles every time a cannon exploded.

The fear on Clander's face told Bass what he hadn't paused to conceive, since the Lord had always been with him. The Lord, for an unfathomable reason, wasn't with Clander. Clander would die today, Bass realized just before they charged to follow the charge. Just before they rode from the last of the trees, the trees already thinning, across a stream of blood slush and the corpses of a brown roan, looking like McIntosh's, and of a general not really looking like McIntosh, but it must have been him, lying facedown and feet-down in the snow, half-buried and flat-like. Looking like little more than an armload of boards that had been chucked from a wagon and tucked inside some clothes.

Bass galloped over another corpse, another general, also face-down, who was as dead as a buzzard shot meanly from the sky. His black preacher hat resting an arm's length away, as if neatly set aside to be picked up later.

Not until the first break in the battle, when Pike rallied all but those who had already deserted to retreat around Big Mountain in order to unite with Price's division, would Bass overhear what had happened. McCulloch had been picked off while surveying the enemy line, and McIntosh, who had just assumed command of the division, had impulsively led a charge with the First Arkansas Cavalry to retrieve McCulloch's corpse and was shot dead, too, along with his mount. The dissolution of leadership only worsened the state of the division when Hébert, now the highest-ranking officer, got disoriented in the woods by the chaotic fighting around him, mistook foe for friend, and was captured.

The litany of errors superior people could make was stupefying. Bass quit listening. The slaves had their own reports to share. Clander had fallen too, but no one had a story of how. Clander was dead. He was just dead.

22

Closer

Price's division fared much better on the eastern side of Pea Ridge, repulsing the Federals southward past Elkhorn Tavern and Ford Road, past Cox's Field and Ruddick's Field, until the evening became too dark for Price's Missourians to keep pushing. Van Dorn called for the officers to headquarter in the tavern.

Once the color bearers had planted a battle flag outside the tavern's front door, the officers filed in. They convened in the dining hall, among racks of mounted elk antlers, while Bass followed the cooks to the kitchen.

The meeting's first numbers for the day drew cheers: two hundred prisoners and seven captured cannons. The next numbers silenced and then rankled them: 325 casualties and 788 missing (with McCulloch's division accounting for all but two). The broken pieces of McCulloch's division meanwhile rested at the rear of the army, along Huntsville Road, from where Bass and the master had just hiked, a long way away.

There was no mention yet of Pike's Indian brigade other than where they were camped—north of everyone else, behind the wounded, the prisoners, and the livestock. Bass knew where—where they could desert the army at any time, because that appeared to be every white man's preference. Even Pike's. Perhaps Bass needed to wear the uniform of an Indian.

Bass reached into his coat pocket to finger the elk antler spearpoint, a gift from one of the very Cherokees these white men had no more use for. He had no use for it either until he tied a stick to it. One day he would tie a stick to it. He hoped it would remind him of all the things he would do.

Once the coffee was ready, he walked into the dining hall.

While the officers devised plans for the morning's engagement, Master Reeves stewed, wanting his cup refilled more times than ever. A bizarre thought occurred to Bass. *What if the master wasn't thirsty? What if Colonel Hébert never was much atall either? What if they don't hate us or believe us stupid but hold us dear like we is something they got to hold to and keep near, something so beautiful and holy like, like a mansion or a flag or one a them antler racks or some basket of marble eggs you got to polish every day because we's maybe a thing they'd just crumble over for losing? Saying in their way of not saying anything but meaning, "Please, climb into my tent here, boy, and keep me warm. A little more closer. Please, I'm just so thirsty for a little closer."*

Bass looked for Colonel Hébert's outstretched cup, expecting to see the colonel's shaved face, like the bottom of a cup, until he remembered that the colonel had been captured. That he was as close to being a slave as a white man ever got. That shouldn't have saddened Bass, but it did some. He couldn't help it.

The discussion among the officers shifted to their reserve artillery as Bass left for the kitchen to retrieve a fresh pot of coffee. With no back door to the room, he had no choice but to return. He stopped at the fireplace first to turn over the half-charred logs and to add fresh ones. The sparks off the turned wood reminded him of the fireplace in his grandparents' cabin. It was half the size of this one. He'd seen fire for the first time there. The moon too. And dirt.

The reserve artillery, they decided, would be staged right here, in front of the tavern. Bass walked back in among the officers, and Master Reeves raised his cup.

"All right," Van Dorn said, "let's adjourn for dinner."

"First, sir, if you don't mind," Master Reeves said, remaining in his chair with his legs crossed, "inform us of when the supply wagons will be arriving."

The crackling of fire and the wind whistling into the chimney were all Bass heard. Van Dorn's face was right for a hanging. Bass didn't want to breathe. He hurriedly filled the master's cup and backed away to stand behind the officers.

Van Dorn turned to Price, on his right. "Have they not arrived already?"

"I'm not aware of it," Price said.

Van Dorn consulted Pike on his left, but Pike shut his eyes and shook his head.

Van Dorn searched out Colonels Young and Little, but both shook their heads as well.

Master Reeves sipped his coffee, set his cup in the cradle of its saucer, and stood from his chair. "On Walpurgisnacht, sir," he said, "you made the decision to leave the supply train behind. To advantage our swift flight and goal of surprise."

"Major, that's enough," Young said.

"Major," Van Dorn said, clasping his hands into a single fist that more closely resembled the natural size of one of Bass's, "that may be an unfortunate oversight. *My* oversight, indeed. But that is merely another challenge we must overcome, but nothing we can't, by Jove."

"Yes, General, yours indeed," Master Reeves said. "But I won't be eating if my men won't be." Master Reeves tipped his head and turned, pressing his way out with his hat in his hand.

"So if your men run out of ammunition," Van Dorn said, "you'll refuse to use yours?"

The master stopped to turn around. "Oh, no, sir," the master said. "I'm not a dog that returns to its vomit. In fact, I'm no baby that freezes. I'm a tail."

The dining hall billowed with asides. Bass looked down at the pot warming his hands.

"Are you finished?" Van Dorn asked.

"I hear that you like poetry, sir. Is that right?"

Van Dorn raised his eyebrows. "A poet typically does, Major."

A few men sniggered. Most were silent.

"I do as well," Master Reeves said. He brushed his coat open to set his hands on his hips. "Though, I prefer poetry dressed in slaves' clothes. When it's working and singing and not just singing. When you least expect it. You know, slipped into life with a grunt. You've read *Moby-Dick*, I reckon."

Van Dorn grinned and slightly bounced as if from laughter but was soundless. "Major," he said, looking to others, "where did you manage to find a copy?"

A few officers laughed, but the laughter was nervous slave laughter.

"And how," Van Dorn continued, "did you manage to find the time? You could build a fine house with a load of those. Let me inform you, Major, my rank doesn't afford me such leisure."

The slave laughter rose again but died swiftly, as slave laughter will, and Master Reeves projected his voice like a preacher, nearly singing: "'Other poets have warbled the praises of the soft eye of the antelope, and the lovely plumage of the bird that never alights; less celestial, I celebrate a tail.' As do I, gentlemen."

"He's nuttier than a damn squirrel turd," Young said. "Never mind him."

"Get your rest, Major," Van Dorn said.

Master Reeves turned to continue walking, and Bass followed.

When Bass bent to grab his hat off the floor by the door, he remembered the pot he was carrying and thought of setting it down, but where? Master Reeves only paused to put on his gloves and hat, then plowed ahead, not waiting for Bass to open the door for him, so Bass followed with a jump.

They passed through a sea of sagging soldiers, around one campfire, on one slope, in one grove after another. The master turned, briefly without speaking, as if only to verify that Bass was still behind him. As they neared the camp for the Eleventh, the master turned again, and this time he stopped, letting Bass catch up to the range of his voice.

"I'm glad you brought the coffee."

◆ ◆ ◆

Cartridges were pooled and redistributed so that every soldier had two each, one loaded and one in the pocket. As instructed, the army slept on their weapons. It was quite an embrace all over, the hope of warm muskets filling the void in their guts. Perhaps everyone was touched with love too. Bass prayed so. The limitation of supplies left slaves unarmed, but Bass felt safe and complete with the love of God and with the coffee the master let him have. He was comforted also by what he knew. The end of life as Bass knew it was coming, beginning in the morning, and that satisfied him—that and the love of God and the coffee the master let him have, along with the warmth of a tent.

◆ ◆ ◆

Every morning for the last four days, since the valley of apple, Van Dorn's Army of the West had broken camp and marched. This time, on March 8, in a defensive posture, the troops simply woke and watched the sun rise serenely over the frosted trees and ridge. Very few of the men even needed to evacuate their bowels. Cardinals and finches chirped and flittered in a dance among the branches. A few in the cavalry passed the time by throwing rocks at birds whenever one alighted on the ground. Most of the slaves slept or lazed, since they were allowed to. But Bass spent his time digging through crusted snow for hog peanuts. He'd crack their black shells for the white bean-shaped peanuts and make two piles, two peanuts for Master Reeves for every one he ate, while the master smoked his red mahogany pipe and read from his red-leather book.

Eventually, Curtis realized the Confederates wouldn't be attacking. Eventually, in the late morning, the Federals began mobilizing and struck Van Dorn's front lines with artillery. For two hours, the volleys never ceased. Then, from his blind station at the rear of the army, Bass heard the musket fire of defense against a Federal charge. He moaned, and it seemed everyone moaned with him. Then came what felt or sounded like a stampede of cattle.

"Quick," Master Reeves said, running across the snow, his pipe clamped in the corner of his mouth. He untied his Morgan, and Bass untied Strawberry.

Even in the saddle, a body could feel the shudder of retreat.

Master Reeves shouted for the men not to panic and waste a shot. Young repeated the master's message. All the officers repeated the master's message.

Within minutes, over twelve thousand men had bottled up around Elkhorn Tavern, terrified to be out of ammunition or too close to it, and cried news of one more dead general among them, William Slack of the Missouri State Guard. Their fourth lost commander in twenty-four hours.

Van Dorn called for an officers' meeting inside the tavern. Bass waited outside with Strawberry and the Morgan, where he wondered if he was the only happy man among them. Maybe other slaves were. Bass asked Joe Joe, "You happy?" But Joe Joe looked at him without answering, as though he didn't understand the meaning of the words. As though Bass were speaking underwater.

Moments later the officers appeared on the second-floor balcony and shouted orders over the rails for an evacuation east on Huntsville Road. Bass had no idea what lay east of them but wanted none of it. He wanted what lay west, back where left was.

When Master Reeves returned from the tavern, he took the Morgan's reins from Bass and climbed onto his saddle, stewing as he had the night before. Without a word, he rode off. Instead of flowing with the tide eastward, he headed north on Telegraph Road, as if to assist the evacuation of the wounded or the livestock or the Cherokees, but the master rode right past all of them as if he intended to circle Big Mountain to get back to Bentonville Detour, going back the way they had come.

If that was the way they were going, back to Indian Territory, then Bass believed God was a slave, too, by Jove, because God was positively working for him. Perhaps the master had decided he'd had enough of the war and was deserting, too, to avoid capture. Or maybe he knew the war was within days of ending anyway.

Bass smelled the air to see if God had put a smell on it for him. But he only smelled gunpowder, still packed in his nose from yesterday's battle. Last night and this morning his nose had only blown black.

◆ ◆ ◆

On the far side of Big Mountain, they rode up on a file of Confederate deserters, who limped off the road and hid among the trees.

"I ain't interested in y'all," the master shouted.

Once he and Bass had passed the spot in the trees where the soldiers had darted, one stepped out, followed by the other four, limping again along the road.

"Shit," the master said to himself, unrolling his blanket and hanging it over his Hardee hat and around the shoulders of his uniform. He still hadn't spoken to Bass yet, and Bass was content with that.

The familiarity continued as they made their way, and long after Big Mountain had faded from view, nearing nightfall they reached Sugar Creek. From the impossible number of hoof and boot marks along the frozen banks of where the Army of the West had crossed two days ago, they could have been riding horses on the moon. Bass liked that thought—him and the master riding horses on the moon. It had to be cold up there. Bass looked and found the moon. Yep, that one. That one that glowed like one of Jennie's teeth under bottle light. And these banks, like her lips.

Master Reeves again turned the way they had turned before, off the main road, down a path into a valley where the army had camped for two hours. Where the hills slowed the winds while the cooks had cooked hardtack. Master Reeves even led them to the ribbed remains of their old fire and tied the Morgan where he'd tied him before. After Bass tied Strawberry, he built a fire from branch scraps, then uncinched the saddles and planted them by the fire.

The master spread his blanket on the ground next to his saddle and sat down. Bass spread his, but instead of sitting, he walked toward the tall dead grass sprouting out of a drift of snow at the edge of the clearing.

"Where in God's name do you think you're headed, Mr. Nighttime?"

Bass spun and was so taken aback by the master's quick temper and gleaming, unholstered pistol that he stuttered. "To, to get the horses a little that grass yonder, sir. They hadn't had a bite since morning."

The flames in the wind made the light wave like water. Master Reeves floated there above the surface of light, then was gone. Vanished. Then was there again, then gone again.

"Boy, do you mistake me for a cowardly deserter?"

"No, sir, you is Master Reeves through and through."

"I got permission from Van Dorn—*Damn Born*, more like it. He's calling it sick leave. You didn't know that. Now you do."

"Yes, sir." Bass took a good breath, thinking any second the master would lower his pistol, thinking either they trusted each other or they didn't. You couldn't go back and forth with a thing like trust, giving and then taking it away. Friends and family and whatever was between them could put time on a seesaw, or songs or things like food, but not trust. What was the master thinking?

"I don't believe that dandy ass wanted my company anyhow," the master said, leaning back against his saddle and laying his pistol in his lap. "Said I could have a few days. As if a few days will give me a competent commander. Hell, he gave Albert and his whole scalping outfit a permanent break from the war. Said for him to stay put in Indian Territory and leave the fighting to us decent people. He's right, but the son of a bitch is wrong too. Shit, that idiot won't know where he'll be in a few days. He's heading east without one clue of an idea. Will probably end up leading the Army of the West all the way to the Atlantic to dig for oysters or some such shit."

If Bass charged the master this very moment, even if slow across the snow, the master would flurry with fear. Of course he would. His hand would stutter. He might even lose the sidearm on his blanket or in the snow, before finding it and gripping it, maybe in time to aim and shoot this big, ungrateful n—— down, but maybe not.

The light waved. And the master paused. "Well," he said, "go get your grass."

"Yes, sir," Bass said. He watched his shadow in the water light. He watched it stretch as if he were a fish leaping free of the water to chomp that grass yonder. As if right now, at last, he was becoming who he was meant to be. If only that shadow could keep on stretching.

What if the war wasn't at its end? That's what he asked himself, point-blank, face-to-face, as he knelt with shame and began ripping grass to make an armful. What then? What now, if once the Union got a foot up, they fell to pieces, too, and began deserting and taking sick leave and digging for oysters themselves? What now, if the war could go on another year or two, maybe seesawing for the rest of his life?

The master had fallen back into his quiet, reading his red book, though without smoking his red pipe. Bass had begun to believe that the master had to do both at the same time, but apparently not.

He split the grass fairly between Strawberry and the Morgan, and with a hand for each, he stroked their faces. He remembered what General McIntosh had said in the officers' tent as a last word when they were camped in the valley of apple, while tugging his beard, petting it: "If them Yankees are hankering for another Bloody Hill, I say we give it to them right quick before they change their mind." Bass thought on that. *Before they change their mind.* Or *right quick* before you changed yours.

"Farewell, O Hiawatha!" the master blustered. Bass turned from the horses to watch the master still seated on his blanket but rearing way back as if to throw something far, and then he threw it—the red book—and it ruffled through the air as gracefully as a chicken. It landed no more than fifteen feet away, out of the light but still visible, splayed on the snow.

"Fuck Longfellow, Bass! I can't believe we lost the fight. We had the numbers to win the damn thing but not the leadership. Not the stuff." He turned his gaze on Bass and hammered his own temple this time in a rage so that Bass felt it too. "Not the stuff. Fuck supplies. Not that supplies don't matter. But fuck supplies, Bass. None of it matters without the stuff, here," he said, hammering his temple again and making Bass blink at the sight of it. "You remember that gift I gave you? You remember to think, boy."

"Yes, sir."

"I wish I had some whiskey, goddammit."

Bass continued to stroke the horses, both at once.

"We could play poker if I could think straight, but I'm so goddamn unsettled, Bass, I don't think I can right now." He scooched away from the saddle and reclined with only his head propped. But then he kicked his feet. "Goddammit, I can't sleep against a saddle. Never could. Goddammit, I sure wish we had some whiskey."

Bass waited. Once the master showed he'd settled down, had finally stopped fussing and hammering, Bass left the horses and lay down on his blanket too. It wasn't like he wanted to be on his feet.

Bass looked up to the sky. There were so many stars, and the moon was so big. If he closed his eyes before the master did, the master might rile in the mood he was in, mistaking that Bass was trying to outsleep him, when he only wished to outthink him. So without closing his eyes, he tried to think it through. How he should take the master's pistol from him and shoot him dead or not shoot him. How a shot might attract the attention of any number of those 788 deserters scattered high and low for miles. Them with nothing suddenly finding something wouldn't go well. He might not have enough cartridges to kill them all.

"Don't think you're going to sleep while I lie here watching you."

"Oh, no, sir. Just admiring God's creation."

After a long moment of hopeful silence, Master Reeves said, "Have you ever thought God could be our creation instead? You know, so we always have something that is ours? You know, like an evacuation plan? Something to fall back on, like this fucking saddle-for-a-pillow bullshit?"

Bass thought twice but said what he wanted. "No, sir."

"Well, isn't that sweet? You and Longfellow have something in common. And who knows, you two could be right—there could be life later. But you're not thinking n——s go to the good part of heaven, are you? You see that big separation up there? You're looking at all those pretty twinkling lights, but if you're going anywhere, you're going where there's nothing. Just black airy nothing. That shit you aren't even looking at. Only white folks go to the big dance, boy. If anybody's going anywhere."

Bass let a moment pass to think.

"You have nothing to say?" Master Reeves said.

"Well, sir," Bass said, "where you suppose Indians and Chinamen go?"

Master Reeves snickered. "Of course, they're stealing on rainbows and climbing up. Shit, wouldn't that be something!" He snickered some more. "Exactly. Nobody's going anywhere."

Bass kept his eyes up. He didn't just study the white. He studied the black too. How could you have the white without the black to make it look pretty, to point to it? What was there in the white was on clear display. It was white, with lace and spark, but white all the same. But what was in the black? No black man and no white man could possibly know, because there wasn't enough light in the world to throw on it for us to see. If nobody across the whole world wanted what was in the black just because they couldn't see it, that was fine with him to be alone in the wanting. Then it was his to claim. He'd take it. Already, he considered it all his.

"I was messing with you, you know," Master Reeves said. "I'm a better Christian than you might believe. I can quote Colossians for you, if you like."

"Or I can read it myself if you will teach me how," Bass said.

"N——, now you're messing with me. I was a lawman once, remember. The career is in my blood. My heart is a badge. Just no money in that kind of work." His saddle leather creaked as he turned to Bass, but Bass continued to keep his eyes up, watching the stars cloud behind his white breath. "Jennie must have told you that the mistress taught her how, but you keep that shit to yourself. You hear me?"

"Oh, yes, sir."

"Maybe the mistress will teach you one day, too, but I have to respect the law."

"Yes, sir. I'd be mighty grateful, Master."

"Listen, if you think you're ready to read, what you're saying to me is you're long past ready to listen and think. Let's see if that's the case. Listen and think on this verse, which is one of my favorites. Colossians is one of the last books in the New Testament, right at the end, so you know it's important. In fact, Apostle Paul repeats the verse in Ephesians, so listen well." He paused by taking a breath or two and licking his lips before he began: "Servants, obey in all things your masters according to the flesh; not with eyeservice, as menpleasers; but singleness of heart, fearing God."

Bass heard the master turn to him again, but Bass was a patient man. He breathed as he always did. He wasn't studying what no Tom, Dick, Harry, or Paul said. Just the Lord.

"That's the Good Book saying I, your master in the flesh, represent the ultimate master. So if you want to make it to that dark space up there between the stars, you've got to serve me heartily as you would Jesus Christ. So of course, I'd be a fool in my position not to be a Christian. You haven't ever seen me throw a bible, have you?"

"No, sir. I never seen that."

"No," the master said.

Silence finally returned, but it sat heavy on Bass, from all those unspeakable thoughts swirling in and out of that master's mad head and now, because of him, his own. Not that the fire stopped crackling or the wind stopped gusting high above. When silence should have been as beautiful as black looked.

Then, far away, from the north, a new sound occurred, like thunder. Like churning horses.

"Master," he said.

"I hear it," the master said. "Could be us. Could be them. Quick!" He jumped to his feet and began shoveling snow with his hands onto the fire.

Bass jumped up to help, and the fire was soon snuffed. Only a tail of smoke remained, stretched high and long, like the breath of something much bigger and darker than Bass, hanging there and blotting stars and fading the moon, shifting, elongating, before pulling away thinner than cheesecloth and disappearing.

"Come on," the master said, running for the horses. The hooves of those distant horses multiplied into an army. Not an army. A mounted regiment. Perhaps a brigade.

Bass searched the ground for what he should grab. The blankets, of course, and the saddles. He looked up to see what the master had in mind with the horses, since he hadn't grabbed his saddle. Did the master actually expect Bass to tack both even now?

"Goddammit, what am I thinking?" the master said, beginning to run back.

Bass tilted his head and saw the master's Colt Dragoon shining on his blanket, the ivory grip looking like a piece of the moon. He lifted his eyes, then lowered them. He could possess it so easily. But if those hooves caught up to him, he'd hang. For killing an officer, he'd hang. Any white-man army would. He lifted his eyes again, to see Master Reeves slide on a slick sheet of crusted snow and fall at his saddle.

Bass moved to help him up, because it was his nature. The cavalry was within a mile now.

"Don't bother with me and mine," the master said, up on his feet and pushing Bass away. "Get yours! Get yours!"

Bass jumped to his blanket to roll it and caught sight of Master Reeves holstering his Colt. He slowed for a moment, thinking of his lost opportunity. Anger swelled, and he grabbed his saddle by the horn with one hand and ran for Strawberry. He tacked with pace, then swung himself into his saddle. Wasn't that some rebellion, sitting high and sitting first?

How many men had he killed? How could anyone ever know? But he hadn't killed one of them in cold blood. He guessed it wasn't his way, because it wasn't God's.

I'm sorry, Granddaddy. I'm sorry, he said over and over. *I didn't, and I can't. I'm sorry. I'm sorry!*

The master was up now, too, and spurring the Morgan for the forest cover, and Bass instantly followed, though not by spurring Strawberry. Strawberry decided for him. Obediently, Strawberry followed, and Bass followed Strawberry. As if they had minds of their own.

23

A Little Red Church

They waited together just inside the darkness of the forest, with nothing to look at but the red book left in the clearing. A little red church that didn't even look red without fire to throw color on it.

They listened to the cavalry approach without torchlight, on the other side of the trees. As if the cavalry knew where to turn, they appeared along the path and entered the clearing, bunched in irregular lines. Not cautiously but boldly. Bass prayed for Federals, but the uniforms proved to be Confederate. And the gelding in the lead was one Bass recognized, and its rider, with his long bristly broom of a beard, was surrounded by men with skin so dark they could have passed in the night for Negroes.

"General Albert?" the master called.

"Major George?" Pike asked.

The master walked his Morgan out of the forest. Once again, Strawberry followed.

"We saw your fire," Pike said. "Why did you put it out?"

"Shit, I didn't know who you were."

"Yeah, well," Pike said, "you should know Curtis is on our trail, thinking the whole army took this route and not just us. Stay here if you want to risk it. But we have safety in numbers."

Bass looked for his friends among the Cherokees, when one he didn't know hopped from his mount and picked up the book.

"The poetry's yours if you want it," the master said. "It's fit for a noble savage, I concede."

The Cherokee held the book up to the light of the sky, turning pages. If he could read, Bass envied him. Any moment, he thought, the music in those words might ring free of their ink for all to hear. The Cherokee lowered the book to his nose, as if to smell it, but clapped it shut and flicked it back on the ground.

The master laughed, and the Cherokee climbed back on his pony. Pike raised a hand, pointing at the closed red church. "Who is it?"

"Longfellow," the master answered.

"Oh," Pike said, his hand melting away in the shadows.

"Let's go then," the master said. "There's nothing here."

◆ ◆ ◆

Strawberry carried Bass south of Bentonville and Springdale and Fayetteville, needling the thread behind the master's thumb on the other side of sleep, and even past Van Buren and Fort Smith and across the Arkansas River, on the ferry and off, and once again along the Butterfield Overland Trail. Strawberry didn't stop taking the lead the entire way to Fort Washita.

Bass was glad to see familiarity when he reached the fort, but his gladness disgusted him. This morning, he wanted to see Jennie, but his want disgusted him too. Somewhere along the Texas Trail, finally alone again with the master, he quit removing his hands from the warmth of his pockets to give Strawberry strokes of encouragement.

Bass was thinking about his masters. How it had been a curse to have a kind one for so long. If this master, the son, had been his master all his life, Bass was certain he would've turned mulish and escaped years ago. The father had been worse, then. Much worse.

They hadn't spoken all day. Not really. Not since leaving Fort Washita soon after dawn. Master Reeves had only given orders, predictable ones that needn't be uttered, and Bass had only said, "Yes, sir." There were many ways to say, "Yes, sir." Countless. Even "No, sir" meant "Yes, sir."

Not even the longhorns lowed, wherever they were.

Snowless, the naked blackjacks reminded Bass of Pike's bristled hair and beard. That morning at the fort, Pike's snores carried over the yard, even to the gate. They reminded Bass of McCulloch and his blackbird preacher suit. Of McIntosh and his stiff-board corpse and horse. Of Master Reeves before his son had convinced him to grow a mustache. Bass decided he would never grow a beard.

Night met night at the iron of the master's gate—the loopy initials of the master's name hanging overhead like nooses. With the moon at a hidden slant, only the Morgan's chest and legs offered any real semblance of light.

"What the hell?" the master said.

Aiming to please, Strawberry followed the master's Morgan in a trot up the lane, which grew no brighter, as it had every time before. As big as a mountain, the big house sat without a flicker at the end of the lane, shiny but dark, like the bottom of a well.

"This is an unusual conservation." The master clicked, speeding the Morgan to a canter, and Strawberry picked up to a canter, too, as any child would.

At the porch, the master reined in fast and hopped down. Bass was staying on, so he kept his hands low, letting Strawberry slow at his own pace.

"Wait here," Master Reeves called, stomping up the steps and across the porch.

"Yes, sir," he said. But what else would he do? What could he do, this late on a hungry, thirsty, panting child mount?

The master opened the front door and called. His bootheels spidered through the house, upstairs and back down. "Rachel?"

The bootheels gradually faded, and the house fell into its previous silence. Bass faced the darkened doorway, waiting, and then he let his eyes rove to the windows—those downstairs, those on the balcony. He expected a candle or lamp somewhere to glow. Eventually, the master's face appeared recessed in the shadows of the doorway, as if he'd been watching Bass for some time, expecting to catch him at something.

"Nobody's here," he told Bass in a heartbreaking tone.

"No, sir?"

Master Reeves stepped from the shadows in slow strides. He mounted the Morgan and clicked.

They took the lane past the stable, around the bearded blackjack bend, to Mr. Hagan's cabin. Gray smoke braided from his chimney. The sticks stood in the clearing—like smokestacks, sure, but also like cannons, once a body learned to see things sideways the way they were.

The master opened Mr. Hagan's door, and the orange of the fire's embers escaped. "Sean?" he said. "Sean, get your ass up!" The master entered and threw the door shut behind him.

Bass waited some more. It was what he'd been trained to do. He'd spent more of his life waiting for masters than sleeping. Than eating or praying, easily. Even more than working.

He looked at where the lane hid behind more blackjacks. No one had heard them ride up. No one was coming. Owls hooted near and far. No other song took to the air. Nothing. Only more smoke braided up above, from the deep slumber of the slave quarters.

The cabin door flung open, and the master threw it to again, against that warm glow and smell of woodsmoke. "Drunk bastard," he said, stepping off the porch. He climbed back into his saddle, then climbed back down again at the stable.

"When you finish," he said, "come find me."

"Yes, sir," Bass said, sliding down from his saddle.

The master removed both of his rifles from their scabbards, while Bass stood aside doing nothing, waiting.

The rifles clacked together in the crook of the master's arm. "Just us tonight. I'll even let you sleep in the house." He arched his eyebrows, as though he thought those puny asshole eyes were pots of gold.

"Thank you, Master, thank you. I'm obliged, yes, sir, Master."

"Yeah, well," the master muttered, walking off toward his big, big house.

◆ ◆ ◆

Maybe if the master had said Jennie was welcome to sleep with him in the master's house, Bass would have felt altogether different about the master's order. Knowing the master, though, he considered his order merely an invitation.

Bass stewed through the feeding and watering and brushing. No kindness was a kindness when a body was a master. No kindness was a kindness when a body was a slave either. All he wanted was to see Jennie—the want no longer disgusting, because he was already here, wasn't he? But tomorrow had to be a different story. He pursed his lips and blew the light off his bottle.

Passing the rosebushes between the outhouse and the big house, he noticed a freckling, a sprouting, and stopped to observe the tiny half leaves and tips of unopened buds not yet fully born. The realization was shocking. Freezing for so long in Arkansas and Indian Territory, he only now realized that the cold in Texas wasn't freezing. It almost wasn't winter.

He reached for the brass knob of the back door and turned it. There was light now in the kitchen and in every room that he could see past the kitchen—the dining room and its cold hearth, the hall that led to the foyer and the staircase and the master's study. "Master?" he called.

He pressed the door behind him until it clicked. He pried his feet from his shoes, dropped his hat on them, and took a few steps on the cold wooden floor. It was coldest where his socks had holes. He stopped prematurely and listened to nothing. "Master Reeves?"

When no sound answered, he proceeded a few more steps onto the cushion of a rug and again stopped his own muted sound. Now in the dining room, he peered down the hall. The closed door on the right, to the master's study, surprised him. He called again. But again there was nothing to hear.

Bass eased forward some more, until he stood at the base of the stairs, below the unlit chandelier, that silent beehive of crystal stingers. His eyes followed the trail of light upstairs, past oval and square gold frames and globed candles along the wall at each step.

"Master Reeves? You up there?"

He listened with stifled breath, then crouched down on all fours. He lowered his ear to the floor and squinted, trying to see under the study's door, but from that distance, at least the length of him, he couldn't be sure there was light.

He crawled closer to the study and lowered again, and this time he did see in, seeing light. He crawled closer yet, until he saw the master's feet—wearing socks without holes and planted across the room beneath his desk chair in front of the desk.

Bass pushed himself up and took a breath before rapping his knuckles on the wood. "Master, you in there?"

"You found me."

Bass waited for his invitation.

He sass-faced the door. "You want me to come in, sir?"

"I said, 'You found me.'"

Bass turned the knob to find Master Reeves sitting slouched, hatless but still in his overcoat. His rifles leaned behind him against the desk, while his arms hung loose, his hands looking dead limp on his legs—one about to let a tipped glass fall.

"Come pour yourself a glass of rye. I couldn't wait."

Bass pushed his thoughts back, answering him with a nod, and walked toward the cherry-leather chest, its lid left open. He bent, and his fingertips touched the raised diamonds of a glass, the grooves, and unsheathed it.

The master was raising his glass to his lips, so Bass poured his own glass halfway before topping off the master's. He corked the bottle and set it back down on the desk with the master's corkscrew and gun belt and hat. He sat to the master's left.

He conceded—a chair felt good.

The master slowly craned to face him. His hair cupped his head from so many days under a hat, looking more like a stitched-on patch of felt. He smiled as Bass sipped. "Do you know what I've been thinking all this time while you were tending to the horses?"

Bass shook his head.

"I was thinking, 'Watch! That n—— will run off before I give him his chance to walk off scot-free.'"

Bass lifted his face almost the full tilt, before he thought better of it. "Master?"

"The whole damn family is off tonight, visiting Rachel's folks. Ain't that some unlucky horseshit?"

Until now, Bass hadn't once considered the possibility that Jennie was not close by. That she could be away tonight with the mistress and sleeping in a strange master's quarters.

"Now, we could ride over there and rouse everybody, or we could stay put so that you and I can have a few drinks and play a round of cards like old times. What do you say?"

Bass nodded. He wanted to walk off scot-free—he sure did. But maybe she was here, so maybe he didn't want to yet. "Yes, sir," he said.

"That's it? That's all you have to say to me?"

Bass leaned back, shaking his head but making sure he didn't slosh his rye. "No, sir. Thank you, sir."

"You act as though you don't believe I'm a man of my word."

"Oh, no, sir," Bass said. "I'm listening to you, sir. Confused, but listening, sure is."

"Don't go getting uppity all of a sudden, as if you're Damn Born."

"Oh, no, sir, I ain't never been that."

"So how am I confusing you, boy?"

"No, sir, I'm not saying *you's* confusing me. I'm saying I'm confused all on my own. About how I can walk outta here scot-free."

The crease of the master's closed lips turned ever so slightly upward, hiding under the overhang of his mustache. He shifted the glass from one hand to the other, as if the glass were freezing cold and he needed to warm his hand in his coat pocket. He touched the rim of the glass to the pink of his lips and swallowed. He licked his lips and the cockeyed ends of his whiskers, then twisted around in his chair to set the glass on the desktop.

"I was getting to that." The master wiped his mouth on the back of his hand, while he withdrew his other hand from his right coat pocket, showing Bass what it held.

Bass recognized the red design on the back of the master's playing cards, like ornate picture frames that had been left in a garden and were now twisted about with blooming vines.

"War can be unpredictable, can't it? You can think you're winning because you have every reason to think so, and then you discover you're losing. And you shouldn't be, by God, but you're losing all the same." He crossed his legs and brought his hands together to cut the cards and straighten them against his knee. "I fully expected you to have the opportunity at some point to play cards with the officers, at least once. So many refuse to believe a n—— can be smart, especially a big one like you." He shuffled the cards with a rip and straightened the pile against his knee. "I believe it, Bass. Oh, I believe it. But we never lacked players. Never once. That hardly makes sense." He lined the halves up and ripped them back into a disheveled whole. "There's always the next battle, though, right?"

"Yes, sir," Bass said.

The master ran his fingers along each side of the deck until the cards made a neat little cabin. Then he set the cabin on the corner of the desk between them. A cabin with a garden with vines with flowers around picture frames.

Bass lifted a hand off his lap and pressed his fingertips to the side of the cabin, his hand making a roof for it, but he didn't like the chewed edges of his nails against the dirty white side of the cards. He needed long, tapered nails like the master's. The master had a little file to prune them just so, as if the hulling of a pea or bean at a moment's notice might one day become a matter of life or death.

He took away the top half and set it beside the bottom half and removed his hand. He watched as the master's hand and his shapely nails set the bottom now on the top.

"So here's my offer," the master said, "and you get only one chance at this. War is war that way, you know, fair or not, and this is war, what we're always in." His eyes swelled, and Bass found himself breathing faster. "If you win," the master said, "this is what I'll do. Pop and I won't set you free at the end of the war. I'll set you free tonight. That's right—I'll write out a letter of manumission you can carry with you at all times." He turned away and plucked a blank sheet of paper from a cubbyhole and laid it beside what all else rested there on his desk. Then he slid his inkwell and a fountain pen next to the paper. "That's my white-man promise." He stretched out a hand, inviting Bass to shake it.

"Thank you, Master. That sound awfully sweet," he said, knowing he could beat him. "Yes, sir, it do. Thank you, sir." He inched his hand out there and held his open, too, like the other half of a deck, the other half of a prayer—being sure, just in case, to keep it a little lower than the master's hand, to let the master come downstream to him.

The master smirked and took Bass's hand in a fast grip and shook it, as if Bass couldn't crush the master's hand if he wanted. "You've been an awfully good servant," he said.

"Thank you, sir," Bass said. He smiled and felt a little ashamed he'd started to doubt that something between friends and family had been growing between them, built on enough trust after all.

They looked into each other's eyes, brown to brown, as if they knew what they were looking for. Without lingering, both looked away to the deck of cards, as if they'd found what it was.

The master slid the deck into his hand and dealt five cards each before setting the deck again on the desk.

Bass waited for the master to collect his cards all at once before he collected his, one at a time. The first one wouldn't look at him straight on. Like a slave, the jack showed one eye but off the other way. The second card made him count—one, two, three, four, five, six, seven spades. Which, he realized, was like the jack—a spade too. The third card made him count even higher—nine of spades this time.

"Hurry up," the master said, his cards fanned in front him like a red latticed fence he was peering over.

Bass glanced. "Yes, sir," he said, pulling up his fourth card. Another spade, with so much to count, counting ten of those shovels, two big Xs of them. He recounted to be sure.

"I can tell you're counting, boy," the master said.

"Sorry, sir," Bass said. "Got to."

"Jesus." The master collapsed his cards into a single pile on his lap. He reached a hand into his coat pocket and withdrew his red pipe.

Bass pulled his fifth card, pleading with God to give him an eight of spades to complete the straight flush. He wasn't in a hurry to look at his lot. No, he had never been one to hurry the Lord. Let the master fill his pipe with tobacco. Let him say the Lord's name in vain. Bass, in his own natural time, would turn his last card over, as if he were shoveling dirt, and he did. And his lot was not the eight of spades. It was the ivory-white queen of hearts. As if he were shoveling snow.

"I can't draw cards until you do."

"Yes, sir, I'm a-hurrying. I'm a-hurrying," Bass said, glancing up at the master and glancing back.

The master struck a match off his desk and stoked his pipe.

Bass rearranged his cards, then rearranged them again. The garlic smell burning off the master's match was trying to distract him by making him hungry. He could discard the seven and pray God would give him an eight of any suit because he could go for the plain straight instead—eight, nine, ten, jack, and queen. Or he could discard the queen and keep his faith in God that he'd receive the lot he'd begun to believe was his—the best hand in the game. Maybe not the best straight flush, not a royal flush, but it would be close and of the darkest suit there was. The suit of diggers. Of doers. Of happy, peaceful, singing, busy people, free as dirt. All of them.

The master waved the flame off his match and tossed the stick onto his desk. "Ready now?"

"Thereabouts," Bass said, weighing his decision against likely outcomes. If he didn't receive an eight of spades, he'd probably lose. If the card happened to be another seven, nine, ten, or jack, he'd at least have a pair, but he doubted that a pair would be enough. He didn't know why exactly he leaned away from the queen. Because she wasn't a spade? He slid her down on the desk and flexed his toes, the big ones sticking out of holes, then offered up another prayer. "Ready, Master."

"Oh, you think you're ready?" the master growled around the stem of his pipe.

Bass nodded. "Yes, sir, I think so," he said, and he reached for his glass to sip the color of rye for good luck.

"Your hand's almost perfect, is it? One card and you're free? It's that simple?"

Bass pressed his cards to his chest. "Only if God will it."

"Uh-huh," the master said, fingering the top card on the deck and placing it on the desk in front of Bass.

"Thank you, sir. I appreciate this chance you giving me—I sure do."

"Well, pick it up," the master said.

"Oh, yes, sir." Bass reached for the card and added it to the others in his hand without looking at it.

"Boy, you aren't afraid to look at it now, are you?"

Bass nodded. "Might be."

"N——, please," the master scoffed. He raked the cards out of his lap, fanned them quickly, and plucked one from the end, flicking it aside with Bass's discard. He then smiled at Bass, baring teeth. "My hand's not bad either." He fingered the top card of the deck, and without looking at it, he added it to his hand. "You look at yours first."

Bass shook his head. "Druther not."

"What did you say?"

"No disrespect, sir, but won't do me no good. Won't change it none, looking at it, so I druther not."

"Don't you rob the fun from the game. Go on now. I want to see the look on your black face when you realize that God favors your master."

"Oh, sir, I be happy with whatever lot God give me." Bass pointed a jagged nail at the master's hand. "You ready to turn over, too, and let's see together if I'm free or not?"

The master leaped up out of his chair and stomped a foot. "I'm ordering you to look, Bass. Do you hear me? I'm still your goddamn master, goddamn slave you!"

Bass tipped his head and thumbed his cards apart. *One last order*, he told himself, to simmer himself. His eyes landed first on the cards he knew he had and scanned slowly across, and before they had even reached his draw card, the master spun away, saying, "Yes, yes, yes!" to the bookcase on the opposite wall. He thrust his left hand up, his fist around his cards, while he dropped his right hand, hidden, making his coattails fly. With a spin, he turned back to Bass, his pipe still clenched in the corner of his mouth.

The master suppressed his grin. He walked back to his chair, raising his right hand and the draw card in it. "God was good to me," he said. He tucked it with the cards in his other hand and sat. "Okay, Bass, let's see what lot God has given you."

Bass took a breath and spread his cards on the desk. A three, seeing it now. A three and not the eight he'd prayed for.

"That can't be, boy."

Bass sought out the three again, realizing only now that it was a spade. They were all spades. Not making a straight flush but a flush. He'd forgotten about the plain flush. A plain flush of the darkest suit there was.

"Do you realize what you have?" the master asked.

"Yes, sir, a plain flush."

"I have to congratulate you, I guess." He slapped Bass on the arm. "That beats a lot of hands, a lot of good hands. It doesn't beat a full house. No, and it doesn't beat four of a kind." The master spread his cards on the desk—an ace, a queen, a queen, a queen, and a queen.

The master unbuttoned the top button on his coat, letting the button dangle by gold thread. He chewed the stem of his pipe and shook his head. "That was a close one. You don't play cards like you shoot, but that was a good game. Good try." He leaned out, gave Bass another slap, and swept the cards into a pile—the discards, the flush, the four of a kind, the entire deck—and rising out of his chair, he set them out of reach in one of the cubbyholes of the desk. Clutching his glass, he dropped back down in his chair. He drank down the rest of his rye and released a moan of relief.

"Now, Bass, since I won," he said, facing Bass straight on, "you need to do something for me. Fair is fair." He stood up, as if he couldn't stay seated, and poured himself another glass. He sat down again and crossed his legs. "Whenever we return to Damn Born's

Army of the West That Lost the West, wherever he holes up, you'll need to kill him for me." He slid the pipe from his mouth and motioned with open arms. "Simple. Just fire a shot off when everybody is firing a shot off, and nobody will ever know where it came from. Really, what should it matter to you? One fewer anguished white man, right? If you do that, not only will I free you after this godforsaken war, but I'll free whichever gal you like. You like Winnie, right? Hell, I'll free her too. You and her both. How's that?"

Bass could hardly utter the word. His lips moved, but his lungs failed.

"Speak up, boy."

Bass felt as though he were in a hole or underwater and couldn't get out but had to. He gazed at that brass coat button hanging by gold thread. "Master?" he said, but the word was little more than a mutter.

"What is it, boy? This is a good day for us both. And for the South, for damn sure. For the South *and* the West. And for Winnie, too, don't forget."

"Master?" Bass said, gazing at that brass coat button, that gold thread. He had to, he told himself. He had to. "I," he tried. "I," he tried again.

"Look," the master said, "you need to be more elastic here, show some flexibility, Bass, if you're going to be the tail to my whale a little longer. Fair is fair."

Bass kept gazing at that gold thread holding that button. He refused to listen. "Master," he blurted.

"Spit it, boy!"

"Master," he said, "I discarded a queen. The queen a hearts."

The master's eyebrows peaked. He tucked the pipe back in the corner of his mouth. "You think you did what?"

"Master," he said, flexing his toes, "I discarded the queen a hearts. I had it. How come you was to have it?"

The master stuck his chin out. "There's only one queen of hearts in the deck. Only one of anything—I've explained that to you. I had one, you saw it, so you couldn't have, understand?" He folded his arms and stared at Bass as if he expected an answer. "I guess you don't know what a queen looks like. You wouldn't know one of those fine things if she was to walk up on you in the middle of the night wearing only a chemise, and you best not, n——."

Bass lowered his eyes to the master's coat pockets. "Master, you cheated me. How could you?" He let his eyes dart to the master's eyes, which were doubling in size. The master's face was flaming. And then the master's jaw slacked, and the red pipe dropped down like a bird pecking seed.

"Oh, hell, no," the master said, and he whirled in a gust toward the desk, knocking a glass and spilling it onto the floor, where it splashed Bass's feet.

Bass sprang out of his chair, balling his fists, hardly believing that the time had come but witnessing it. The master's fingers grew around the ivory grips of his revolver.

Bass threw a fist where the master's hair cupped the back of his head, and it made the sound of a melon splitting. Grunting, the master buckled, as if to fall across the desk, but instead he wobbled backward, hands empty, eyes rolling. And Bass threw another, crushing the master's jaw and sending that pipe flying, spit flying, maybe a tooth, and the master crumpled down fast, as if melting in all his splendid gray at Bass's feet.

Bass took a step back. Head hung, he studied the master, who was still as still could be but not dead—pulsing with breath, and that was it. The house was silent, like nothing Bass had ever heard. He looked across the desktop, at the revolver half-unholstered, the sheet of paper, the ink and pen, the bottle of rye still standing beside the master's Hardee hat. He realized his fists were balled up tight as ever, so he opened them, but stiffly, and reached for the ivory handle and finished unholstering the Colt Dragoon. He turned the .44 around in his hands until the nickel-plated barrel pointed between his eyes. He rolled the cylinder and watched. It was fully loaded.

He pressed the long pistol into his coat pocket, while his other hand reached for the paper and pen and stuffed them into his other pocket. And he grabbed the inkwell. Jennie would know what to do.

He tipped his head again to see the master once more, when fright struck him, and he bolted from the room.

At the back door, he saw his hat and remembered his feet needed shoes, and he stopped to put them on. Remembering the inkwell, he grabbed it back up and threw the door open, lighting the path along the rosebushes.

He didn't feel the heft or jostle of every step. He was almost flying. His head almost light without thought.

He led Strawberry to the water manger. "We gotta ride, gotta ride," he told him as he tacked. "So drink up," he said. "Drink up, and let's go."

He set the inkwell inside the saddle rider, then cinched and clicked, and together they split the lane in a gallop. The blackjacks became a cloudy memory, erased by the clearing and the returning smell of woodsmoke.

If he hadn't known that Mr. Hagan was drunk, he would have proceeded differently. He might have ridden straight out the gate. But he did know, so he rode right to the overseer's porch, and with a flourish, as if he were the master himself. He pulled the Colt out and threw the door back in a clap. The orange glow showed Mr. Hagan stirring but nothing more. Being dragged could rouse, so Bass reared back and gave him a good one in the mouth. He felt the bite of teeth against his knuckles and heard the corn shucks in the mattress rasping about it.

"You feel that, Mr. Hagan?"

Mr. Hagan didn't have an answer.

Mr. Hagan slept in his day clothes, even wearing his coat and shoes to bed. Bass put the Colt away, back in the right coat pocket, and reached for Mr. Hagan's smaller and darker .22 Smith and Wesson, curled like a shadow on a table with a dirty plate and fork by the bed. He unlatched the barrel and saw two percussion caps in the seven-round cylinder. He latched the barrel back down, dropped the revolver into his left pocket with the paper and pen and the elk antler spearpoint, and then reached for the coiled whip hanging on a nail. He tucked it inside his coat, in the waist of his trousers.

He gave the cabin another quick look around. But there was only Mr. Hagan to grab, so he grabbed him by the collar of his coat and dragged him off the bed and out of the cabin and down the steps to the yard, where he dragged him some more.

A thin voice almost like a woman's called his name.

Bass searched farther down the lane, at the bend, where he saw a silhouette of Henry's height. "Run along, Henry," he said.

"That Mr. Hagan there?"

"It's him. Is Jennie yonder, or she gone?"

"Yes, sir. She sick, but she here."

"Okay, now run along. I mean it. Stay clear a here."

"Yes, sir!" Henry turned and churned his legs back the other way.

Bass heaved Mr. Hagan onto the ground between the sticks before he realized he shouldn't follow through. "I ought to," he said. He snatched Mr. Hagan's collar and dragged him back to the cabin, up the steps, and back onto his bed, where being warm could keep him passed out a whole lot longer. He hadn't noticed the egg smell before, for the fire, but now he did and held his breath.

Bass strode out quickly and rode Strawberry hard around the bend, almost running up on everyone spilling from the quarters. Henry, Rub, Winnie, everyone but Jennie was outside in their long underwear and underdresses. Winnie and another woman giggled and danced, holding hands, but some stared with blank looks, holding themselves, while Rub gave him a sour face.

"You gonna get us all killed," Rub said as Bass charged past.

She was sitting up in bed, her shirt like a gravestone.

He stepped fast, and she opened her arms.

"Bass," she said, her voice like somebody else's, "you kill Master Reeves?" Her hands so good on his back.

"I ain't killed nobody," he said. "I beat him, though. And Mr. Hagan too."

She pressed her head, her hair, against his chin.

"Bass, you even know where you're going?" Her voice dragged out like a saw across dry wood.

"I know," he said.

"But do you know how to get there? There's a difference."

"I know." He pulled away from her and showed her the master's inkwell. He showed her the paper and pen. "In case I get run up on and need a pass to be out alone. Will you?"

She coughed and told him where to find a candle and to slide the crate next to her bed.

She laid the paper across one of the slats of the crate. She dipped the pen but held it in delay.

"I don't know how to start, Bass. What do I say?"

"It don't matter," he said.

"It does matter." Her eyes were loud, because her voice couldn't be.

He held her shoulders to make her believe. "It don't," he said. "Half the white people out there is dumber than the dumbest one a us. I seen it! Just make it look good. Put words down. Really scratch it up."

"Oh, Bass," she said.

He waited, but she waited too. He lowered his hands to pat her legs over her covers. "How about I'm on the road to visit my sick mama?"

"And where're you from? What's your name?"

"I'm Bass. Bass Reeves. From right here."

She took a long breath and coughed. "I suppose." She bent to the paper, the ink really scrolling right out of her, pretty like the outlines of the littlest flowers.

He held it up. "I like it." He smiled at the paper, at her. "I be back to get you, you hear?" He folded the paper and put it in his pocket with the Smith and Wesson and the spearpoint. He remembered his necklace and wished he could give it to her. She could turn it around her neck while thinking of him and counting the beads as days or weeks. But he leaned in and hugged her and kissed her warm forehead and her warm cheek and lips. He shut his eyes, then opened them. He plucked up the pen and stoppered the inkwell, but Jennie clasped her hands down on his.

"Leave them," she said.

"Can't," he said. "You ever found with these, you'll hang."

She eased her hands away, and he eased from the bed.

"Get to feeling better now, cause I be back, hear?"

She smiled, and he nodded from the doorway and strode past Rub.

"You gonna get us all killed."

"Nah," Bass said. He emptied his hands of the letter-writing materials into a saddle rider and buckled the saddle rider. He climbed up Strawberry and turned Strawberry in a circle to see everybody. "Y'all best act like y'all don't know nothing. Go back to sleep. Like it's just another night." Seeing the lane ahead of him, he realized that the hoofprints in the dirt all the way around the bend would tell something different.

He rallied them to follow. "Come on, scuff the hooves, everyone. I weren't here cause y'all wiped them all away, understand? Get rid of 'em all. Kick 'em all gone," he said, and Henry skipped behind him, leading the others, laughing, kicking dirt. Even Rub joined in.

Once they reached Mr. Hagan's cabin, he told them to get gone. Winnie ran up to reach up for his hand. He gave it a squeeze but was short about it. "Now go on back to sleep," he told her. To the others, to all of them, he demanded that they go and not talk anymore. "Don't let nobody hear you speak a word about me or nothing, not a whisper, cause I expect they won't admit a bit of it anyhow. So go now. Go!"

He spun Strawberry around, and Strawberry kicked into a gallop, passing the stable, the rosebushes, the mansion. The lane almost came to its end. And then it did.

24

Left

Bass watched the blur of blackjacks for distant torchlight and horse shapes, patroller shapes, but he couldn't hear ahead for Strawberry's thunder. He and Strawberry bore down hard.

Theirs not to make reply, he remembered, telling himself. He remembered the way to the Texas Trail without thinking of the way.

Theirs not to reason why, he remembered next.

Theirs but to do and die.

He thought about that. He liked that. So he said it all again. Then he thought, *Theirs means mine's.*

Sometimes the road ran straight and the moon was good for seeing, but not when the road slowed down in its crooks. In its crooks, he feared ambush, expecting it, though telling himself he had the pass. He had the right pistol that was full and the left one that wasn't empty. They wouldn't even expect a slave to have a horse. He'd have the jump.

He'd been riding for a half hour before he saw the first person out in the night. At first he didn't know it was a person. He thought it was a rock set off between the road and the trees, but as Bass got closer, what looked like a rock was actually a crouching child firing a pistol straight up in the air. Bass saw from the sparks of the blast the white face of a grinning kid.

With more crooks coming up, with the trail coming up soon beyond them and then the Red River and Indian Territory just across it, Bass slowed. He supposed more white folks would show before they fell off the earth, believing it was time.

A glow sure enough pierced the trees, the fabric of limbs cross-ing and crossing between the crooks. Bass took a deep breath and slowed Strawberry to a trot, praying for the Lord to keep him free, and then remembered the pen and inkwell. He unbuckled the saddle rider and tossed what he wouldn't have wanted to be caught with into the brush. He thanked the Lord for reminding him. Maybe he asked for too much. He didn't pray to be free a little longer. He made that clear. *For good, Lord*, he said. *Forgive me, for good.*

The trees eventually removed their veil, and the light someone was holding showed the stick it was burning on. It gradually showed three men sitting on horses and blocking the road. One held a shot-gun at the trigger but without aim, standing it up casually against his shoulder. The one to his left was the one with the torchlight. The one to his right was slowly climbing down off his mount.

Strawberry halted himself.

"How do, gentlemen," Bass said.

"Get off that damn horse," the man with the shotgun said.

"Yes, sir," Bass said, dismounting. "Do y'all need to see my pass, sir?"

The man on the ground stepping up to Bass was so heavy that his fat face made his beard look like a coon curled up. He tugged a revolver from his waist as if it wasn't an easy thing to do. "Why you getting shot at?"

"Oh, not at me, sir," Bass said. "Don't know why he did it. A kid. But I didn't do nothing." He shook his head. "No, sir."

"You like scaring children?" the man with the shotgun asked.

"Oh, no, sir," Bass said. "Was just passing by, and he fired up. I'm heading to see my mama. All I'm doing." He nodded low and shifted his feet a little to turn his right pocket to the dark. "She sick, not good atall, not atall."

"Well, gimme that pass," the fat man said with wheezed breath.

"Who's your master?" asked the man with the shotgun, which still leaned against his shoulder as if to point out the moon.

Bass reached into his left coat pocket. "Major George Reeves. He a major in the Eleventh Texas Cavalry. Maybe you heard of him. A member of the Texas House of Representatives too." He pulled out the pass and slipped his right hand into his coat pocket.

"Well, he important, ain't he?" the man with the shotgun said.

"Oh, yes, sir," Bass said, holding the pass out to the fat man with the coon beard and the revolver aimed from the waist, but the man kept his free hand at the end of his short arm down by his side. "I be passing back this way tomorrow." Bass kept his hand out, but the fat man kept still, wheezing.

Strawberry snorted.

The fat man raised his hand finally and took the pass and carried it to the man with the shotgun.

Bass slid the Colt free of his pocket and squeezed the ivory grips, the pistol feeling his. He glanced at the one holding the torch—a dumb-eyed young man with an unfinished mustache, probably only there to hold the torch.

The man with the shotgun took the pass and squinted at it, while the fat man turned around to face Bass and walk toward him again.

"Lean that light this way some," the man with the shotgun said, lifting the pass closer to his eyes, and the man with the torch stretched it closer to him. "A little closer," he said, and when the torch was stretched closer, the man with the shotgun removed the pass from before his eyes and touched it to the torch, letting it catch. "Oh, my," he said. He flicked the pass, and it fluttered moth-like to the ground. "I don't reckon that major master of yourn will cotton to that."

The dumb-eyed man giggled, shaking his light.

The fat man turned to see what he'd missed, and Bass swung his arm around, cocking the hammer. The fat man must have heard that, too, spinning back to face Bass one last time. Bass pulled the trigger and watched the fat man's head blow back against the men on horses.

The man with the shotgun grunted something as he fought his rearing mount and tried to level an aim.

Bass thumbed the hammer back and fired into his chest, and the shotgun tumbled. He glanced at the dumb-eyed one, who was only fighting to hold on to his mount and torch, but the man who'd lost his shotgun remained upright, alive, and quiet, with his hands reaching. Bass thumbed the hammer back again and shot him in the mouth, which exploded as if filled with ink before he flopped over the flank of his horse.

Bass cocked the hammer and aimed at the dumb-eyed one left, whose face had been sprayed with blood.

"Don't shoot," he shrieked, his torch shaking worse.

"Is you anguished too?" Bass asked.

"I'm just along."

"Throw down your guns."

"I ain't got any."

Bass took a step forward. "Get down off your horse."

"Yours—take it," he said, jumping down and buckling in the knees.

"I ain't a thief," Bass spat. "I just want what's due."

A patter of feet sounded behind Bass, and before he could see past the blur of turning, a pistol fired.

The bullet whistled wide, and Bass leaped for cover behind the dumb-eyed one, wringing an arm around his neck, making him gurgle and drop his torch.

The kid he'd seen earlier crouching like a rock stood now at Henry's height, twenty feet away, cocking the hammer on his pistol and peeking down the sight.

"Take your dirty black hands off my brother," the kid shouted.

"Boy, you want me to shoot him dead and you too? Throw it down, and I'll let you both live."

"Don't you *boy* me, boy. Listen here, no n—— can kill me. You kidding me? You? Can't be done!"

Bass plunged forward, shoving the dumb-eyed one at the kid, who jumped back and fired, hitting his brother in the gut. And the dumb-eyed one dropped to the ground, squealing like a hog, his squeals getting higher and higher pitched as he writhed, pulling at his clothes and kicking.

The kid gawked in horror, lowering his pistol.

Bass aimed the Colt. "You gonna drop it or die?"

The kid raised his eyes at Bass and then raised his pistol, trying to fix an aim and taking his sweet time, as if he had all the time in the world. As if Bass really couldn't kill him, ever.

"Don't," Bass said. He would wait. He didn't want to. The Lord knew he didn't.

"It ain't your fault," Bass said, "but it will be."

The kid's barrel swayed, and the kid peeked and peeked down its sight.

The dumb-eyed one stopped kicking and squealing and began grunting and sucking air through gritted teeth. His torch burned on beyond his reach but smaller there on the ground, the flames flickering sort of tenderly as if trying to lick his wounds.

"God loves both us, kid. How can you look up at the moon and stars and all that space between and not believe he loves all us? You *and* me. *Both?*"

The kid cracked the hammer back, so Bass had to.

His bullet threw the kid as if he were a rock. As if he were skipping away on water.

Bass hadn't noticed the smell of smoke or the rise of it before his eyes, until now.

The dumb-eyed one whimpered. His blood had spread to Bass's shoes.

Bass backed away. "God help you, you anguished people." He slipped the hot pistol into his pocket and spun, already whistling for Strawberry to walk over to him, but Strawberry was already there, whisking his tail.

"Lordy, ain't you a doer!"

He wiped his shoes in the clean dirt, then stepped on up.

25

Thataway

Once Strawberry had broken free of the blackjacks and was racing up the open Texas Trail, it seemed no one had heard the shootout. There was no alarm, so there was no one who could take anything away. There was just beautiful clear air in the broad space they were riding through, which was filled on most days with a herd or on others with a regiment, but it was now a stream of free and clear blackness for Bass and Strawberry to claim for the moment as theirs.

He saw himself as a child grasping at the air about him and asking his mother why there was nothing there or there or there, no body or cabin or tree, but why? Why was nothing so much a part of something? Then ahead in the far distance, he saw two spots of torchlight in flight, coming from the direction of Colbert's Ferry.

He turned Strawberry off the trail with a leap into the grass, toward the blackjacks banking the trail, and as they slowed, their dust cloud caught up and passed them. He could hear the men's horses now. He watched their torchlight grow, from puny to less puny—their clouds of dust announced three or four riders, maybe five.

Bass could charge Strawberry into the trees for a slow chase, or he could stand like a dog refusing to return to his vomit.

"We gotta live, Straw," he decided, backing Strawberry into a thicket of blackjacks where he could see the trail and the men not there yet but coming, riding in two columns at a gallop and shouting clearly now, "Thataway, thataway!"

One, two, three, four, save Jesus, he thought as he counted them, two per column—not soldiers in formation but patrollers in farm clothes. The lead riders held torches, bearing what little light the wind allowed, while the ones in the rear waved pistols.

Bass let go of the reins and held the .44 Colt Dragoon in his right hand and the .22 Smith and Wesson in his left. He had two rounds in each. He'd kill whom he could as they rode up or rode past, before they spotted him, and he couldn't miss. That was as far as his plan got.

He thumbed the hammers back and took a breath. He held it to listen to the hoofbeats. He watched, but he wasn't sure what he was watching—how they tore up to his plot on the trail with a belief he couldn't be hidden there only because they hadn't considered it.

He let the first one of the closer column go by, then aimed the Colt at the one behind him, who could return fire. It was just another anguished white man with a beard and some buttons. The man never even looked his way.

Bass pulled the trigger and, through the smoke, watched the rider swing slow and steady as a pendulum off his mount. The mount cried and bucked for its loss, and Bass followed the first rider as he circled back, throwing down his torch and drawing a sidearm, yelling, "Where? Where?"

Bass shot him in the buttons with the quieter .22 and thumbed both hammers back to begin again.

The other two patrollers were galloping toward Bass, answering, "There! There!" The one without the torch fired but was way wide of him, so Bass found him with the Colt at twenty yards and pulled the trigger.

The man's hat flew away, a smart thing, while the man clung on, rolling under his steed with his feet caught in the stirrups and getting trampled. Bass lowered the Colt and aimed the .22 at the last one, who tossed his torch and turned his mount back the way they'd come, back to the river and the ferry, as if Bass weren't headed there too.

There were no buttons on the back of the man's black coat, so Bass imagined them. He imagined that he was a Cherokee and that those buttons twinkled as black water can twinkle, as if he could really see them now. As if he were just shooting into water.

Bass squeezed the trigger, and the man kept riding as if the revolver hadn't sparked or coughed, as if the man hadn't been hit. He rode as if Bass had completely missed, staying balled up but sitting straight, his sorrel mount digging just as fast up the trail. Bass slipped the spent pistols back into his coat pockets as if he thought he'd reload later somehow in his future. He clutched the reins and clicked, and Strawberry bolted from the blackjacks.

If Bass didn't catch the man, he didn't know how he'd make it to the river and cross it. All along he had vaguely believed that he would leave Strawberry at the river and swim across. He would have been on foot and freezing wet, slow but free, but now he wanted to take Strawberry with him, to somehow steal the ferry across and ride fast and dry away from here.

This patroller racing ahead of him would rouse everyone sleeping for the night at Ben Colbert's place, and there would be no ferry to steal if Bass didn't catch him, though without a loaded weapon, he didn't know how he would. Maybe he'd learn to dive from horse to horse and strangle a man to the ground. The man was sure to have a loaded one himself, but he hadn't once turned to use it—intent only to give chase and win it.

Catching him was as far as Bass's plan seriously got.

Strawberry cut the distance between them to twenty yards but was slow to bridge the rest. The sorrel ahead was nearly as strong, was digging and digging. The man, half of Bass, stayed balled up in the saddle and never turned, as if Bass had never seen the buttons on his back or as if Bass had seen them and struck them right but the man only wanted to die where he wanted—at the river, at the border, with the last of his people.

Ben Colbert, the ferryman, was a tribal chief who lived on the Chickasaw Nation side of the river, up on the bluff with an inn. Bass doubted anyone milled on this side of the river at this time of night, or else they would have already stirred. The man balled on the sorrel would have to reach the river and fire his weapon to attract the attention of anyone on the other side. If he had a weapon.

The sorrels rocked and steamed in the cold night, one after the other, drifting closer together and farther away and then closer again, as if on a loose tether. The big sky poured down on Bass with the pressure of things soon ending. He watched the trail sloping down to the river coming up, the blackest thing in the night, with the Indian Territory bluff and the inn and its chimney sitting like one shadow breathing.

Strawberry lacked ten yards and had no space left to close it. Bass drew the Colt, thinking a man could never know what was inside it and what wasn't.

But the man had no stop. He raced for the river as if he believed his sorrel could leap it or race across it like Jesus walking. But then the sorrel stopped itself short with a quick drop of its head, and the balled man flew forward off the saddle and hung there, as if weightless, before splashing down.

Bass let Strawberry halt himself, and he watched the balled man bob facedown without a thrash, his black coat billowing like a sail.

He hadn't missed.

Strawberry blew and was out of breath.

Bass scanned up and down the river and across it, then gazed at the man beginning to unball, sailing out. He turned to see the trail behind him and looked across the river once more, where the ferry was tied to an anchor rope strung over the river from a tree on the territory side to a tree on the Texas side. The rope hung like a clothesline about ten feet off the ground and then off the water and then off the ground again, to keep the ferry from drifting away like that man as it passed back and forth.

Bass slid the Colt into his pocket and steered Strawberry to the tree on this side and reached up for the rope. It was as hardy as a tree branch. He could climb across and bring the ferry over to pick Strawberry up, but he couldn't even finish the thought, because it was such a poor one.

He stroked Strawberry's ears and leaned down and rubbed his nose. "Straw," he said. It saddened him to abandon a thing so much like himself, what he couldn't own but wanted to and maybe for that reason loved.

He reached for the rope with both hands and looked across the river once more, where only smoke seemed to stir. The river stirred—and the unballed man with it, sailing out of sight. Strawberry stirred, too, quivering and catching his breath, while the other sorrel drank at the water's edge.

Bass heaved himself up as if he were simply climbing a tree, and then he climbed some more, reaching out and pulling in more rope while keeping the rope hugged between his legs. Once he was over ground again, free ground, he uncrossed his legs and dropped.

He looked up at the inn, which wasn't as dark close up but was still just as still, with nothing stirring but smoke. A stable with a horse to steal was just a jot away. He looked across the river once more at Strawberry waiting for him by the tree, beneath the rope, whisking his tail.

Before he could stop himself, Bass raised a hand to wave, and Strawberry's ears, stiff as summer leaves, began to twitch with sorrow and God's blessing.

Acknowledgments

I am especially indebted to the following:

Art T. Burton, the historian who rescued Bass from one hundred years of obscurity. For a decade, while I researched and conceived and revised a novel that has now grown into a trilogy, as I traveled from Alabama to Texas to do it right, as I earned my PhD in American fiction, with a secondary area of specialization in African American narratives, as I moved from one desk, one university, one conference, to another, I carried my singular constant, my bible: Art's *Black Gun, Silver Star*.

Morgan Freeman, for his 2010 clarion call on CNN: "You ain't hear a lot of stuff about Bass Reeves," he said, appearing already to slip into character. "Nobody's ever tackled him. He was one of the most well-known deputy marshals in the West in his time. I want to do Bass Reeves."

The shrewd and dedicated staff at the University of Nebraska Press. I am immensely grateful to this impressive lot, from corner to corner.

Miroslav Penkov, Laila Amine, and Barbara Rodman, professors and friends at the University of North Texas. I continue to hear their echoes in the clouds.

Robert F. and Bette Barsanti Sherman, for funding the Inspiration Award at the University of North Texas, which an early draft of this book received.

Western Literature Association, for giving me a platform to present excerpts of this book at annual conferences and for honoring "Thataway" with the 2018 Creative Writing Award.

Clapboard House and *Ostrich Review*, for publishing "The Wallows" and "Shoo" (as "Ice"), respectively.

Courtney Craggett, Ashley Reis, Cynthia Shearer, Steve Sherwood, and Erin Stalcup, for their unwavering faith and acute observations.

My mother, for giving me the ticket to go West and the pluck to persevere.

Sara, for being an angel, a dove, and a jackpot, no matter how many times I pull the arm: for Shania, Josh, Emme, and Owen, too, whose collective love, support, patience, and time allowed me to chase this dream. And for welcoming Bass as a member of the family.

My father, for always asking if I'd spoken yet to Morgan Freeman.

And Bass Reeves, who will forever move freely in my mind, from tree to tree and horse to tree.

Printed in the USA
CPSIA information can be obtained
at www.ICGtesting.com
CBHW031733140624
10088CB00002B/53